The books in
THE LOST T
THE ONE-EYED MULE SKINNER: BOOK TWO
THE BLACK PEARL TREASURE: BOOK THREE
THE HIDDEN FORTRESS: BOOK FOUR

ALSO BY ERIC T KNIGHT
IMMORTALITY AND CHAOS
(epic fantasy series)
Wreckers Gate: Book One
Landsend Plateau: Book Two
Guardians Watch: Book Three
Hunger's Reach: Book Four
Oblivion's Grasp: Book Five

CHAOS AND RETRIBUTION
(sequel to Immortality and Chaos)
Stone Bound: Book One
Sky Touched: Book Two
Sea Born: Book Three
Chaos Trapped: Book Four
Shadow Hunted: Book Five
Book Six – Winter 2018

THE ACTION THRILLER
WATCHING THE END OF THE WORLD

Follow me at:
ericTknight.com

All books available on
Amazon.com

ACE LONE WOLF
and the
Black Pearl Treasure

by

Eric T Knight

ISBN-13: 978-1546474425
ISBN-10: 1546474420

Author's Note: The Lone Wolf Howls *series does not need
to be read in order.*

1

I wake up to the sound of a pistol being cocked near my head.

There's no sound quite like it. I come awake instantly and reach for one of my Colt .44s.

A boot comes down on my wrist, pinning it to the ground.

"It ain't there no more, half-breed," a voice rasps.

I turn my head and blink the sleep out of my eyes. In the early dawn light I can see that the man staring down at me has washed-out blue eyes. They're utterly cold, those eyes, and they're staring down the sights of a Colt Dragoon right at me.

"What do you want?" I ask him.

"Why you, of course."

I see that he isn't alone. There's at least four more men with him, all pointing guns at me. One of them is grinning at me like he just won first prize at the county fair.

I look back at the one standing on my wrist. "Do I know you?"

"You may know *of* me," he says and smiles. He has a gold tooth. His beard is thin and neatly trimmed and he has a heavy ring on one finger. "But I don't believe you *know* me."

I'm starting to get irate. I don't like having a gun shoved in my face and I don't like being called a half-breed, even if it's what I am, what with my mother being a full-blood Chiricahua Apache and my father being a white man. "Get off my damn hand already."

"Don't you talk like that," one of the others says.

He's got a pinched-up face and a narrow chin that disappears into his neck. He's got a mustache but no beard. If I was missing my chin like he is, I'd grow a beard. If I could grow one anyway, which I can't.

"I'll shoot you right here and now," he says. "Say I won't."

"Say you won't what?" I ask, not sure what he just said.

"Say I won't do it!" he crows. "Go on, say it!" He's hopping from one foot to another like he's got ants crawling up his legs. I figure he's about two shakes away from shooting me.

"Dial it back, Jesse," the cold-eyed one says.

"You ain't spoiling the fun again like last time!" one of the others blurts out. This one's hat is pushed back so I can see the front of his head has all gone bald. One of his eyes is squinched about halfway shut like maybe a hornet stung him or something. "You always do this, Jesse, go off all half-cocked and start spraying lead everywhere. Not this time, I'm telling you. Not this time!"

"Shut up, Cole," the cold-eyed one says. "You don't talk to my brother like that or I'll shoot the damned Injun right here and now."

Okay, I don't like the way this whole palaver is going. I might as well speak up, get my say in while I still can.

"Before anyone shoots me, I want to know why."

"Your horse," the cold-eyed one says. "It's stolen. Though why anyone would steal such an ugly horse is beyond me."

"Watch what you say about Coyote," I warn him. "That horse is twice the man you are."

I have a deep fondness for Coyote. I can't deny that he *is* ugly though, with his jug head and short legs.

"Besides, I paid for that horse." Not just in money either, but with my own blood.

"If that's so," Jesse says, waving his gun at me. "Then show us the bill of sale."

"What kind of fool talk is that? I don't have a bill of sale. Do you have a bill of sale for your horse? He's mine and that's all there is to it."

"That Rocking R brand on his hip says otherwise," the cold-eyed one says.

"Yeah, we heard they're having real trouble with rustlers and horse thieves and here you show up with one of their horses and no bill of sale," Jesse says. "It don't take a genius to put two and two together."

"And what's two and two make?" I ask him. I know it's stupid to provoke him, but hell, I'm probably going to die anyway. Might as well get in what I can.

"Two and two?" he says, his forehead wrinkling. He puzzles this for a second. "Ain't that just a saying, Frank?" he says, turning to the one with the cold eyes. "Ain't it? How'm I supposed to know what it means?"

"I don't cotton much to those who pick on my brother," Frank says, his eyes slitting down.

"So that means what? That you're going to kill me? Aren't you planning on doing that anyway?" I know. I have a problem. I can't keep my mouth shut.

Frank grinds my wrist under his boot. It hurts, but I won't give him the satisfaction of showing it.

"What we have here," Frank says to the others, "is a gen-yoo-ine horse thief. And what do we do with horse thieves?"

"We string 'em up!" Cole hoots. He's all kinds of excited. This is the part of the show he's been waiting for.

"This isn't about stealing a horse, is it?" I ask Frank. Seems clear to me he's the only one with enough sense in his head to buy a penny candy.

"Well, sure it is," he says. "What else would it be?"

"Because this is Wyoming. And the Rocking R is a New Mexico brand. Probably you've never even been there."

"I hear it's warm," Jesse says, shivering a little.

It's a cold morning, winter just reaching its end. There's frost on the ground and our breath leaves little clouds in front of our faces.

Suddenly it all makes sense. "You followed me from Virginia City, didn't you?"

"We saw the coin you were spending," Jesse says. "Only one way a half-breed like you gets hold of that kind of scratch and that's by stealin'!"

"Or I got it by spending the winter cowboying on the Double X Ranch, up in Montana. I earned every penny of it." And I did too. Coldest goddamned winter I ever spent in my life. Snow up to my eyebrows. Wind that cut like a knife, coming down from Canada. Feeding hay to cows in the dark and the snow. Rescuing calves with the bad sense to be born in the winter.

When I came north I aimed to get far away from anything that could remind me of Annie. Now I just want to get south as fast as I can and get warm.

3

Except I hadn't counted on getting hung.

"It doesn't matter what I say, does it?" I ask.

Frank gives a little smile and shows that gold tooth again. "No. It don't." He shoves his Dragoon right up to my face. "Bring the rope, Jim. It's time to fix our friend a little going-away party."

Hands grab me and drag me to my feet. My hands are bound behind my back and a noose is dropped over my head.

It's hanging time.

2

"Ain't you caught his horse yet?" Jesse yells.

"Damned critter won't let me get close to it!" a voice yells back. "It keeps running off."

"Use your rope!" Jesse yells back. He grins at me, showing off a pretty impressive snaggle tooth. "We're going to hang you using your own horse. How do you like that?"

"Good luck with that," I tell him.

"Luck ain't got nothing to do with it."

"You're right there."

He scowls at me, trying to figure out if I'm making fun of him.

"You won't catch Coyote unless he wants to be caught," I say. "And I guarantee you he doesn't want to be caught." I hear running hooves and a man cursing off in the trees behind me and smile. Coyote's too smart for these clowns.

"Maybe we'll just shoot the damned horse then," Jesse says.

I fix him with my coldest, dead-eye stare. "You shoot that horse and I promise you I will hunt you down and torture you. When I'm done with you there won't be enough left for the buzzards to eat."

He starts to make a smart comment but a shadow comes over his face and he looks uncertain instead.

Frank backhands me. "Empty words, coming from a dead man."

"I'm Apache," I tell him. "Grandson of the great chief Cochise. You ever fight Apaches before, pale face?" That gets his attention.

"We don't have Apaches in Missouri," Jesse says.

"I heard of Apaches before. They're reckoned to be fierce fighters," Cole says and the man next to him nods in agreement. The man is ugly enough that I reckon he's Cole's brother.

I spit some Apache at them, fast and angry. Jesse, Cole and his brother flinch a little. Only Frank seems unmoved.

5

"We don't die like ordinary men," I say. "Kill an Apache and he'll crawl out of his grave and gut you in your sleep."

"I don't believe in haunts," Jesse says, but his eyes are wide and there's a quiver in his voice says it's a lie.

"Don't listen to him," Frank says. "He's just trying to rattle you. A man's dead and that's that."

I rattle off some more Apache and bare my teeth at them.

"What's that?" Jesse says. "What'd you say?"

I smile at him real cold. "It's an Apache death curse." Which it isn't, since there's no such thing, but what do I have to lose? They're already planning to kill me and dead's dead, like Frank said.

"Let's just kill him and get it over with," Cole says. That swole-up eye of his is twitching. "This ain't fun anymore." He points his gun at me. His hand is shaking a little.

"Climb down," Frank hisses. "I say we're hanging him and that means we're hanging him." His voice goes low and deadly. "Unless you're thinking maybe you should be the leader of this gang now, Cole?"

Cole starts shaking his head, babbling how it ain't like that at all. I can't blame him all that much. Frank is clearly a bad hombre. If I live through this, that's something I'm going to remember.

"Bring your horse over here, Bob," Frank says to Cole's brother. "We'll use it."

"He ain't gonna shit on my saddle, is he?" Bob yelps. "I seen plenty of men crap themselves when they hang."

"Really?" Frank says. "How hard is this to figure? He isn't going to be in your saddle anymore once he's hanging."

"Oh," Bob says. "That's right." He hustles off to fetch his horse.

Another man shows up then, all out of breath. He's got the same vacant look in his eyes that tells me he's another brother to Cole and Bob. I guess it's true what they say, about good things coming in threes. Or is that bad things? I can never remember.

"I had to give up. The horse run off."

"Forget it, Jim," Frank says. He sounds disgusted.

"That ain't no natural horse," Jim says. "There's something in his eyes. It's like he was reading my mind."

"I said forget it," Frank snaps. He's holding the rope that is tied around my neck and now he tosses the other end up at a pine tree limb overhead.

The throw falls short. So does the next one. It's harder than it looks, tossing a rope over a tree limb.

"Shinny up there and loop this over that limb," Frank snaps at Cole, who puts up his hands and steps back.

"You know I fell out of a tree as a kid, Frank," he protests. "It's how I got this eye like it is."

Frank curses under his breath and turns to Jim. "Since you can't manage to catch one ugly horse, maybe you can do this."

Okay, now I'm mad. No one calls Coyote ugly but me. The fact that he *is* ugly has nothing to do with it.

Jim scoots up the tree, cursing now and then when he scratches himself. He slips the rope over the limb and slides back down. Halfway down he puts his foot on a limb that snaps clean away and he falls the rest of the way, landing with a thud. Jesse giggles.

Bob comes up with his horse. Together they hoist me onto its back. I don't fight them. An idea has been coming to me.

I just might survive this.

Frank pulls the rope snug and ties off the other end to the tree. I look around at a fine Wyoming morning, birds coming out, squirrel racing up a nearby tree, snow-capped peaks in the distance. If I'm going to die here, there's worse places.

"Any last words?" Frank says.

"My spirit's coming after you. It won't rest until you're all dead."

Jesse pales and makes the sign of the cross, except he gets it backward. I'm not Catholic and even I know that.

"Goddamn it," Frank says to me in a low voice. "Would you knock that shit off? You already scared him. He's going to be up half the night shivering in his blankets now and I'll have to sit up with him."

I spit some Apache at him.

Frank shakes his head. "In the days to come, when I'm bored or tired, I'm going to think about your body, hanging here from this tree, the crows eating your eyes."

7

"The crows are smart enough to stay away from the body of an Apache warrior."

Frank shrugs and steps back. "I'm done with you." He looks at the others. "You got all his gear?"

"All loaded up," Cole says.

"Then mount up. We've got places to go and we've wasted enough time with this Injun."

Once they're all mounted up he smiles at me, showing me that gold tooth one more time. "Be seeing you," he says.

He swats the horse on the butt and it jerks forward. Suddenly there's nothing but air underneath my boots.

3

There's this thing about hanging.

It hurts. A lot.

And you can't breathe.

Lucky for me they didn't drop me, so my neck isn't broken. I also sucked in a big lungful of air right before, so I'm not going to die right away.

But it's sure as hell mighty unpleasant, that rope digging into my neck, backed with the knowledge that if my plan doesn't work, I've got only a couple minutes of life left.

With catcalls and other general signs of idiocy, my attackers gallop off. That was important. If they'd stuck around this would get real messy.

It might anyway.

Once I'm sure they're out of earshot, I can put my plan into action. I whistle for Coyote.

At least I try to. It doesn't work so well the first time. All that comes out is a rasping noise. Turns out whistling and hanging don't go together all that well.

This might not work.

I try again. It sounds a little more like a whistle this time, but it's sure not very loud. I listen, but I don't hear the sound of Coyote's hoofbeats.

How far away did he run?

I'm running out of time. Breath too. Whistling is cutting into what little air I have left. I maybe have one good try left in me.

It would be harder to think if my neck didn't hurt so much.

I try again, putting everything I have into it.

Then I wait, listening.

Nothing.

The world starts going black around the edges. I have a terrible desire to panic, to thrash about and fight with everything I have. It's all I can do not to give into it. Fighting will only kill me faster.

All at once Coyote is there, walking casually up to me like he's got all the time in the world. He shoves his nose into my chest, which starts me swinging, and gives me a look. I know what's in that look. He wants to know what crazy thing I'm doing now.

Waves of blackness are crashing over me. I'm almost out of time. I concentrate with everything I've got left, staring at him, willing him to understand.

Help me out here, brother. You're my only chance.

He lifts his head and shows me his teeth. That's Coyote. Sometimes he forgets he's a horse. I've told him over and over that horses don't do that, but he never listens.

There's a roaring in my ears and my vision has narrowed down to almost nothing.

Goodbye, brother. I'll see you on the great hunting grounds.

Coyote whickers, drops his head and walks underneath me, then stands there.

With the last of my strength I bring my knees together and push up. The rope loosens a tiny bit and air, beautiful air, rushes into my lungs. I suck it in greedily. Nothing will ever taste finer.

Coyote swishes his tail and takes a little sidestep. I nearly lose my balance and fall off.

He's not a patient horse.

"Hold on, Coyote," I rasp. "Give me a minute."

The air is bringing life back to my limbs. I pull my legs up so I'm crouching on his back.

The next part is going to be tricky.

I have to get my bound hands from behind me to in front of me. I'm going to have to jump up and at the same time swing my hands under my feet and bring them around front. I've done this before, but never half-strangled and standing on the back of an impatient horse.

I gather myself, flex the muscles in my legs, then jump and tuck, bringing my hands forward at the same time.

It works. I get my hands around in front of me. But Coyote spooks and jumps away and now I'm hanging again and this time I got a little drop to make it all worse. It feels like my head damn near gets pulled off.

But my hands are in front now and hands are wonderful things. I reach up and grab the rope. I feel weak—turns out hanging takes a lot out of a man—but I'm also desperate, and desperation is a powerful motivator.

I lift myself up a few inches, then a few inches more. Bit by bit, more slack, more air.

And now what?

I can't hang here forever and there's no way I can get the rope off my neck with my hands tied like this. A knife sure would come in handy at a time like this, but those weasels took mine.

There's nothing left but to climb.

Which I do. Hand over hand. A couple inches at a time, since the rope binding my hands won't allow any more.

It's slow, agonizing, and I want to give up a dozen times, but finally I reach that tree limb and with one last, painful effort, I pull myself up onto it.

What do you know? It's starting to look like I'm not gonna die today after all.

4

Lying there, clinging to that tree limb, I have a realization.

Hanging's a terrible thing.

I mean, I already knew that. But only in a distant kind of way. Now I know close up how terrible it is. I make a promise to myself to avoid it in the future.

I work my hands around and start on the knots with my teeth. It takes a while, but I've got nothing else to do and I finally get them loose. It feels good to have my hands back.

I pull the rope off my neck and toss it aside. Then I climb down the tree and after a minute I'm standing on solid ground once again. It's a powerfully good feeling, I have to say.

Coyote comes walking up and nuzzles me. He's never done that before. Coyote's not what you'd call an affectionate animal. He's more the biting and kicking type.

"It would've been easier if you stood still," I tell him.

And I already know his answer.

Why don't you try not getting yourself hung?

I hang onto his neck for a minute then, gathering my strength.

"We're going after them," I tell Coyote. "I got an angry spirit that needs some payback."

Those men got almost everything I own in the world. My Colt pistols. My Winchester Model 1873 rifle. The Spencer rifle. The money I earned over the winter. They even took my saddle and bridle.

But I still have Coyote, so I'm a long ways from done. I climb onto his back. I don't even need a saddle or a bridle for him. I can guide him with my knees and he'll go where I want.

Unless he's feeling cantankerous.

It's easy to pick up their trail, especially because they're not expecting anyone to follow them. They're going more or less south, which is good because I was heading that way.

I take it slow. I'm in no hurry to catch up to them. One unarmed man against five armed men?

"They don't have a chance," I tell Coyote. He swivels his ears back.

"This makes us even now, you know." He shakes his head and snorts. That may or may not mean he agrees with me. I saved Coyote a few years back from a man who was fixing to ride him to death. Now he saved me. It seems pretty clear to me that we're even, but there's no telling with Coyote. The horse gets peculiar ideas.

We follow their trail through the day. Along about dark I see the glow of their campfire. I slip down off Coyote and give him a pat on the rump.

"Stay out of sight," I tell him, even though I don't need to. He hates other horses almost as much as he hates people. He's not going to go try and make friends.

I soft foot it over to their camp. It would be nice to have my moccasins for this, but those are still in my saddlebags. They better not have thrown them away. My mother made those.

They're sitting around the fire, passing a clay jug around. The first thing I notice is there's only three of them. Frank and one of the idiot brothers are missing. I wonder where they went.

Jesse is cooking something in a pot hanging over the fire.

"I told you not to shoot that bird," Cole says.

"Good thing I didn't listen to you, or we'd be eating a whole lot of nothing," Jesse replies.

"You can't eat crow," Cole says. He takes a drink off the jug and passes it to his brother. It's either Bob or Jim, I can't remember which. Not that it probably matters all that much.

Jesse stirs the pot and gives Cole a hard look. "The hell you can't. Where'd you hear something stupid like that?"

"I heard it from my granny, back in Mississippi. You speaking ill of my granny?"

"I will when she says foolishness like that. Can't eat crow. What kind of nonsense is that?"

"It'll give you bad dreams. That's the straight truth."

"We et crow all the time back in Missouri," Jesse says. "Didn't we, Frank?" He looks around. "Oh, I forgot Frank and Jim went to town."

"I hope to hell they get back soon," Cole says. "With a whole load a supplies. Then we could toss out that damned crow and eat some real food."

"I thought I heard something a while ago," Bob says hopefully. He looks straight at me, but of course he can't see me, not with his night vision ruined by staring into the fire. Plus I'm hunkered down.

"No way they'd be back this soon," Jesse says. "An' if I know Frank, they won't be back at all tonight. He'll be drinking in the saloon all night." He sounds downright sad. "I still don't see why he took Jim instead of me."

"Weren't you listening?" Cole asks. "He said it plain as day. You're Frank and Jesse James. Half the country's looking for you. You show up together and the sheriff's sure to notice."

"I ain't afraid of no tinpot sheriff."

"He better not drink up all our coin," Cole says. "Better come back with some proper grub. I won't stand for eating trash birds."

You mean *my* coin, I think. It galls me, thinking about them going to town on my dime. I worked hard for that money.

"You don't quit complaining, you won't get any bird at all. Bob and I will eat it all."

"That suits me just fine." Cole looks at Bob. "Quit sucking on that jug. It ain't Mama's teat. Pass it on."

Bob scowls at him, but passes the jug along. "Tastes like kerosene anyhow. I wouldn't be surprised if that's what the old man sold us."

"What'd you expect for two bits?" Cole says. "Fine champagne?"

"Maybe something that won't kill me by morning." Bob thumps his chest. "There's something burning in here."

"You think you feel bad now, wait till you eat some of that crow," Cole says, taking a slug off the jug and grimacing.

Jesse pulls the spoon out of the pot and points it at him. "One more word, Cole. Just one more and you'll go hungry."

Cole glares at him but doesn't say anything. A few minutes pass and out of nowhere Jesse says, "You think it's true, what that Injun we hung said? You think he put an Apache death curse on us?"

"I don't want to talk about it," Cole says, taking another slug off the jug and choking. "It's just superstitious bullshit."

But he doesn't sound too sure about that and it gives me an idea.

5

I melt back into the bushes a bit. I haven't done this in a while. I hope I can still remember how.

I cup my hands around my mouth in a way I learned long ago and let loose.

What comes out sounds quite a lot like a great horned owl. I do it a couple more times then creep back closer to the fire.

It's working.

"Did you all hear that?" Jesse says, looking around with big eyes.

"I heard an owl," Bob says. "Is that what you're talking about?"

"Yes that's what I'm talking about, you idiot!" Jesse snaps.

"It's just an owl," Cole says, but he doesn't sound too confident.

While they're talking I creep around to the other side of their fire and let off a few more hoots.

"There's another one!" Jesse says, his head swiveling toward the new sound. "My grandma always said great horned owls is the messengers of death."

"Shut up," Cole says. "It ain't nothing but an owl. Maybe you ought to shoot it and add it to the pot too."

He talks brave, but I can see how tightly he's gripping that jug.

I creep around to a new spot and call some more.

"Goddamn!" Jesse yells, whirling to face the new sound. "They're all around us!"

"You cut that out, Jesse. You're getting Bob here all worked up," Cole says. But he's just as wide-eyed as Bob is.

I creep to a new spot and call some more.

Jesse drops the spoon, draws his pistol, and starts firing wild into the darkness. I'm stashed behind a tree so I'm safe, especially since he's firing up into the tops of the trees.

"Cut that out!" Cole yells. "You'll hit the horses!"

But Jesse doesn't quit until his gun is empty. He stands there, staring this way and that, his mouth open wide enough I could just about chuck a pine cone in there.

He turns back to the others. "You think it's that Apache, coming to haunt us?"

"Why would an Apache ghost make a sound like an owl?"

It's a reasonable question, but Jesse's past the reasonable stage. I think Cole is too, though he's trying to hide it. He takes a hasty gulp off the jug and wipes his mouth with the back of his hand.

"Remember that Cajun what moved into that shack in the hills when we was kids?" Bob asks. "He swore up and down there was spirits in the woods at night. He said they was Spaniards from the old days, what couldn't find rest and was looking for the flesh of the living to feed on."

"He was just saying that to scare you!" Cole barks, but he's got the jug pressed up tight to his chest and he's looking around like a mouse that knows the cat is coming.

I let off with a few more calls, then circle around and call some more.

Now they're all on their feet, guns in hand, staring off into the darkness.

"Psst," Jesse whispers. "Pass me that jug."

"Why you whispering?" Cole asks, but his voice is pitched real low too. "You think ghosts can't hear you if you whisper?"

"I didn't know ghosts had ears," Bob says, but the others ignore him.

"Ha! You think it's a spirit now too!" Jesse hisses. "Gimme that jug. I'm parched."

They stand there huddled together, passing the jug steadily. Now and then I let off with some more hoots, enough to keep them on edge. I hope Frank doesn't return about now. I've a feeling he wouldn't be so easy to fool.

An hour passes. No one eats any of the crow stew. They just keep passing the jug. They get a little woozy and tired and sit down.

I can't believe how easy they're making this for me. They're drunk enough now I could probably wait until they pass out and

17

walk in and take everything they got, my gear and their gear. That would be the smart thing to do.

But they've gone and gotten me all riled up. Bad enough they tried to hang me, but they insulted Coyote. I'm not letting that pass. I want these boys to pay. I aim to teach them a lesson they won't soon forget.

"Damn it," Jesse says.

"What?"

"I got to piss."

Cole looks at him blearily. "So go take a piss already."

Jesse stands up. He's weaving pretty good and almost falls on Bob, has to put his hand on Bob's head to steady himself. When he does he pushes the Bob's hat down over his eyes. Bob curses and pushes him away.

But Jesse doesn't go anywhere. He takes a half turn, unbuttons his trousers and lets fly.

"What in tarnation are you doing?" Cole squawks.

"It's running back this way!" Bob yells, trying to crawl away. "I got some on me!"

"I ain't going out there in the dark to piss," Jesse wails. "Not with that spirit roaming around."

"I was gonna sleep there," Cole complains. "Land sakes! I can't for the life of me figger out why yore mama didn't strangle you in your crib."

"You take that back!" Jesse yells, turning his head to glare at Cole. Unfortunately, this causes him to lose his balance and he topples over, still peeing.

"Aauughh!" Bob hollers. "He peed on my back!" He tries to get up but falls straight back down. Jesse is thrashing around, piss spraying everywhere and both brothers are fighting to get away from him.

It's all I can do to not bust out laughing. I have to move away a bit until I get a hold of myself.

When I sneak back up to the fire both brothers are glaring at Jesse.

"I'm gonna hafta take a bath now," Bob says. "I hate baths."

"It coulda happened to anybody," Jesse protests.

"If it wasn't for what Frank would do, I'd shoot you right now," Cole says. He's rubbing at his leg, which has a big wet spot on it. "Swear to god, I never seen anybody piss so much in my life. Was your mama a horse?"

"Told you I had to go," Jesse says sullenly.

After a bit they get themselves sorted out, put some more wood on the fire and slump down around it. It isn't long before they're all snoring peacefully. Seems whatever is in that jug is stronger than their fear.

I stand up and walk into their camp. It's time for the fun part of my plan.

6

First thing I do is take their shooting irons. I don't think any of these boys are going to be waking up anytime soon, but it's best to be sure.

Then I dig around in the pile of gear until I find my gun belt and buckle it on. I check the loads in my Colts and drop them back in their holsters.

I dig out my saddle and saddlebags. I go through the saddlebags. It looks like all they took was my cash and a handful of jerky I had. Both my rifles are in the pile too. I carry my gear back into the trees and whistle for Coyote, then saddle him up and tie everything into place.

Hanging off my gun belt behind the right holster is the sheath holding my knife. It's a big knife, of the type some call an Arkansas toothpick and others call a Bowie knife. Whatever you call it, it's a fearsome-looking weapon.

It also has a variety of uses.

I go back over to the fire and add a little wood so the flames come up. Then I sit down and empty the cartridges from all three of their guns. It takes a little while, but I pry the slugs out of every one of those cartridges. Then I put them back into the pistols and give the boys their guns back.

Only one thing left to do.

I dig a handful of cold ashes up from the edge of the fire and go to work, smearing them on my face and neck and hands, wherever the skin is showing. I also pat some into my clothes and hat.

Now all I need to do is wait. I want the fire to die down a bit and I want to let the boys sleep off some of their drunk. The way they're snoring, I'm not sure I could wake them up right now if I tried.

I use the extra time to take care of some other details. I go take the hobbles off their horses and chouse them until they run off into the darkness. Then I gather up their saddles, saddlebags, bed rolls, everything I can lay hands on and haul it all off into the darkness.

It's not far to the stream I heard off on the other side of their camp. It's down in the bottom of this sharp-sided little gulch. I pitch their gear off over the edge and watch it wash away.

I look at the stars and when it's a couple hours after midnight I reckon it's time to get started. Just one more detail. I bust open a couple cartridges, pull out the wadding holding the gunpowder in, and dump the gunpowder into my hand. That should add a little extra flair to the show.

The fire has died down too much, so I add a few twigs, enough so that they can see dimly, but not enough for them to really see well.

With a pistol in one hand and that wicked big knife in the other I stand at the edge of their camp, throw my head back and let loose with the most bloodcurdling war cry I know. I really let them have it, putting everything I got into it.

They start and jerk upright, looking around them. Dazed by sleep and alcohol as they are, at first they don't see me.

I give another wild howl and follow it with the most evil laugh I can muster. I toss the gunpowder in my hand into the fire, so it hisses and flares up.

They all look up at me at once, their eyes as big around as dinner plates.

"Time to die!" I yell at them, waving the pistol and the knife around. I must look like a proper ghost to them, gray as death.

"It's that Injun!" Jesse hollers. "He's come for vengeance!"

I stalk toward them, giving them my fiercest, craziest look. They thrash about, making frightened puppy noises. Cole is the first one to lay his hands on his gun.

He picks it up and points it at me. His hands are shaking like mad and he can barely cock it.

"You ain't taking me, foul spirit!" he yells, and cuts loose.

The shots are loud, but of course they do nothing, since the lead is all gone. More shots follow as the other two take up their weapons and unload too.

Through it all I laugh and laugh.

When their guns click on empty I wave circles in the air with that damn big knife. "You think mere bullets can stop me?" I yell. "Nothing can stop me! Tonight I will feast on your hearts!"

I charge at them.

What little courage they still had left deserts them then. They squall like stuck pigs, throw their guns down and run.

The problem is they still have quite a lot of that poison liquor in their guts and they can't quite get their limbs to do what they tell them to. Jesse falls down twice. The second time Bob steps right in the center of his back, then also falls down.

Cole makes it about three steps and runs smack into a tree. He topples over, then jumps back up. There's blood streaming down his face and he's yelling bloody murder. He doesn't make it far before he runs into another tree.

Jesse and Bob make it to their feet about the same time. Jesse shoves Bob, making him fall down. But Bob's not going without a fight and as soon as he hits the ground he kicks out with both legs, tripping Jesse up before he can get away.

I howl and fire my gun into the air a couple of times and that gets them worked up even more.

Cole is crying and moaning, his face an awful, bloody mess. He runs bent over, his face in his hands, and right away trips over a fallen tree. He goes down hard, his shirt catching on one of the fallen tree's limbs and ripping badly.

Jesse shrieks and jumps back to his feet, colliding with Bob who has just done the same. They go down in a tangle and start clawing at each other. I take up a half-burned limb from the fire and throw it at them.

"The spirit's got me!" Jesse yells, swinging his arms wildly.

Bob leaps to his feet and takes off screaming. Jesse follows and right behind him is Cole.

I let them go. It's probably best to get on down the road, put some miles between me and them before Frank gets back and talks some sense into them.

I whistle for Coyote and we ride off into the night.

7

I don't think I'll have any more trouble with those fools, but to be safe I ride on through the night and don't stop until the end of the next day. I make sure I set up camp in an area with lots of pine needles on the ground and no streams nearby. It's next to impossible to sneak through those needles without making noise and it's quiet enough that I can hear if someone tries. The problem with my last camp is I got careless and set up too close to a stream. The water drowned out the noise of them sneaking up on me.

"Aren't you supposed to warn me when someone is coming?" I ask Coyote as I pull the saddle off him.

Coyote twitches his ears at me. He's made it clear all along that he's not responsible for my health and welfare.

"You're right," I say, giving him a pat on the neck. "There's no need to rub it in."

Coyote wanders off to graze and I head on down the hillside toward a beaver dam I can see in the bottom of the canyon. There should be some fat trout in there and if I can catch a couple I'll have a fine dinner.

I pass a quiet night and continue on south the next day. I'm following the spine of the Rocky Mountains and by my reckoning I should be into Colorado by now, but it's not like there's any signs or anything.

I'm heading for Leadville. Now that all my coin is gone I'm going to need a new grubstake. I can live off the land all right, but there's some things I can't get on my own, like ammo and new shoes for Coyote. Heck, I could use some new shoes myself. The left boot has a big old hole in the sole and the newspaper I folded up and stuck in there is about worn through too.

Leadville is a rip-snorting place, a true mining boom town, and I should be able to find work there. Strangely enough, though you wouldn't know it from the name, Leadville is built on just about the richest silver deposits ever found. Why they didn't name it Silverville is beyond me. Maybe that name was already taken.

I get to Leadville a couple days later in the late afternoon. The town sits high up in the mountains and there's lots of snow still on the ground. Smoke and tailings piles mark the numerous mines dotting the surrounding mountainsides. There's a steady hum of heavy machinery that kind of rumbles through the ground underfoot. From what I hear that machinery runs night and day. Gotta get that silver out before it melts away, I guess.

I ride on into the town proper and it doesn't take long to figure out Leadville's reputation as a hardscrabble place is well-earned.

The main street is mostly saloons, one after the other. Music and drunken laughter spill out of them. Drunks stumble up and down the street and though it's early there's already a couple lying motionless in the gutters, drunk or dead I can't tell.

I come on a small building wedged between two saloons. The rough sign on the front says "Laundry." As I ride by the door opens and two men come out, dragging a third man between them. They throw him into the street, practically at Coyote's feet. One of them rips the sign down off the wall and throws it on top of the man, who's lying there groaning.

"Don't try coming back, neither," one of the men hisses. "Or it's…" He draws his thumb across his throat.

The other man looks up at me. He's got so much hair I can barely see his face but his eyes are hard. "What are you looking at? You want some of what he got?"

I shake my head and pull back my duster, letting him see my twin Colts. He glares at them for a second, then kicks the man on the ground and follows his partner back into the building.

The man on the ground comes unsteadily to his feet. He's kind of a little guy, going bald, wearing a stained apron. He picks up the sign.

"Just like that, they stole my place," he says. He wipes his eyes. "I built that with my own two hands."

That surprises me. I've heard of horses being stolen, cattle, guns, money, basically anything a body can move or carry, but I never heard of someone stealing a whole building. "What about the sheriff?" I ask.

"The sheriff," the man snorts. "Unless your name's Horace Tabor or you got a fistful of silver, Bill Hickey don't give a good goddamn what happens to you." He looks at the sign again and shakes his head sadly. "It's all gone." He tucks the sign under one arm and wanders off down the street.

A bit further on is a bank. In the door is a man in a suit. He's got a gold watch chain running across his stomach and he's smoking a cigar. Next to him is a rough-looking character toting a shotgun, probably a bank guard.

Standing out in the street in front of the bank is a miner, his beard white and full. Based on the funny suspenders he's wearing, I'd guess he's a Dutchman, and when he starts yelling I know for sure from his accent.

"The devil take your hide, Smithson! Vos it your money or mine?" the old Dutchman yells. He's weaving as he stands there, clearly blind drunk.

"It's your money, Hans," the banker says calmly.

"Then open the safe and give me some."

The banker puffs on his cigar. "No."

"Damn your soul! You gif me my money!"

"Not until you're sober," the banker says.

"So I drink a little." Hans holds up his hand, fingers an inch apart. "What difference does that make?"

"You told me very clearly not to let you withdraw any of your money when you're drunk, Hans, because you'd only waste it. As your banker I intend to honor those conditions."

"That's it!" Hans yells. "I shoot you so full of holes you leak like a busted pot!" Hans has a truly ancient pistol stuck in his waistband and he pulls it out and promptly drops it in the mud.

He picks it up but he's too drunk to draw back the hammer. Furious, he throws the gun at the banker, but misses badly. He peers up at me.

"You shoot him I make you rich man."

"I don't think so, old-timer," I say and continue on.

Maybe stopping here isn't such a good idea. But it's not like I have a lot of options. I hate the thought of it, but I know there's work to be had in those mines and I've heard the pay is better than cowboying. If I can put up with it for a couple of weeks, I should end up with enough for a decent grubstake. At least enough to get on down the road a piece.

I come to a mercantile. That seems like a good place to get some information, find out who to talk to about a job. I get down and loop Coyote's reins over the hitching post.

I never tie Coyote or hobble him. I put him in a corral now and then when I'm in town, but that's so he can get some hay and oats and I know he can break out of just about any corral ever built if he's of a mind to.

What people don't get is that Coyote isn't mine in the usual sense. I don't own him. I bailed him out of a tough situation, when a man was fixing to kill him in the name of breaking him. I busted the man up before he could carry through with it and paid the owner of the ranch for Coyote. In return, Coyote seems to have agreed to carry me around when I need to get places. I say "seems to" because I can't always be sure of what Coyote's thinking. He's tricky, even for a horse.

No, the way I see it, me and Coyote, we're partners. I help him and he helps me. But if he wants out, I won't stop him. He can leave whenever he wants.

I pull his head close before I head on into the store. "I'd appreciate it if you didn't pick today to pull up stakes and leave without me. I don't believe this is a good town to get stranded in."

Coyote makes a sort of whuffing sound which I hope means he agrees with me.

Tacked to the wall of the mercantile is a wanted poster, but it's not like any wanted poster I've ever seen. It's for a bear, instead of a man. My reading isn't the best, but I can muddle through when I want and from what I pick up the bear is a grizzly and they call him Old Mose. It seems Old Mose has been killing livestock and the odd hunter sent after him.

I can't blame Old Mose. Probably that old bear doesn't understand the whole idea of livestock ownership. As for the dead hunters? Well, even a bear's got a right to defend himself.

Still, it's something to keep in mind. The three hundred dollars they're offering as a reward would go a long ways.

I'm reaching for the door knob when someone calls out behind me.

"Hey you! With the ugly horse! Your kind ain't welcome around here!"

8

I turn around slowly, at the same time easing my duster back so I can get at my pistols. I'm thinking anyone stupid enough to call Coyote ugly probably needs shooting.

There's two men standing in the street, hats pulled down low, guns slung even lower and tied down. The one on the right's chewing on a matchstick. It looks like he's been trying to grow a beard, but it's just a wispy thing, hardly worthy of the name, more like peach fuzz. His partner doesn't even have that, but he sure has a lot of pimples. They're both young, younger even than I am, and I peg them right away.

I know this type. They fancy themselves gunslicks and they're out to make a name for themselves. They have an idea they can speed the whole thing up by starting a fight with me.

They're wrong.

"What kind is that?" I ask them.

"Injuns," Peach Fuzz says.

"We don't like 'em," Pimples adds.

"And so you aim to run me out of town?"

"Or put you down. It's your choice." They're acting tough, but I can see the tremor in Peach Fuzz's hands and Pimple's voice sounds a little high. They're new at this and finding out it's maybe a little harder than they thought.

"But first we'll take those fancy shootin' irons you're packing," Peach Fuzz says.

"You mean these?" I say, and draw.

Just like that the Colts are in my hands, pointing at them. Their eyes fairly bug out of their heads. It happened so fast they didn't even have a chance to go for their guns. They were thinking there's be a bit more talking before it got to that stage, I guess.

"How'd you do that?" Pimples says.

"Maybe I was just lucky. You want to try again?"

I drop the Colts back into my holsters.

"Are you ready this time?"

They look at each other, then at me. Peach Fuzz nods, but I can see his heart's no longer in it.

I draw again, both guns pointing at them before they can so much as get a good hold on their weapons. Now they're both looking pretty pasty.

"Maybe you fellows made a mistake," I suggest.

"You may be right," Peach Fuzz allows.

"I think we have you confused with someone else," Pimples adds. "The light's not too good, this time of day."

Peach Fuzz looks at him. "I think we left the candle burning in our room. We don't want to be responsible for burning the whole hotel down." He starts backing away.

"You're right," Pimples says, backing up too. "I just remembered that too. We better go take care of that right away."

"Have a nice day," Peach Fuzz says, touching his hat brim.

"Enjoy your stay in Leadville," Pimples adds. They both turn tail and high step it out of there.

I chuckle and put my guns away. Hopefully those boys learned something that will keep them alive long enough to realize how dumb they really are. Most folks in this town probably wouldn't go so easy on them.

Across the street is a real fancy place, five stories tall and made of red brick. It's painted up in all kinds of bright red and gold colors. It has pillars out front and fancy swirls and such along the top. The sign out front says Tabor Hotel and Fine Restaurant.

What draws my attention to it is the door just opened and a man has come out. He's clearly heading for me and from the serious look on his face he means business.

I step out into the street and watch him come. He's a thick-bodied feller, solid top to bottom. The kind who at first looks fat, but when you look closer you can see all kinds of muscle packed underneath. He's got no neck that I can see and deep set, angry-looking eyes. He's bald and has a bowler hat perched on top of his head. He's wearing a black suit. He's got a gun on his hip, but from the looks of him, this is a man who'd rather use his hands on you.

"You there," he says when he gets close. "The boss wants to talk to you. Come on."

29

9

I don't move. "Who says I want to talk to your boss?"

No-Neck is so sure I'll come when he calls that he's already turning away. Now he freezes and turns slowly back to face me. His eyes slit down so they almost disappear completely.

"In that case it will go very bad for you, mister." He cracks his knuckles. He has very large hands. "What Mr. Tabor wants, Mr. Tabor gets."

"So you work for Mr. Tabor. By any chance is he the same Tabor whose name is on the sign?"

"One and the same."

"And he wants to talk to me. Why?"

"That's for him to tell you."

I look at the building again. The bottom floor is mostly big, gilt-edged windows. The sun has gone down by now and I can see through those windows. I'm looking at some kind of first-class restaurant, way beyond anything I've ever been in. There's a man sitting alone at a table by the window, watching us.

"Is that him there?"

No-Neck nods. Or tries to. Without a neck it's hard to tell. I'll take it as a nod.

I consider this. It's not like I have a lot going on right now. A job in the mine holds no appeal. It seems unlikely that this Mr. Tabor would be having me come into his restaurant just to murder me. I'd get blood all over the fancy tablecloths, which would probably be bad for business.

Besides which, saying no likely means I'd have to fight No-Neck here and that looks like a real iffy proposition.

"Okay, let's go talk to Mr. Tabor then."

No-Neck looks a mite disappointed at this. Maybe Mr. Tabor hasn't fed him yet today and he was hoping to take a few bites out of me. He swings around and stumps off toward the hotel.

"You could have just said please," I say to his back, which is wide enough to hang several signs off of, while still leaving room for a wanted poster or two.

He stops abruptly and swings around to face me. He looks me up and down and what he sees makes the corners of his thick mouth turn down.

"A smart ass, eh? Is that what you are?"

"My momma always said, 'Better a smart ass than a dumb ass.'" Which isn't true, but I like the saying.

The tip of his tongue pokes out of those fleshy lips, swipes around a bit, then pulls back. "I'm of a mind to tear you in half right now."

"But you won't, because it's Sunday and you promised your dying mother you wouldn't get yourself killed on a Sunday." As soon as the words leave my mouth I wonder why I said them. Why rile this walking brick shithouse any more than he already is? Do I not have enough enemies already?

He nods and a little smile hits his doughy face. "I won't because Mr. Tabor hasn't said to yet." He points a sausage finger at me. "But when he does..."

"I'll be waiting for you with flowers." Oops, there I go again.

I follow No-Neck through the door. Inside, the place is even fancier than I thought. There's a fountain bubbling away in the middle of the room, an actual fountain. Fancy wallpaper thick with flowers. The ceiling is pressed tin painted gold. Or maybe it actually is gold. Against the back wall is a bar with a big mirror behind it. In front of the mirror are more kinds of liquor than I thought existed in the whole world. The rugs on the floor are deep and thick and waiters wearing red vests scurry everywhere.

"I brought him, boss," No-Neck says when we reach the table where Mr. Tabor is sitting.

"It's hardly necessary to tell him," I say. "He can plainly see me standing here beside you." Why do I keep needling the man? It's like poking a bear to see if it will maul you.

"Thank you, Wallace," Tabor says. "Go get yourself a drink while I have a chat with my guest."

Wallace gives me a pig-eyed glare and stumps off to the bar. The floor shakes with each step. It's like being in the same room with a bull.

"Please, have a seat," Tabor says, gesturing to an empty chair. "Would you care for a drink?" He holds up a hand and a waiter darts forward.

31

I drag out a chair and sit down. "Sure. A drink sounds good."

"What will you have, sir?" the waiter asks.

"Whatever you have, so long as it's not rotgut."

"I assure you we do not have such a spirit here."

"Bring him a mint julep," Tabor says. As the waiter scurries away he says to me, "It's a hot-weather drink that is popular in the South. On these cold days when it seems spring will never arrive I like to drink them. It reminds me that somewhere it is actually warm."

"I just spent the winter in Montana."

"The winds there blow straight down from the North Pole I hear." He shivers as he says this. Tabor isn't a big man, with narrow shoulders and a neck that's too long and thin, like someone tried to hang him and didn't finish the job. The thought makes my hand go to my neck. The skin is still raw. Tabor notices, but says nothing about it.

The waiter brings the drink and I take a slug. It tastes weird, with none of the burning I've learned to associate with liquor. Maybe it's not an alcoholic drink at all. I set it down.

"Unless you're in the habit of buying drinks for random drifters, I guess you called me in here for a reason," I tell Tabor.

"Straightforward and direct. I like that," Tabor says, steepling his fingers. His suit looks like it's made of silk, if such a thing is possible. I've only ever seen hankies made of the stuff. His hair is black, neatly trimmed, parted in the middle and heavily slicked down with a thick layer of pomade. His mustache is bushy, the ends hanging down past his chin.

I finish the drink.

"Another?" Tabor asks.

"Maybe something with alcohol in it this time?"

Tabor smiles. It's not a friendly smile, so much as the smile of a man who is used to having whatever he wants and now has found something new he wants.

"Bring Mr...." He hesitates, looking for my name.

"Ace."

"Mr. Ace—"

"Not Mr. Ace, just Ace."

His smile broadens. "Excellent! Bring Ace a scotch. Neat." He raises an eyebrow at me. "Will that do?"

I don't know what scotch is, and I don't know what's neat about it, but I nod. I might as well try new things while I have the chance.

"Ace, I am Horace Tabor."

"The man on the sign."

"Indeed." He doesn't offer his hand. "I was fortunate enough to have a fine seat from which to watch your performance out there." He waves a hand at the street, which is quickly growing dark. There are two gas lamps on iron stands out front of the hotel and a man is lifting the glass chimneys and lighting them.

"You're quite the hand with those pistols, Ace," he continues.

I shrug. "I've had some practice."

"Ah, your modesty becomes you. Truly I have never seen anyone so fast. The word lightning comes to mind."

"Is there a point to this?"

A frown crosses his face and is quickly gone. He leans forward. His hands are very small, the nails polished so they shine.

"Ace, I would like to offer you a job."

10

That perks me right up. "What sort of job?"

Tabor smiles happily and leans back in his chair. "As my bodyguard, of course."

I glance over at Wallace, who is standing stiffly at the bar, glaring at me. "Don't you already have a bodyguard?"

"I have five of them, to be precise."

"But you want another?"

"I do." There's that smug look on his face again. Maybe being rich makes you want things just for the sake of having them.

"Why?"

"They are so boring, so ordinary. But you, you are exotic, dashing. With your long hair and your noble features you cut quite a figure. I assume you are a half-breed? What tribe?"

"My mother is Apache." As soon as I say the words, I regret them. The way he's looking at me, like I'm some kind of animal he's never seen before, I don't like it much.

He claps his hands together. "Perfect! Even better than I'd hoped! My own Apache bodyguard."

"I never said I'd take the job."

"But of course you will, Ace. Look at you." His gesture takes in my general shabbiness. "Your hat has seen better days, to put it mildly. Your shirt is little more than rags. Your boots, well, I would be willing to wager at least one of them has a hole in the bottom. When you crossed the street, did you perhaps step in any mud? And did some enter into your boot uninvited?"

He's right. I did get some mud in my boot through the hole in the bottom. But that doesn't make me like him any more. I don't like the feeling of being somebody's prize pony.

"In short, Ace, my Apache friend, you are a man down on his luck. Why would you not consent to hire on as my bodyguard? It pays sixty dollars a week."

Sixty dollars a week? That's twice what I made in a month cowboying over the winter.

He wags a finger at me. "But that's not all. You will also receive a room in this fine hotel, free of charge. Meals and drinks here in the restaurant as well."

My stomach has the very bad timing to growl right then. I haven't eaten all day and whatever they're cooking in the kitchen smells heavenly.

Tabor's smile grows even bigger. If it gets any larger his face is going to split in half.

"One more benefit, before you give me your answer. Your new position will, of course, come with a brand new wardrobe. Hat, boots, gun belt, everything." He laces his hands over his stomach. "What do you say now?"

I don't know what to say. In truth, it sounds mighty fine. I still don't much like the idea of this man parading me around like a pet monkey, but I do like the sound of the pay and the new clothes. The idea of sleeping on a real bed and doing a little fattening up at this fine restaurant makes it all the sweeter.

"You just got yourself a new hand, Tabor."

"Splendid! And please, call me Mr. Tabor."

He's still smiling, but there's a glint in his eye. It occurs to me then that he may look soft, he may look foolish, but there's more to him than that. No man gets to where he's at without some claws. I would be smart to remember that.

"No problem, Mr. Tabor."

He waves Wallace over. "Wallace here will show you to your room and the maid will set you up with a bath. Order whatever you like to eat and drink and someone from the wait staff will bring it by your room. Tomorrow we'll get you set up with a new wardrobe and then you can begin your duties. Don't worry about your horse. I'll have a man take him to the livery."

"Tell him to watch his hands," I say. "Coyote likes to bite."

"Follow me," Wallace says. If it's possible, he looks even unhappier than he did before. This has got to stick in his craw. I, of course, have to push it down a bit further.

"It must be rough," I tell him as we walk down a hallway paneled richly in dark wood, "losing your position so quickly to a complete stranger. But I promise you I will not hold it over you."

35

He turns to look at me. Without a neck, this requires turning his whole upper body. He bares his teeth. Strangely, one of them has been sharpened.

"I've lost nothing to you," he growls. "You're a novelty and he'll grow tired of you."

"How do you know he hasn't grown tired of you? Gorillas make awful pets I hear. So hard to house break." I saw a picture of a gorilla once and I'd say Wallace is at least a close relative.

We go around a corner. I'm on the inside of the turn and as we make it Wallace takes a step to the side and basically flattens me against the wall. I lose most of the air in my lungs.

"Oops," he says.

"I really should watch where I'm going."

"Careless people get hurt all the time."

"I'll keep that in mind."

We start up some stairs. They're not the main stairs I saw when I came in. These are narrow and at the back of the hotel. Probably for staff. The stairs are steep, the stairwell dimly lit.

"A man fell down these a while back," Wallace says conversationally. "Bounced all the way to the bottom. Broke his neck."

"He should have been more careful."

"They weren't sure if the broken neck killed him, or the knife wound in his back."

"Somehow he fell on his own knife on the way down? Is that what you're saying?"

"Something like that."

"Was he a friend of yours?"

"Not anymore."

We go all the way to the fourth floor. There's only one more floor above us. Wallace points up at it. "The top floor belongs to the boss and his missus. Never go up there."

We walk down the hall. There's a half dozen doors. The hall is richly carpeted and brightly lit with gas lamps. The wood is highly polished. He leads me to the last door and fishes a key out of his pocket. He unlocks the door and pushes it open.

"This room is yours."

I poke my head inside. It's even nicer than I'd expected. A big, four-poster bed with a canopy. Crystal lamps. A glass door leading out to a small balcony. "I guess it will do for now," I say.

"Don't wander off," he rumbles and starts to leave.

"Hey!" He turns ponderously. I hold out my hand. "The key?"

He shakes his head. The way he does it puts me in mind of a bull shaking his head before charging. "I'll hang onto it for now." He drops it back in his coat pocket and lumbers away. "Sweet dreams," he calls over his shoulder. "Maybe I'll look in on you later, make sure you haven't had an unfortunate accident."

"You mean like falling out the window?"

"Something like that." An odd rumbling sound comes from him and it takes me a moment to realize he's laughing.

11

I eat good, get all cleaned up, sleep like the dead on that big, soft bed and in the morning here comes Wallace to fetch me. He stands in the doorway and fills it completely. The bowler hat he's wearing looks no bigger than a thimble against the sheer mass of his head.

"Come," he says. His face looks like it's chipped out of granite.

"Good morning!" I say cheerily, but he doesn't respond, only backs out of the room and stands waiting in the hall. I put on my duster. "So I guess you're not a morning person then?" No response. No expression.

He stumps on down the stairs. His coat is stretched so tight over his shoulders that I wouldn't be surprised to see all the seams suddenly pop at once.

"Before I leave town, you simply have to give me the name of the tentmaker who sews all your clothes," I say.

Nothing.

"This is no fun if we don't both play," I tell him. He doesn't seem to care either way. Or maybe he's deeply upset and doesn't know how to show it.

We reach the ground floor and walk right on by the entrance to the restaurant without slowing down. "Hey!" I say. "What about breakfast?"

Without breaking stride, one ham hand shoots out and grabs onto the scruff of my duster. Just like that I find myself being dragged along beside him like a puppy.

"Didn't your mother ever teach you to keep your hands to yourself?" I ask.

He opens the front door and shoves me outside. I slip on the ice and nearly fall down. It's cold and my breath freezes in my lungs. There aren't any clouds and the sun is blindingly bright.

"Where are we off to?"

His answer is a shove. This time I'm ready so at least I don't slip on the ice.

38

We go down the street, around a corner, and I discover that Leadville has more than one street. That makes it one of the biggest towns I've ever been in. Maybe the biggest.

We come to a building with "Haberdashery" painted on the window. Wallace jerks the door open and shoves me inside.

The place is full of men's clothes and such. Hats, belts, boots, ties. Other stuff I don't recognize.

"So this is a haberdashery," I say. "Who knew there was such a thing?"

The shopkeeper is evidently expecting me because he leaves the man he is helping and hustles me to the back of the shop where has me stand on this little stool. The man he was helping is standing there in a jacket without any sleeves and a bunch of pins sticking out everywhere. He looks irate, but then glances at Wallace and shuts his mouth.

The shopkeeper is a little guy with a bald head and tiny, round spectacles. He's wearing suspenders and has a cloth measuring tape around his neck and a bunch of pins sticking out the corner of his mouth.

Right away he starts measuring my arms and shoulders. He measures my neck. Then down the outside of my leg. But when he starts measuring the inside of my leg he gets a little too up close and personal and I push him back.

"Now hold on there, pardner," I tell him. "You and I haven't even been properly introduced yet."

He looks alarmed and his head swivels toward Wallace who has pulled a copy of the Leadville newspaper out of his pocket and is sitting in a chair by the window reading it. Without looking up, Wallace rumbles, "Quit your yapping. He's measuring your in-seam."

Right. Like that means anything to me. "What's an in-seam?" I ask the little man. "And why do you need to know how long mine is?"

"It's the length of the inside seam on your pant leg. So I can make your pants the right length."

I look around and see a pair on a hanger nearby. "There's no need for all that. That pair there looks like it will do fine."

The little man looks shocked at my suggestion. "Not for Mr. Tabor, it's not."

With a sigh, Wallace gets up, shoves the paper back in his pocket and lumbers over to me. Hands that would fit better on a bear clamp down on my shoulders. "Now there, Mr. Adler," he says to the little man. "Measure away."

The little man finishes with my in-seam and then measures my foot. He scribbles some numbers on a little pad of paper and says, "Very good, very good. I will have everything ready by the end of the day."

"What's all this?" the other customer says. "You told me it would be two days before my coat was ready and now he gets the works in one day?"

"You're not Mr. Tabor," the little man says, as if that explains everything.

And apparently it does, because the other customer shuts right up. The fact that Wallace looks like he could eat him whole probably helps him make up his mind.

Wallace grabs my arm and shoves me out the door of the shop. "Use your words, Wallace," I tell him firmly.

He scowls at me.

"You know, words? Those sounds you make with your mouth?"

He shoves me again.

"I'm glad we could have this little talk," I tell him as we make our way back to the hotel, my progress aided by a periodic shove. "I think we're going to be friends."

Once again we pass the restaurant and go up the stairs. He shoves me into my room.

"A maid will bring you food," he says. "You wait here until I come get you at the end of the day." He closes the door and I hear the key turn in the lock.

Did he really just lock me in here?

I try the door knob. Sure enough he did.

Damned if I'll sit in here all day. I open the door that leads out onto the little balcony and look out over the edge. Up or down, I'm getting out of here.

12

There's a ledge along the face of the building. It's only a couple of inches wide, but that's all I need. More than I need, actually. I spent a lot of my youth climbing on the cliffs around Pa-Gotzin-Kay, the stronghold where my clan is holed up in northern Mexico. I reckon I can climb just about anything. Making it even easier is a row of bricks about head high that sticks out an inch or so.

Before I can spend too much time thinking about it and maybe change my mind, I go over the railing and out onto that ledge. I cling there, thinking it seems a little narrower than it looked. But I'm in now and I'm too stubborn to turn back. Which is probably one of my larger failings as a man.

I scoot along to the corner of the building and ease around it, which is a little tricky because the wind picks up right about then. But I don't fall and die so all is well.

At the back corner of the hotel I can see an outside staircase leading down to the street. It's good to know I have a way down.

What's not so good is that the ledge I'm on runs out about ten feet short of the staircase.

I really need to start thinking things through a bit more before I act. In my defense, though, Wallace made me angry. All that shoving gets under a feller's skin, you know?

I go to the end of the ledge and study my options. There's some kind of drain spout sticking out about halfway to the staircase. It looks pretty solid.

I hope it's solid.

I jump and grab onto it. Naturally, it rips away from the building. But in the half second while it's still attached, I kind of scrabble on the wall and manage to push off again, giving me just enough to get to the stairs. I stand there for a moment to calm down a bit, then try the door leading inside. It's locked so I head on down. Probably better this way. I won't have to worry about running into Wallace.

I get to ground level and look up and down the street. Time to explore Leadville.

Lots of saloons. I mean, lots of saloons. Just about every building on the main street houses a saloon, even ones that don't look like it. I stick my head into one place, not much bigger than a shoebox. The sign on the outside says "Dry Goods", but inside they're only selling wet goods, of the kind you drink.

The laundry I passed yesterday, where the men threw the owner out into the street? It's now a saloon too, with a rough counter nailed up against one of the walls and the oldest man I've ever seen carrying trays of drinks to an unruly crowd of loud, dirty, unshaven miners.

The saloons don't interest me. For one thing I've got no money to spend in them. For another it's barely midmorning. I've learned that when I start drinking this early the day generally doesn't turn out all that well. Too many hours to make a damn fool out of myself.

I turn up one of the side streets and step into the first shop I see. The sign says "Dresses" but my short time in Leadville has made me skeptical. More than likely it's another saloon.

Surprisingly enough, it's full of dresses. Big, frilly hats too. A woman bustles over when she hears the door open. Her eyes take me in and the big smile on her face fades. "Oh," she says. "If it's a saloon you're looking for, you'll have to go next door."

I remember my manners and take off my hat. "No, ma'am. I'm not."

She frowns a little. "You're looking to buy a dress?"

"Not at the moment, no."

She puts one hand to her throat. "Then I must confess I am at a loss as to why you are here."

"I'm new to town. Just looking to get the lay of the place." I hook a thumb over my shoulder. "Your main street seems to be nothing but saloons."

She sighs and nods. "It's no fit place for any lady, that's for sure."

"I saw a man take a donkey into one."

"That's Milo," she says. "You won't believe it to look at him, but he's worth hundreds of thousands of dollars. He owns the Surefire Mine. He claims the donkey is the one who found the

42

mine and has made the animal half owner. Therefore, suitable to take anywhere he pleases. Why, just last week he brought the creature into the church!"

"I guess that explains why the donkey was wearing a top hat then."

"If you'll take my advice, Mr...."

"Ace. But no mister. Just Ace."

"If you'll take my advice, Mr. Ace, you'll head on out of this vile place, this nest of vipers. You'll go and never look back, that's what you'll do."

"That's surely good advice, ma'am, but I'm broke and I just took a job working for Mr. Tabor."

Her eyes grow very wide and she pulls out a lacy kerchief and flutters it around her face. "Sakes alive, Mr. Ace! But he is the beating heart of all this wickedness and evil you see around you. How can you work for the likes of him?"

"Uh...broke?"

"You don't know what you signed up for. Come here. Look." She takes me to the window and pushes a dress aside so I can see out. "You see that woman over there?"

On the other side of the street, sitting on a bench in front of a shop is a woman. She looks to be in her fifties somewhere. She's wearing a bonnet tied down tight to her head and a voluminous dress with more petticoats than a dog has fleas. Over the dress is a thick, quilted jacket.

"That is Augusta Tabor."

"As in Horace Tabor? His wife?"

"The same."

"I haven't seen her around the hotel."

"And you won't. Horace divorced her last year to marry a young hussy by the name of Baby Doe! Oh, it was a proper scandal, absolutely rocked Leadville society, it did!"

She looks terribly shocked, nostrils flaring, hanky waving like mad. I can see she wants me to join her so I do my best to look concerned, though I can't see any reason why either of us should care who Horace does or doesn't marry.

"Why he would toss aside a fine, upstanding woman like Augusta is beyond me," she says.

I look back at Augusta. Her mouth is hard and grim and the look in her eyes says she hasn't wasted much of her life on such foolishness as smiling. So off-hand I can think of at least one reason why a body wouldn't want to be married to her, but I keep it to myself.

"Now, you see, that's the man you'll be working for. Flee from this den of iniquity before it's too late!"

I'm thinking it's time to mosey on. I thank her nicely for the advice and start backing out the door. She follows me, still yammering about Augusta and Horace, how they were the very flower of Leadville society before that young tramp rolled into town. I keep nodding and backing. She's still going at it when I close the door in her face.

Is that what shopping for dresses is like? I wonder. Suddenly the haberdashery doesn't seem so bad, even with the measuring and all.

The door pops open and she leans out and starts in again. There's no quit in this woman.

Fortunately, right then a thick, meaty hand clamps down on my shoulder and I am forcibly turned around. It's Wallace, of course.

"You're just in time, Wallace. Please save me."

13

Wallace marches me back to the hotel and shoves me into my room.

"Will you stay put this time?" he asks. "Or do I get to chain you to the bed?"

"Calm down, Wallace. I just went out for a breath of fresh air."

He glowers at me.

"Okay, I'll stay." I sit down in a chair and put my feet up on the table.

With nothing else to do, I spend most of the day sleeping. Along about sunset, here comes the haberdashery man with my clothes, just like he promised. Wallace stands in the doorway like a jailer.

I take the clothes from the man. He stands there, blinking at me from behind his spectacles. "What?" I ask him.

"I need to make sure they fit properly," he says in this small, miserable voice.

I hold them up and have a gander. "They look fine."

"Please," he says softly. "It's Mr. Tabor. He's very particular. If they're not just right..." He flutters his hands.

So then I have to get dressed with both of them watching me. I have to admit they're some awfully nice duds. Everything is black except the white shirt. There's a vest and a tight-fitting, waist-length jacket to go over it. The boots are shiny as a mirror, with silver inlaid on the tips of the toes. The hat is high-crowned with a big brim. There's even a new gun belt, like Mr. Tabor promised, made of black leather with silver studs set into it.

I turn and look at myself in the mirror and I have to admit I look pretty impressive.

The little guy fusses over the clothes for a bit, tugging on this and that, but finally allows that it all fits right and bows his way out of the room.

"What do you think, Wallace?" I say, turning slowly, my arms out. "Feeling a little shabby now, are you?"

"Like putting a dress on a pig," he grunts. "Waste of time and good cotton."

"Now that's downright hurtful, Wallace. I'd expected more of you."

He turns. "Come. Mr. Tabor is waiting."

I follow him down to the restaurant. Mr. Tabor is standing at the bar beside a young woman. He's wearing a cream-colored suit this evening and carrying a cane with a silver head. He turns when we approach and his face lights up.

"Ace, as I live and breathe. Don't you look fancy." He turns to the woman beside him. "Sweetness, this is Ace, the new Apache bodyguard I was telling you about. Isn't he something?"

She looks to be about twenty-five. Her hair is a blonde mass of curls and she's wearing a big, floppy hat. Her face is painted up with colors I didn't know existed and she has this slinky red dress on that doesn't leave much to the imagination. She holds out a hand with a giant diamond on it.

I stare at it, not sure what I'm supposed to do.

Wallace elbows me. "Kiss the lady's hand."

I take her hand and give it a quick kiss, wondering if this is something rich people do or if Tabor and Baby Doe are just a special kind of crazy.

"Why, he's as pretty as a little red heifer," she says in a slow, smoky voice. She flutters her eyelashes at me and right away I know she's ten pounds of trouble in a five-pound bag.

Tabor doesn't seem to notice. He's already going on. "Timms and Forbes will be green with envy. I can't wait to show him off at the opera." He looks me up and down like I'm a prize bull he just bought.

This is going to be a long evening.

Tabor pulls out his gold pocket watch. "Look at the time! If we're going to be on time for the opera, we had better get going." He grabs his top hat off the bar and sets it on his head.

Wallace and I follow as he and Baby Doe head for the door. Outside a shiny, enclosed carriage pulled by a pair of matched white horses is waiting. The driver, wearing a suit and a top hat, smiles and opens the door of the carriage for them.

Tabor comes to a halt and turns on the man. "What is this?" he demands angrily.

The poor man looks around like a trapped rabbit. "It's your carriage, sir. Come to fetch you for the opera." He's clearly confused and looks close to bolting.

"You're wearing a top hat, just as I am."

The man's eyes dart this way and that. "I am?" he says tentatively.

"I won't have you looking like me!" Tabor snaps, and slaps the hat off the man's head.

The man lowers his head. "Very good, sir."

Seemingly appeased, Tabor pats him on his bare head. "You couldn't have known. Have a coin for your troubles." He tosses a coin to the man carelessly. It bounces under the carriage. The man looks at him fearfully, not sure what to do.

"Too proud to crawl for a coin, are you?" Tabor says.

"Not at all, sir." The man gets down on his knees and crawls under the carriage.

I look at Wallace to see what he thinks of all this, but his face is made of stone.

Tabor climbs into the carriage and holds his hand out for Baby Doe, but she ignores it and turns to me.

"It's quite a step up," she says breathlessly. "If you would be so kind, Ace?"

This is *really* going to be a long evening.

14

It's only a block to the opera house. Wallace and I get there on foot about the same time they get there in the carriage. Seems pointless to me to get into a carriage for such a short distance, but maybe that's just another one of those things peculiar to rich folks.

For some reason I'm not surprised to discover Tabor's name on the opera house as well. I guess when you have more money than sense you can get your name on all kinds of things.

Inside the opera house is like nothing I've ever seen. Tiled floors so shiny you can almost see yourself in them. Marble columns thirty feet tall. A massive bar that reaches clear across the room, with a brass footrail and about an acre of polished wood. The mirror behind the bar is about ten feet high and has gilt edges.

But what really draws the eye is all the people. There's about forty of them in here and they're all dressed in a way that makes it clear they're trying to outdo each other in some kind of race with no end and no point to it.

The men are wearing top hats and silk jackets with long tails in the back. About half are sporting canes that it's clear they don't actually need. The women are dressed in every color imaginable, yards and yards of shiny, brightly-colored fabric. They're wearing the most outlandish hats, from tiny little things about the size of a pillbox, up to monstrous affairs that will surely lead to some sore necks by the end of the night. Ribbons and feathers are everywhere.

Mr. Tabor and Baby Doe flow right on into the rest of them like they were born to it. Everywhere they turn glasses are raised to them, greetings tossed, bright smiles flashed.

And every single one of them completely fake.

I may not know a lot of things, but one thing I know for sure is not a one of them likes any of the others. There are teeth underneath those smiles and I know for a fact that any one of them would wipe his feet on Tabor's bleeding body without so much as blinking.

No wonder he needs so many bodyguards.

"Ace, Ace, come here," Tabor says, waving me closer. He's standing with an older man wearing a white suit and a funny sort of spectacles that only has one lens, like his glasses broke in half and he lost the other piece.

"Show Mr. Addison what you can do."

I draw my Colts, spin them a couple times on my fingers and drop them back in their holsters.

Mr. Addison beams and the young woman next to him laughs and claps her hands.

"Splendid," Addison says. "Simply splendid. And you say he is Apache?"

"Straight from the savage wastes of the Arizona Territory," Tabor replies.

Now that's a little irritating, being talked about like maybe I don't have the power of speech, but I keep my expression impassive. For sixty dollars a week I reckon I can tolerate quite a lot.

"Do it again, do it again!" the young woman squeals. She's young enough to be his daughter, but from the placement of his hand, I'd say she isn't.

Tabor nods at me and I oblige, throwing in a few extra twirls.

"I say, he could be in one of the wild west shows," Addison says. "With Buffalo Bill and that lot."

"Now don't give him any ideas," Tabor says with a laugh. "He works for me. I don't want him running off."

Others crowd around then and there's nothing for it but to repeat my tricks a few more times.

"Can he shoot, too?" someone calls out.

"Of course he can!" Tabor yells back. He leans in close to me. "You better be able to shoot."

To the crowd he says, "Who wants a demonstration?" Cheers follow. "Everybody grab a bottle and follow me outside!" he yells.

People start grabbing bottles off the bar—most of which aren't anywhere near empty—and heading for the door. For a moment I stand there in disbelief. Is this really happening again? What is it with people and shooting?

I head outside with the rest of them. There's quite a bit of light from the gas lamps that line the street, something no other town I've ever seen has. It should be enough for shooting.

"You ready, Ace?" Tabor asks.

I nod. "Would you see that they throw them high enough so I don't accidentally shoot anyone over there?" The other side of the street is lined with saloons packed with miners.

"Did you hear that?" Tabor crows. "He's worried about shooting some of the miners by accident!"

They all laugh like accidentally shooting someone for sport is hilarious.

Fortunately, no one gets shot. I blast a dozen bottles or so and then everyone heads back inside.

As we crowd through the doors I hear a woman's voice in my ear. "Are you as good with your other gun as you are with those?"

It's Baby Doe and she squeezes my leg as she says it and flashes me a big smile.

Damn it. I was really hoping to keep this job for a spell.

15

We head on into the opera itself. Tabor has a booth all his own way up on one side where he can look down over the rest of them. He and Baby Doe take seats in the front of the booth and Wallace and I station ourselves in the back.

What follows is two hours of the most nonsensical, misguided, confusing thing I've ever seen. It seems to be one of those plays old one-eyed Lou was always going on about, but it's all in some language I never heard before and most of it's singing. And not the good kind of singing either. More the kind that sets dogs to howling and sours the milk cow.

Partway through I slide over next to Wallace and in a low voice I ask him, "Is it always like this?"

"No," he says, without looking at me. "Sometimes it's worse."

I see then that he has cotton stuffed in his ears. Old Wallace isn't as dumb as he looks.

Finally, some fat lady in a too-small dress comes out and sings one last song, then slumps over at the end like she's dead.

Everyone stands up and starts clapping and whistling and cheering. I want to cheer too, but mostly because it's over.

When we walk out into the lobby, Tabor turns to Wallace. "I'm going to my card game. You two escort Baby Doe back to our rooms." I see the angry look Baby Doe gives Tabor when he says this, but he either misses it or doesn't care because he gives her a kiss on the cheek and heads off for a back room.

We get Baby Doe to her door and then head back down to our floor. "Don't even think about it," I tell Wallace. "I'm not a prisoner and you're not locking me in again." He shrugs and goes to his room.

I consider going back out for a walk around, but it's late and I still don't have any money to spend, so instead I start getting undressed for bed. I take off the boots first. They're sharp, but need a whole lot more breaking in before they get comfortable. Next goes the coat, the tie and the shirt.

I'm down to nothing but my trousers when the door opens.

Of course it's Baby Doe. I know it's her before I see her.

I sigh. Can't things ever be simple?

The thing she's wearing couldn't rightly be called a dress. It seems to be nothing but lace and feathers. It looks like she added another, very thick, layer of red lipstick and she has a bottle of champagne and two glasses in one hand.

"You shouldn't be here," I say, careful to keep my voice down. The last thing I need is Wallace to come barging in.

She pouts. "Horace has his card game. Why can't I have a little fun?"

"Because you're married."

"Being married means I can't have any fun?"

"Can't say. I've never been married."

"Don't you want me?" she says in this little girl voice.

The truth? No, I don't. I still hurt for Annie. And while I'm sure lots of men would draw to the hand she's showing, the fact is there's way too much paint and glitter there for me.

But I'm smarter than that. I may not know women, but I know enough that when they throw themselves at you, scorning them makes the wildcat come out. I'll be lucky if I don't lose an eye.

"It's not about whether I want you or not," I say. I figure that sounds pretty good.

She comes closer and runs a finger across my chest. I step back, watching her warily. I have an inkling she can turn all claws and teeth in a heartbeat.

"You've seen that toad I'm married to," she says in a sulky voice. "Don't I deserve something better now and then?"

"That toad you're talking about is the richest man in town."

"He's still a toad."

"If he's a toad, why did you marry him?"

"I was bored. I was young and stupid."

"And the money?"

She shrugs and gives me an impish smile. "Money never hurts."

I put my hand on her shoulder and try to steer her to the door.

"Ooh, you have such strong hands," she says breathlessly.

"You have to leave."

She gives me a cross look. "You try to make me and I'll yell rape."

"Lady, you're in *my* room."

"You think that will make any difference?"

She has a point.

"What will it take to get you out of here?"

"Just give me a little kiss. I'm so terribly lonely."

"Then you'll leave?"

She draws an X on her chest. "I promise."

She sets the champagne and glasses down on the table and holds her arms wide. With all kinds of misgivings I let her wrap me up. She pulls me in close. She's got on about a gallon of some perfume that's so strong it makes my eyes water. I'm blinking the tears back when suddenly she puts her tongue in my ear.

That startles me and I give a sort of yelp and jerk backward. When I do, my elbow hits the champagne and knocks it to the floor where it smashes in a great spray of foam.

We both stare at each other. Her eyes are wide and bright, her red lips turned up in a smile.

The door opens again and, sure enough, Wallace has come to join the party.

16

Wallace has this big evil grin on his face and he's cracking his knuckles. "I can't tell you how badly I've been hoping you'd do something stupid like this," he chuckles.

I take a couple steps back to give myself some room. I sure wish I was wearing my guns. Even my boots would be nice.

"I don't suppose it would do any good to point out that she's in my room, that I was trying to get her to leave?"

"Not even a little bit," he says.

"Is there going to be a fight?" Baby Doe says breathlessly, her eyes sparkling.

"There's going to be something," Wallace says, "but I don't know if you'd call it a fight or just a beating."

"Now don't be so hard on yourself, Wallace," I say. "I'm sure you'll put up a bit of a struggle." Why do I say things like that? I wonder. Aren't things bad enough without making them worse?

"Please move aside, Mrs. Tabor," Wallace says. He puts his big hands on her shoulders and slides her out of the way. "I don't want you to get hurt."

"You know I don't like being called Mrs. Tabor," she pouts. "That's the name of the old hag Horace used to be married to. I'm Baby Doe."

"What you are is trouble," I tell her.

She flares up instantly. "Why you filthy little man. I was going to feel sorry for you. Now I hope he breaks you in half. Go get him, Wallace!"

"With pleasure," he says, and bull rushes me.

I tag him twice on the way in, my best punches with all my strength behind them. They don't even slow him down.

He hits me like a runaway locomotive, slamming me back into the wall so hard that we smash clear through it and tumble into the room on the other side.

It hurts. More than a lot. And it drives most of the air out of my lungs so that for a moment I'm stunned. I can't think, can barely see.

Wallace is fine, though. He picks me up, I have a brief sensation of being over his head, and then he throws me.

Back through the wall.

Now I'm back in my room. I have a vague image of Baby Doe squealing with delight and clapping her hands while she watches. "You're fighting over me! I love it!"

I roll over, make it to my knees and then up on my feet, though I have to hold onto the bedpost to manage it.

Shaking my head to clear out the stars I tell her, "You're crazy as a bedbug, lady, you know that?"

Wallace charges me again, driving me back onto the bed, which collapses under me. The punches I throw at him don't have any real force and he ignores them. He rears up and clocks me in the temple, which doesn't help with the stars any.

When he draws back to hit me again, I manage to get hold of one of the blankets and wrap his fist in it. While he's getting free, I squirm out of his grip and wrap the other end of the blanket around his head, blinding him for a second. I slug him a couple times while I have the chance and then take off running for my gun belt, which is hanging over the back of one of the chairs.

But I forgot about the champagne bottle broken all over the floor. The glass cuts my feet. It slows me enough that Wallace gets a hold of me before I can get my gun free. A hand like an anvil clamps on my wrist and he spins and throws me across the room, right into the wardrobe, smashing in the doors.

I'm getting really tired of being thrown around.

I pull myself out of the wreckage of the wardrobe and stand there trying to gather myself. Wallace is staring at me like a cat about to stop playing with the mouse and eat it. He licks his lips and charges me.

This time I do a little better. I manage to duck under his outstretched arms. I snatch the kerosene lamp out of its wall sconce and smash it down on the back of his head before he can recover.

The lamp smashes and kerosene spills all over his bald head. Now half his head's on fire, but he pays it no mind and comes after me again.

This time I'm not quick enough and he gets me in a big bear hug, though I do manage to get one hand free. He lifts me into the air and squeezes me hard enough that I hear ribs crack. But what really worries me is the flames still flickering across his skull. They're way too close to my face and I start slapping at them with my free hand, trying to put them out before I get burned.

"Don't you care that your head is on fire?" I yell.

He just squeezes me harder.

Okay, that's enough. If he keeps this up my ribs will all be poking out the wrong places.

So I bite his ear. Hard. Finally, Wallace lets go. He gives me an openhanded smack that rocks my head back and I lose my hold on his ear, though I can still taste it.

I stagger back, trying to catch my breath. Wallace follows. He looks pretty bad now, burns all over his scalp, blood running down the side of his head, but he doesn't seem to care about any of it.

"Time to finish this," he grunts.

I take another step back. There's nowhere really to go. Between the wreckage of the wardrobe and the bed, there's no way I can get past him. The glass door to the balcony is at my back. I could maybe crash through it, jump off the balcony for that little ledge I was walking on earlier. I'll probably fall to my death, but at least I'll get away from him.

Too late.

He rushes me again.

"Don't you know how to do anything else?" I yell at him. I kick about where a normal person's balls would be but whatever I hit it's either not them or he doesn't care about that part of his body either.

He smashes me back through the glass door. It splinters, glass flying everywhere. He drives me across the balcony and back against the railing which, being metal, fortunately holds.

"You're going down," he grunts. He grabs hold of my torso with his ridiculously big hands and picks me up.

He's going to throw me over the railing.

I swing my legs up and around and lock them around what little neck he has. "Throw me over if you want," I gasp, "but I'm not going alone."

He hammers me with his big fists, but I don't loosen my grip. It's not like I have a lot of choices here. It's hang on tight or fall and die. Pretty straightforward really.

He stops trying to hit me and settles for trying to pry my legs free. But he can't really get a good grip on anything and the whole time I'm squeezing tighter and tighter. Fear of dying makes a man wonderfully strong, you know?

Bit by bit his struggles get a little weaker. Even a monster like him needs air, I guess, and I'm making sure he doesn't get any.

He slumps to his knees, then sags to the floor and goes limp. I unlock my legs and roll away from him.

"Well, that was something to see," a man says.

Tabor is standing over me, pointing a pistol at me.

17

I look up at Tabor. The adrenaline is fading and the pain is starting to set in. I think I'm going to be sore for a while.

"That man needs to be on a chain," I say.

He motions with the pistol. "Get up."

Stifling a groan, I make it to my feet and stagger back into the room.

"It looks like I won't be able to rent this room for a spell," Tabor says, surveying the damage. It looks pretty bad. There's two giant holes in the wall. The bed is flattened. The wardrobe is destroyed. There's broken glass everywhere and the smell of smoke and kerosene. Somehow the table survived and one of the chairs.

There's no sign of Baby Doe.

"Have a seat," Tabor says. "Mind the glass."

I pick my way through the glass and sit down. I hurt in places I didn't know I had. I feel like a mountain fell on me.

"I didn't touch her," I say.

"Hold on a second," Tabor says, and goes through one of the holes in the wall to fetch a chair from the other room. The other one that was in here is matchsticks.

I watch him go, thinking now's my chance, that I should grab my guns and either run for the door or shoot Tabor down. But somehow it all seems like too much trouble right then, so I settle for laying my head on the table.

Tabor pulls up the other chair and sits down. That's when I notice he's holding a bottle of whiskey. He pulls the cork with his teeth and passes the bottle to me.

The whiskey tastes heavenly. It runs to all the cracks and lays its numbing fingers on me. When I set the bottle down a good bit of it is gone. I slide it back over to Tabor, who takes a drink and hands it back.

He looks out at Wallace, still snoozing peacefully on the balcony. "I didn't know anyone could beat him," he says thoughtfully.

"I think I'm the one who took most of the beating."

He turns back to me and looks me up and down. "I've seen corpses that look better than you."

"They probably felt better too." I take another drink of the whiskey. I wish I could sink into a tub of the stuff. "Are you planning on shooting me?" I ask him.

He looks down at the pistol like he forgot he was holding it. "Oh," he says, putting it down. "Probably not."

"I was getting ready for bed and she waltzed on in. I didn't ask her to."

"What?" For a moment he looks confused, then he nods. "Oh, you're talking about Baby Doe." He scrubs his face with his hands. "Hand me that bottle back, will you?"

I give it to him. He takes a long drink, burps, and looks at me. "You think I don't know how she is?" he asks.

I don't like the question. There's too many ways to answer it wrong. "How is that?" I say cautiously.

"Young and pretty and flighty," he says, waving his hands. "She bats her eyes at every young buck that crosses her path. She thinks I don't see it, but I do. I knew this would happen tonight." He looks around the room speculatively and his eyes fall on the ruined wardrobe. "That piece right there looks pretty expensive. I wish you wouldn't have smashed it."

"I wish Wallace wouldn't have smashed me."

He nods, then changes the subject. "You know how I got this rich? I was nothing but a shopkeeper, you know. Augusta and I got here during the first rush, which was all about gold. I tried my hand at mining, but I was never cut out for it. I don't have the patience, I suppose. Also I hate anything that resembles work.

"We had a little money from Augusta's father and I used it to open a store, but I didn't like that much either. Lucky for me I had one good idea, just one. You want to know what it was?"

I shrug and take another drink off the bottle.

"I didn't get it right away. It was later, when the silver rush started, that it came to me. One day I figured, why go out and look for a vein of ore that I'll probably never find? Why not let others do the looking? I started grubstaking every miner who came through, setting them up with a pick, a donkey and a bag of rice. All for free. All I asked in exchange was a signature on a piece of paper giving me half of whatever they found."

His eyes go distant, remembering. "The Little Pittsburgh mine was the first one that struck, but it was the Matchless where I really made the big money. Do you know one day we took a hundred thousand dollars in silver out of it? In *one day*!"

In one day. And here I was hoping to pick up sixty bucks for a week's work.

"Once the money started coming in you decided you'd had enough of Augusta." I probably shouldn't say it. He still has a gun in front of him after all. Maybe it's the whiskey that has me talking that way.

"I'd had enough of her long before that," Tabor admits, shaking his head. "You know what a Puritan is, Ace?"

"No."

"Then you're lucky. Because they're the most miserable, fun-hating people on God's green earth. It's their religion that makes them that way. The way they see it, if a person's happy, even a little bit, he must be a sinner and he's heading straight for the gates of hell. Twenty-six years I was married to that miserable woman."

He bangs his fist on the table. "I won't apologize for divorcing her. I gave her plenty of money, God knows. Getting her out of my life was the best thing I ever did. It was divorce her or kill her, so I say I did the right thing, don't you?" The look he turns on me is kind of pleading.

He sighs and strokes his mustache. "Maybe I shouldn't have married Baby Doe. Probably I've made better decisions. Being rich doesn't make you immune to stupid."

I shift my position in the chair, which hurts a lot more than it should. "Where does that leave us, Mr. Tabor?"

"Where, indeed?" he replies. "You'll have to leave town, of course. Tonight." He looks out to the balcony. Wallace groans and shifts slightly. "Wallace will wake up soon and you don't want to be here when he does."

"You're letting me go?"

"Of course I am. I regret that I'll no longer have my own Apache bodyguard, but I'll find something else I suppose. That's the thing about having lots of money. There's always something else to buy."

He waves his hand. "Go. Quickly. Wallace is an excitable man and I don't know what he'll do if he wakes up and you're still here. I may not be able to control him."

18

A few minutes later I'm riding out of town just as broke as I rode into town, though a whole lot more beat up. On the bright side, I did manage to get some new duds, but riding through the cold darkness, hurting with every breath, it doesn't seem all that bright to me. I'm about as low as I've ever been.

I make camp a few miles out of town and spend a long, miserable night trying to find some side to lie down on that doesn't hurt like hell. It snows too, so there's that. Finally I give up on sleep and huddle by the fire waiting for the sun to come up.

In the morning I crawl on Coyote's back and more or less let him have his head. If he wants to take us both off the edge of a cliff, well, at least it'll stop the hurting.

But I don't get that lucky. Coyote follows the wagon road that leads south from Leadville, along the Arkansas River, and about midday we ride on into a tiny little town with a hand-painted sign sitting on a rock proclaiming it to be Granite, Colorado.

I get off in front of the post office and out of habit I scan the wanted posters tacked up to the wall outside, hoping I don't see any with my face on them. There isn't one, but I do see one that's familiar. It's for the grizzly bear, the one they call Old Mose. Three hundred dollars they're offering for his hide. That's enough money to get a man thinking.

While I'm standing there, studying the poster, the postmaster comes out. He's a plump little guy with a starched white shirt, suspenders and an eyeshade. He sticks his thumbs in his suspenders, rocks back on his heels and says, "You fixin' to go after Old Mose?"

"Maybe."

"Mister, you'd make a powerful lot of friends in this area if'n you was to get that monster's hide."

"It's not the friends that interest me as much as the three hundred dollars."

"Seems high for one ol' bear, don't it?"

"I was thinking that."

"But then, this ain't just any ol' bear. It's Old Mose and his look would pucker a hog's butt." He puts his hands up over his head. "Old Mose is twelve foot tall if he's an inch, the biggest, meanest grizzly bear to ever live."

I give him a skeptical look. "Twelve foot tall?"

"It's the Lord's truth, so help me god."

"You've seen him yourself?"

He snaps his suspenders and shakes his head. "Can't say I have, actually. But others have, and they all swear he's twelve foot tall, though some say fourteen."

"No bear gets that big."

"They say he's killed near eight hundred head of cattle and horses in the thirty-five years he's been terrorizing this valley. I know a feller swears he seen him drop a running horse with one swipe of his massive paw." He mimes swiping at Coyote, who lays his ears back. This ol' boy needs to worry less about Old Mose and more about Coyote, who's got no problem biting off a piece of his anatomy if he gets too close.

"Eight hundred seems like a lot of cattle and horses," I say.

He squints at me, not quite as friendly now that I'm questioning him. "Why do you think they're offering such a tall price for him?"

Okay, he's got me there. When a cougar pelt gets you ten dollars, three hundred is a lot.

"He killed old Jake Radcliffe, you know."

"Who's Jake Radcliffe?" I ask.

"A local boy, quite the hunter."

"Not that good I expect, if Old Mose killed him."

He continues like he hasn't heard me. "Jake surprised Old Mose while he was out hunting. The bear came after him and he tried to shoot him, but Old Mose slapped away his gun and snapped his legs with his teeth."

"That must have hurt."

"It wasn't over yet. Jake played possum until Old Mose left. Once he figured the bear was good and gone, he started hollerin' for help. But he figgered wrong. Old Mose wasn't gone. The durned bear was waiting just out of sight and he come back and finished the job, chewed up his scalp, bit through his cheek, and tossed him in the bushes."

63

"With Jake dead, how do you know all this?" I ask, thinking I've caught him in his tall tale.

The postmaster takes off his eyeshade sorrowfully. "Jake lived long enough to tell those what found him. But he died afore they could get him back to town." He points up the hillside to a cleared area where there's a number of crude wooden crosses sticking out of the ground. "They buried him up there in boot hill."

I eye him for a bit to see if he's putting me on, but he looks sincere enough. "It seems like this is a bear a man would be wise to stay clear of."

He puts his eyeshade back on and nods his head. "Indeed he would." Then he perks up and slaps me on the shoulder, which causes all kinds of new pains to flash through my body. "But you look like the feller to finish the job. You're Injun, ain't you? You fellers can just about talk to the animals, can't you? Maybe you can hex that old bear or something and finish him off with that Winchester I see on your horse."

Hex the bear? What does that even mean? I wonder.

"Do you know where Old Mose was last seen?" I ask him.

"I do." He points. "Up yonder. Willow Creek. He killed a miner's mule a couple days ago."

Killed a mule? Old Mose can't be all bad then. I've hardly met a mule I didn't want to kill.

I mount up and ride on out of town, heading towards Willow Creek.

It can't hurt to at least take a look at this bear.

19

I don't do much looking at first. Mostly I just try and heal up from the pounding Wallace gave me. I set some rabbit snares, break out some fishing line and hook a few trout. A few days go by, I stop feeling like I'm going to break in half when I sneeze, and I figure it's time to poke around a bit.

Willow Creek cuts between two big peaks in the Rocky Mountains, both of them better than fourteen thousand feet tall. The mountainsides on either side of the creek are steep and thick with fir, pine, aspen and lots of rocks. Willow Creek makes a lot of twists and turns as it heads downhill, crashing through tangles of granite boulders and fallen trees. Plenty of hidden meadows and beaver ponds too. It's pretty country and rough. Coyote and I have to work to pick our way along.

A couple days in I see my first track and get down to have a look at it. Maybe the postmaster was right about how big Old Mose is. It's certainly the biggest bear track I've ever seen by half. I can put my boot in it with plenty of room to spare.

I start following the tracks. It's not difficult. Old Mose clearly doesn't care if anyone follows him. There's sign everywhere, rotted logs torn open, bee hives ripped apart and such. It occurs to me that Old Mose recently woke up from his winter nap and is feeling a might peckish.

I come across one tree with deep gouges in it about twelve feet up, where Old Mose was sharpening his claws. Sitting there, looking at it, I have to ask myself if this is such a good idea.

But then I remember that bad ideas never stopped me before. Take, for example, that whole incident with the Aztec god awhile back. That was a bad idea, but it worked itself out by the end. So I continue on.

I find that old bear the next afternoon. He's in this little meadow, clawing at an old log, digging out the grubs squirming inside it.

I pull on my moccasins and climb down off Coyote, then ease up on Old Mose to get a closer look, careful to stay downwind and real, real quiet.

Up close that bear is one magnificent creature. He ripples with muscle, his teeth are as long as my thumb and his claws longer than my fingers. He is the undisputed chief of this world he lives in, an animal to sing songs about.

Damn it.

I can't kill him. I can't kill anything that impressive. I don't care how many cows and hunters he's killed. He's above any laws or rules we puny humans could possibly put on him. We should bow before him, not shoot him, bounties be damned.

I get a crazy idea then.

When I was a kid, the other young braves and I had this thing we did. The idea was to challenge our stalking skills by seeing if we could sneak up on a grazing deer or antelope and touch it before it noticed us. Not to be too full of myself or anything, but I was the best at it.

I came all this way and I'll leave emptyhanded, but before I go I dearly want to test myself against this bear.

Before I can spend much time pondering the wisdom of this decision, I clamp my new hat down tightly on my head and start creeping forward.

It's actually disappointingly easy to stalk Old Mose. He's making so much noise he probably couldn't hear me if I was playing a fiddle. He's tearing at the log, grunting and snuffling like a hog while he goes after those fat grubs. It only takes me a few minutes to get right up on him. I rise up, whack him on the ass, and then take off running.

It only takes me a couple heartbeats to realize I just made one helluva mistake.

That bear turns a whole lot faster than anything that size has a right to. He whuffs and lights out after me.

I can hear those heavy footsteps right behind me and I know I've only got a couple more seconds to live. Just about enough time to realize I might be the stupidest man alive.

There's no way I can make it back to Coyote. There's a medium-sized pine tree up ahead to my right and I swerve and head for it. I leap when I get close and I'm already climbing before I even touch the tree.

I skitter up that thing like a squirrel, about a hairsbreadth ahead of Big and Nasty. He hits the tree about hard enough to shake me out, but I hang on and get up even higher.

That was close. I peer down through the branches at him, thinking it's a good thing I chose such a small tree. Anything bigger and he might have been able to climb up after me.

"No harm done!" I call down to him. "Now how about you just go on your way and I'll go on mine. You'll never see me again."

He stares at me from eyes that have a little too much thinking going on in them and then he growls, low and mean, making me think he's not going to let this go so easy.

"Before you do anything hasty, remember that I could have shot you but I didn't."

That doesn't seem to clear things up for him any. He growls a couple more times and does not seem inclined to wander off.

Okay, so I guess I'm spending some time up here, waiting for him to get bored and go back to his grubs.

Or maybe not.

Because along about then Old Mose rears back and whacks my tree a good one. I have to hold tight to keep from getting tossed out on my ass.

He can't really knock this tree down, can he? I look up. It's got to be thirty feet tall and a good foot around. One bear, even a big one like this, surely can't knock down a tree this big.

Right?

Then he commences to get serious. He goes after my tree with everything he's got and now it's shaking like the hurricane deck of a buckin' bronco. If this keeps up much longer my teeth will rattle right on out of my head.

And…right about then there's this loud crack and I realize it's not my teeth I'm going to have to worry about.

Old Mose stops pounding on my tree, which I notice to my consternation has developed quite a list. He stands up to his full height and puts both massive paws on the trunk. He looks up at me and I swear he smiles and that smile is all teeth.

He pushes. More cracking and more tilting. His toothy smile gets bigger.

This was most definitely not my best idea.

One more big push and the tree gives up the fight. Right before it hits the ground, I jump off and land on one of those big, moss-covered, granite rocks sticking out of the creek. It's slick and I barely manage to keep from skipping off into the icy, rushing water.

But there's no time to enjoy the view. I barely hit before I'm jumping again to the next rock over. None too soon either, as Old Mose hits the spot where I was about a heartbeat later. He's not so lucky with his footing though and goes skidding off into the creek.

I take advantage of that little break and head for Coyote, who's standing on the far side of the creek watching us with his ears perked forward. But right behind me comes that big, angry bear and Coyote throws his tail up and takes off.

Thanks for nothing, you miserable nag.

There's a big slab of granite that slid down the mountainside during some past avalanche. It's tilted up on one side a foot or two and I dart under there like a rat running from a wolf, wedging myself as far back in as I can.

Old Mose gets there real quick and first he tries reaching for me. I get a whole lot more up close and personal than I'd like with his claws, but he can't quite reach me. It looks like I might have actually found safety this time.

He pulls his paw back out and I figure all I have to do now is wait him out.

How many times in one day can one man be wrong?

A moment later he hooks both paws onto the edge of that slab of rock and starts heaving. It's a big rock, ten, fifteen feet across, but damned if it doesn't shift when he does that.

"What's it going to take for you to quit?" I yell at him.

Judging by how he growls, I'm pretty sure I wouldn't like the answer if I could speak bear.

He gives another heave and the slab of rock tilts up another six inches. A bit more and he'll be able to get under here with me.

Which means it's time to go.

I scoot out the side. The avalanche left a whole long scree slope in its wake, tens of thousands of jumbled rocks of all sizes reaching way up the mountainside and every one of them loose, as I find out when I start running up through them.

Turns out that looseness is the only thing that keeps me alive. Only the smaller rocks move when I step on them. *Every* rock moves under Old Mose's bulk. He spends as much time sliding backwards as chasing me forwards.

That gives me enough time to make it to this big cliff and scurry up the first pitch at the bottom. I make it to this little ledge about six inches wide and crouch there and watch as Old Mose makes it to the bottom of the cliff.

"This is it, bear," I tell him. "Nowhere for me to go from here." From here on up the cliff is sheer and overhanging.

He growls and starts climbing. He only makes it about halfway up before the rocks he's clinging to snap off under his weight and pitch him back down to the bottom. He tries a couple more times. Same result. Then he stands there on his hind legs, paws against the cliff face, staring up at me.

"You made your point, you know," I tell him. "This is one man who has learned good and well not to cross you. You head on off now and you'll never see me again."

He stares at me like he's trying to figure out if I'm telling the truth. Or maybe he's trying to figure out if I'm worth eating.

He whuffs a couple of times, drops down and ambles off.

20

I'm climbing down off the cliff when I hear something I didn't expect.

It's the sound of someone clapping.

I turn and see a man come walking up. He's a little shorter than I am and darker-skinned. He has short, curly black hair that is rapidly turning white. He's wearing a fringed buckskin coat and pants and a beaver-skin hat. There's a rifle jutting up over his shoulder and a pistol stuck in his belt.

"That was quite the show!" he calls out. He walks right up to me and sticks out his hand, a big smile on his face. "James P. Beckwourth, mountaineer, pioneer, scout and chief of the Crow Indian tribe, at your service, sir."

I take his hand, still trying to sort through all those titles. Did he say chief of the Crow Indian tribe? Maybe I heard wrong. "Ace Lone Wolf."

"Pleased to make your acquaintance, Ace Lone Wolf," he booms, pumping my hand with great energy. His voice is very loud. "That right there, what I just witnessed, was either the bravest or stupidest undertaking in the history of this land."

Since he shows no inclination toward returning my hand anytime soon, I pull it out of his grasp. "I was hoping to keep that to myself," I say.

His eyebrows draw together and he gets this confused look on his face. "Why ever would you want to do a thing like that?"

"Because it almost got me killed?"

"I'm not talking about whacking that old bear. I understand doing reckless deeds just because they're there to be done and I applaud your decision to do so. I also applaud your execution of said deed. I don't believe I've ever seen anyone move that fast."

Now I'm the one who's confused. "Did I miss something?"

"What I don't understand, Ace, is this talk about keeping your deed to yourself. What good is an adventure if no one hears about it?"

I look him up and down, trying to get a handle on him. Maybe he's addled. But, even though he has to be somewhere in his sixties, maybe more, he looks fit and lively as a skunk with a bee in its teeth.

"I was planning on keeping it to myself because it was a stupid thing to do. I'm not generally in the habit of giving people reasons to laugh at me."

He shakes his head vigorously. "No, no, no. You can't keep such a deed quiet. I mean, you didn't whack any old bear. You whacked Old Mose himself! Who does that? Wait, let me answer that. *No one does.* Except, apparently, my new friend Ace Lone Wolf. Must be that Indian blood in your veins, am I right? What are you Ute? Pawnee?"

"Apache."

His eyes go wide and his smile gets even bigger. "Apache, is it? Well, don't that beat all? I've met, fought and lived with about every flavor of Indian this land has to offer, but you're my first Apache. Are they all as brave and foolish as you?"

I don't quite know how to answer that so I shrug.

"My point is, you did something legendary. You can't keep such a feat to yourself. You have to share it with the world."

"No sir, I don't. I aim to keep this to myself and I'd see it kindly if you did the same."

He looks at me like I just grew a rooster tail. "You're an odd one, I'll warrant."

That's funny. I was just thinking the same thing about him.

"Well, it's been a pleasure meeting you. I'll be moseying along now," I say and start to walk away.

"Hold on, hold on!" he cries, and hurries after me. "I believe you may be the man I'm looking for."

That puts me on alert. I let a hand drift closer to a gun. Has he seen a wanted poster? After all, this is Colorado and there was a little incident involving a train robbery and a dead U.S. Marshall awhile back.

He sees my hand move and he says, "It's not like that at all. I mean you no harm. You have my word on that. No, what I have in mind is more of a business proposition."

"What sort of proposition?"

71

"If you don't mind, we'll get into that later. Right now I have traps to check and beavers to skin. If I don't get to them quick, Old Mose will eat every one of them."

I start to turn away again. "I'm not really interested anyway."

"Not so quick. You haven't heard me out." He looks up and down the canyon like someone might be listening in, but when he speaks again he's still as loud as ever. "It's a once in a lifetime opportunity," he says earnestly.

"I'm not in need of opportunities. Not at the moment."

"The hell you aren't," he says with a glint in his eye. "Those are fancy duds, but I'd bet my whole cache of beaver pelts you haven't got so much as a wooden nickel to your name."

"You seem awfully sure of yourself."

"Only because I'm right. You came up here chasing Old Mose for the reward, didn't you? Don't deny it. I can see the truth of it in your eyes. You can't hide it from me. I've been dealing with Indians too long to be fooled. Only a penniless man would consider chasing that brute." He scratches the white stubble of beard on his chin. "Though I can't for the life of me figure out what made you decide to slap him instead of shooting him."

He's got me there. I *am* penniless. Maybe it wouldn't be a bad idea to hear him out. "So what is this opportunity you're so hot about?"

He wags a finger at me. "Not here. I'll tell you in camp, later on, when we have time to sit down and discuss it proper like." He points up canyon. "Four or five miles up that way. There's a pot of beans on and a pot of coffee that might or might not taste like turpentine. Help yourself and I'll be along shortly."

He pats me on the shoulder and walks on down the canyon, whistling.

21

I watch him walk out of sight and tell myself the smart thing to do here is get on Coyote and ride away. Whatever this opportunity is, I'd bet a silver dollar to a rattlesnake it involves me risking my life in some harebrained way. You know, like sneaking into an Aztec temple and facing a pissed-off god.

But when I get on Coyote I head upstream. Those beans sound good and even bad coffee beats no coffee which is what I have.

I'm stretched out under a tree getting some shuteye when Beckwourth shows up late that afternoon, toting a bundle of green beaver pelts on his shoulder. He tosses the pelts down and looks at Coyote, grazing nearby.

"I figured you were on rough times, friend, but I didn't know how rough until I laid eyes on that horse of yours. Did you lose a bet or something?"

That gets my back up a little. Why does everyone feel they have to remark on my horse's appearance?

"You wouldn't say that if you could see his heart like I can," I mutter. "Coyote can run all day and night and still have the strength to thrash anything on four legs. He's saved my life too, more than once." My hand goes to my throat, remembering the feel of the rope.

"Look at the way he's looking at me," Beckwourth muses. "If I didn't know better I'd think he knows what I just said and he's planning his revenge on me."

"You've got no notion of half of what Coyote knows. Watch your ears around him. He's prone to biting."

"I'll keep that close to mind." Beckwourth gets out his knife and sets to scraping and stretching the green pelts. After a minute I pitch in. I did eat a lot of his beans after all.

When we're done he takes a turkey out of his pack and cleans it while I build up the fire and set up a spit for cooking. The sun's down by then. He sits down with his back up against a thick tree and takes a small brown bottle out of his pack. He takes a drink off the bottle and puts it away, then pulls a pipe and a pouch of tobacco out of his pocket.

He lights the pipe, blows out a cloud of smoke and looks at me. "Hundreds of years ago the Spaniards came to this new world. They came looking to get rich. They came looking for gold. Down in what we now call Mexico they found a people with gold, the Aztecs."

I know a thing or two about the Aztecs. Can't say I think much of their gods. A bloodthirsty lot.

"The Aztecs had a lot of gold, mountains of the stuff. Those first Spaniards got fabulously rich." He puffs on his pipe a couple of times. "Those who came later? Not so much. Once the Aztecs were tapped out gold proved a lot harder to come by. It took a lot more looking.

"One of those doing the looking was a Spaniard who went by the moniker Juan de Iturbe. De Iturbe was a stubborn cuss. When he saw there was no more gold to be had in Mexico he started sailing south. He landed at every village he found, looking for gold. But he didn't find any, or at least not enough. He picked up some strange things, but the gold he dreamed of eluded him. He wasn't a quitter, though. He kept plugging away. He sailed so far south that finally the land ran out and there was nothing left but to sail north, up the other side of the new world.

"His men weren't happy about it. They were tired of being so far from home. They missed their wives and sweethearts and they were sick with scurvy and malaria and diseases none of them had ever seen. But de Iturbe was crafty and ruthless and every time they tried to mutiny, he sussed them out and beat them back into line. And all the time he kept them moving, knowing the treasure he was looking for had to be around the next bend.

"It was when they were clear up on the west coast of Mexico, almost to California, that he finally found it. Only it wasn't gold he found. It was something no Spaniard had ever seen before. A unique treasure, something worth more than gold.

"All he had to do was take it from the Indians who had it and that was no problem at all. Hell, they had no idea what they had. To them it was just trinkets."

"What treasure are you talking about?"

He waves his pipe at me. "I've got your interest now, don't I?"

"Some."

"You know what pearls are?" I shake my head. "They're little round, white, shiny things. Women favor them in necklaces and such. They grow inside clams in the ocean…" He pauses. "Which you probably don't know what clams are, do you? They're little critters with rock-hard shells, shaped like this."

He shows me with his hands. None of it makes any sense to me at all. Jewelry that grows inside rocks? I wonder if he's making this all up.

"The details don't really matter," he continues. "The point is that pearls are worth money. A lot of money. And black ones, because they're rare, are worth even more."

"That's the treasure de Iturbe found?"

"The very same. Enough to fill a chest." He taps out his pipe and refills it. "This is where the story gets interesting. See, the smart thing would have been to turn around and head back to Spain right then. De Iturbe had his treasure. It was time to go home and spend it.

"But he didn't. He kept going north. Only he didn't realize he wasn't out in the Pacific Ocean anymore. He was in the Sea of Cortez. There was no way out to the north, nothing but the Colorado River where it dumps into the sea.

"He got all the way to that river and he still didn't turn around. For some reason no one will ever know, he sailed up the river. Maybe he was plumb loco by then. Anyway, while he was sailing on that river there was a storm or something out on the Sea of Cortez. It caused a freak tidal wave that went right up the river and picked his ship up like it was a toy. It lifted that ship clean out of the river channel, carried it miles inland and dumped it on the sand." He grins at me. "Where it lies to this day. Waiting for you and me to come claim it."

His eyes are shining in the firelight and he stares at me like he's waiting for me to cheer for him or something. "What do you think?" he asks at last.

I dump out the last dregs of my coffee. "No."

"What do you mean, no?"

"Seems simple enough to me. No."

"You're really going to pass up on all that treasure?"

"Treasure doesn't mean as much to me as it does most folks, I guess."

"But you're broke."

"It's not the first time. It won't be the last time."

"If you won't do it for the treasure, do it for the adventure."

"I get all the adventure I need. I don't need to go looking for it."

"You don't believe my story."

"It does stretch the bounds."

"It's true. I'd stake my life on it."

"You go right ahead and do that. I won't."

"But I can't do this alone. I need a partner. I'm not as spry as I used to be."

"You'll find someone. The world is full of people who'll do anything for money."

"But not you."

"Not me."

"Why?"

"Mister, I've gone searching for lost treasure before. It didn't work out so well."

"You didn't find it?"

"We found it all right. Heaps of it."

"So?"

"So my partners cheated me out of my share. Left me in a tight spot too."

"I would never do that. I'm a man of my word."

I look at him for a bit, then nod. "I believe you are."

"But you still won't go."

"Nope."

"If I may I ask, what was the treasure you and your companions went looking for?"

"The temple of Xipe Totec."

His eyes light up. "The lost temple of Totec?"

"It's not lost anymore."

"That sounds like quite an adventure."

"What it really was, Beckwourth, was a big mistake. One in which I nearly got shot or blown up too many times to remember."

"That must have been incredible," he says in this far off voice. I get the feeling he's sad he wasn't there.

"You don't hear too well, do you? I almost died. Over and over."

"Ah," he says, holding up his pipe as if he has caught me on something important, "but the fact is that you did *not* get killed. You're still very much alive."

"Which makes me determined to stay that way."

"And even though you didn't get the treasure, you did come out of it with a fantastic story. Surely that makes it all worth it?"

"Not even close."

He shakes his head somewhat sadly. "It's because you're young. When you're old, like me, then you'll care. Then you'll see that the story is everything."

"Or maybe not. Maybe I'll see that not getting killed was everything."

He goes to his pack, rummages in it and pulls out something wrapped in oilcloth. It's a thick book bound in leather. "See this?" he says. "This is my life's story. I've been writing it for the last few years. It's filled with all the tales of my wild youth. The things I've done, the places I've seen. It's truly the greatest story ever told." He rewraps the book.

"But it's missing one last tale to finish it off. One grand adventure that they'll talk about for a hundred years to come."

"Who's they? Who are you talking about?"

"Why, my readers, of course. All over this great country. Europe too, I expect. They need excitement in their lives over there."

"So you want to chase this ship that probably never existed and probably get yourself killed, all for a *story*?"

"That is correct."

"I think you've got a few squirrels loose in your attic, Beckwourth."

It doesn't offend him. He smiles. "I saw you whack Old Mose on the ass for no good reason. You'll come around. This is perfect for you. How can you say no?"

I look at him in disbelief. Is he hearing me at all? "Is that turkey done yet?" I ask. "I'm hungry."

"So you'll come?"

77

"I didn't say that."

"Why not? What else do you have to do?"

He's got a point there. My options aren't what you'd call plentiful.

"Do you have any money for supplies, or do I have to risk my life in a card game to stake this fool adventure of yours?"

"I have these pelts. Once I sell them I'll have plenty of money."

I have an idea. "I'll tell you what, Beckwourth. How about if I hire on to get you close?"

"How close?"

"The nearest town."

"I'd rather you went the whole way."

"That's the offer. Take it or leave it."

"It's better than nothing."

"And you're paying me a hundred dollars for this. Up front. Once you sell those pelts."

"You drive a hard bargain, Ace."

"Say no, then. I don't care either way."

"It's a deal." He stands up and holds out his hand.

I stand up as well. "I'm going to regret this, aren't I?"

"Probably more than once."

"You're not making this any easier."

"Oh, it won't be easy, I assure you. A good story takes real sweat and blood to acquire."

I shake his hand, already regretting my decision. Somewhere I think I can hear Lou having a good laugh at my expense right now.

22

"I ever tell you how I came to be made a chief of the Crow Indian tribe?" Beckwourth asks me the next morning.

I open my eyes to see that it's still pretty dark. Last I remember before I fell asleep last night he was telling me some story about a time he faced down a cougar in its den with nothing but a knife and a sack of moldy potatoes. Which can't be right. What would potatoes have to do with anything?

I wonder if maybe he talked clean through the night without stopping.

Beckwourth sits up and takes out his pipe, starts packing tobacco in it. The pipe means I'm getting a story. It also means I'm not going to be getting any more sleep.

"I was up trapping on the Yellow River with a couple dozen others and Captain Bridger, who was as skillful a hunter as I have ever had the good fortune to make acquaintance of. One day a number of Crow Indians came into our camp. This caused us no great consternation, for the Crows were friendly to us as we had more than once assisted them in battles against their mortal enemies, the Cheyennes."

He pauses to light his pipe. "While in camp the Crows saw a great number of scalps that we had taken after a recent battle with the Cheyennes." He pauses for a moment. "I know what you're thinking now, Ace."

No you don't. If you did you'd shut up and let me go back to sleep.

"You are thinking that taking scalps is not something usually associated with the civilized man. I have no defense for our participation in this barbarous custom, other than to say that we spent many months at a time in which the only other people we saw were Indians and over time we came to adopt some of their ways. There is a saying, which you may or may not be aware of. 'When in Rome, do as the Romans do.' We were perhaps as far as one could get from Rome, but the saying was very applicable nonetheless, I assure you."

"Applicable nonetheless"? What does that even mean? I've noticed that when Beckwourth tells stories he uses big words. Also, his voice changes, becoming kind of rhythmic. It's almost hypnotic.

"But on with the story. While the Crows were admiring our scalps it was pointed out to them that the greatest number had been taken by yours truly. At this the Crows became very taken with me and were anxious to speak with me and cultivate my acquaintance. Unfortunately, I could not at that time speak their language so they had to resort to using a man named Greenwood, whose wife was a Crow, to interpret for them. In time, Greenwood became tired of this role and for his own entertainment he invented a fiction, which all found amusing for its ingenuity.

"He told the Crows that I was one of them. They were rightly astonished to hear this news."

I'm a little peeved at being woke up and so I say, "I imagine they were, since you don't look like an Indian at all."

He continues on with his story like he hasn't heard me. Which he probably hasn't. I've known Beckwourth only a short time, but long enough to realize that when he's talking he gets lost in himself and not much else around him matters.

"The Crows wished to know how this could be. Greenwood said, 'You know how you were defeated by the Cheyennes many winters ago, how they killed hundreds of your warriors and carried off a great many of your women and children? Well, Beckwourth here was one of those children. Only, a few moons later some trappers bought him off the Cheyennes and raised him as one of their own.'

"As you can imagine, this caused a great deal of excitement among the Crows. They hastened to their village to spread the joyful news that they had found one of their own people who had been stolen by the Cheyennes but had grown up to become a great white chief, with his lodge pole full of the scalps of his enemies, who had fallen to his gun and battle axe. The old women were the most excited of all, each of them wondering if I might be their own child.

"When I learned of the fiction Greenwood had spread I did nothing to impugn his authenticity. Indeed, I found myself greatly astonished at the inordinate gullibility of the red man and joined in the general laughter of my fellows."

I pull my blanket over my head but it does no good. I can still hear him plainly. I'm not sure it even matters to him whether I'm listening or not. I think he's talking mostly for the sheer pleasure of hearing his own voice. I wonder what Block—I still can't think of him as Blake, whatever he said his name is—would make of Beckwourth. That man hated words like a dog hates ticks. Probably he would have knocked Beckwourth out by now.

"Our party soon broke up and I thought no more of this. After making a plan to re-unite after a certain number of days, we issued from camp to go our separate ways. Several days later, while trapping alone on a small, remote stream, I looked up from my work to find myself surrounded by Indians. Seeing that there were nearly a hundred of them, and therefore too many even for me to fight, I surrendered my arms and my traps and allowed myself to be taken as their prisoner.

"Imagine my surprise when I was taken to their chief's lodge and discovered that in his company were several of the Crows whom Greenwood had told his fiction to, some days before. When they recognized me it caused a great excitement in their village and hundreds soon gathered around the chief's lodge to catch a sight of me, their long-lost son and brother.

"Orders were given to summon all the old women who had suffered a son lost to the depredations of the Cheyennes. The women were breathless with excitement, their eyes wild and protruding, as they crowded around me. Never in my life have I been subject to such an intense scrutiny as I was then. I believe several hours passed while they examined every inch of me, even to the soles of my feet, all of them seeking some sign that would prove I was their dead son, returned to them.

"Finally, one old woman who was missing several fingers on her left hand, said, 'I believe this is my son, but if it is, he will have a mole on his left eyelid.' My eyelid was quickly stretched down and sure enough, there was the mole!"

Beckwourth says this like it's the most extraordinary thing ever spoken but all I can think is what a shame it was they didn't scalp him instead.

"You never heard such shouts of joy," Beckwourth says. "And the greatest joy was the old woman's, but can you blame her? This son she had supposed dead for so many years, who she had mourned silently through weary nights for twenty years, was suddenly returned to her. Not only that, but this son had grown into a great chief, with accolades and honors beyond what any mother could hope for."

I sit up then and glare at Beckwourth. "Is this story going to end soon? Or does it go on and on forever?"

"Oh, there is a great deal more," he assures me. "Only be patient and you will hear the whole of it."

I look at him in disbelief. Is he really so confused as to believe I *want* to hear this story?

But he's already prattling on again, oblivious to the dark looks I'm giving him.

"In their excitement, the Crows fairly carried me to the lodge of the old lady, where she lived with her husband, my presumed father. The news spread through the village like lightning and by the time we got to the lodge it was filled with all degrees of my newly-reunited relatives, who welcomed me nigh unto death, they were so rapturous. The hugs and the kisses which were bestowed upon me were not to be believed, for all firmly believed that I was who the old woman said I was.

"I was soon outfitted with new leggings, moccasins and other garments all ornamented with shells and feathers according to the Crow fashion. A bed was prepared for me in the lodge in a place of honor and like that I became a full member of their family. In short fashion I was presented a wide array of young Indian maidens from which to choose as a wife, all of the greatest braves of the tribe fairly wrestling with each other for the honor of having their daughter chosen by me. Once this was accomplished a great feast was laid out and several days of merrymaking followed."

Seeing that this isn't going to stop, might never truly stop, I grumble and get up. I roll up my bedroll and tie it to my saddle. Meanwhile, Beckwourth goes on and on, only pausing to take a drink off the same small brown bottle he took a drink off the night before. He gets up and packs his gear while he talks.

"I must take a short aside here, Ace, and relate events which were happening concurrently with these, but at a distance. Events which I was not to know until years later after I had returned to live among my own kind.

"Captain Bridger was on a nearby hill, thinking to come join me, when he saw the Crows surrounding me. Not realizing they were Crows, but believing they were Cheyennes, he supposed my death to be imminent. Nor was there any aid he could offer me, there being such a large number of them. Accordingly, he hurried back to the general camp and communicated to the other trappers and traders the painful news of my demise. All who heard it assumed that I was being sacrificed in the most painful manner the savages could invent and were plunged into gloom at the tragic news. They pronounced my funeral eulogy, my daring encounters were spoken of with the highest praise and they lamented the loss of their best hunter, their kind and ever-obliging friend."

Beckwourth chuckles. "Little did they dream that while they were lamenting my untimely death I was being hugged and kissed by a lodge filled with relatives and welcomed with a public reception of equal intensity to that accorded the victor of Waterloo when he marched triumphantly into Paris."

I'm making no pretense of listening, but it's not slowing him down at all. I saddle up Coyote and he saddles up his horse, taking steadily the whole time, telling me about one battle after another in which he led the Crows to victories over their enemies. Most of it washes over me unheard.

When my gear is packed, I mount up and start down the canyon. He's not quite ready and calls after me to wait but I ignore him. I have to have a few minutes of peace. Otherwise I'm afraid I will hurt him.

He catches up to me a few minutes later and picks up his story where he left off, telling me how finally the Crows had no choice but to make him a chief, he led them to so many tremendous victories through his skill and ferocity in battle. I begin to wish I had some cotton to stuff into my ears.

23

"But enough of my tale," Beckwourth says sometime that afternoon. "I wish to hear more of yours."

I give him a sidelong look. "Don't you think you talk enough for the both of us?"

He laughs like this is a great joke and once again presses me to tell my story. In the hope that he will leave me alone after, I give in.

"My mother found my father by a watering hole, nearly dead from a couple bullets he'd taken, going away presents from some men who didn't like being cheated at cards. She brought him back to my clan and nursed him back to health. He survived, I was born, a few years later he ran off to chase a card game and here I am."

Beckwourth shakes his head sadly. "You have a great deal of room for improvement in the art of story-telling, my friend."

"What if I don't care about the 'art of story-telling'?"

But it's too late. Beckwourth has already gotten the bit between his teeth and is going on again.

"Like you, I am a child of mixed parentage. My father was a white man, a slave owner in Tennessee, and my mother was one of his slaves. When I was quite young he packed up his family and moved to Missouri to further his fortunes. By birth my brothers and sisters and I were slaves like my mother, but before too long he freed all of us and thereafter raised us as his own with all the care of any natural father."

He digs out his pipe and packs some tobacco in it. He takes a match out of a small wooden box and lights the pipe, then continues.

"He never did free my mother. His first wife had run off with a patent medicine man and because of that he had come to the belief that the only way to truly secure a woman's love was to make sure she could not run off when she had a mind to.

"Father was a strict man, as is necessary when raising children, but he didn't whip us overmuch and my brothers and I grew up feisty and strong. When I was but a stripling, he apprenticed me out to a blacksmith and I went to live with the man, believing that blacksmithing would be my trade for the remainder of my God-given life. I suppose it would have been too, had not the man such a terrible problem with drink and a temper to match. After some months of regular beatings, I knew I would have to leave or face the sheriff after I had killed him. So it was I took my leave in the dead of night.

"Knowing my father would not be understanding of my decision, I shipped out the next morning on a boat full of trappers heading upriver into the wilderness. Very soon I began to make myself noticed by the others, due to the accuracy of my shooting and my natural bravery in the face of dangers most grown men would quail before."

I decide to cut in before he picks up too much of a head of steam. "I thought you wanted to hear my story."

"I did," he says, giving me a gentle smile. "And quite a story it was too. Someday you will have to share the whole of it. Now, as I was saying..."

I tune him out after that, only checking back in now and then to determine whether he is still talking. It's a nice day, with the sun warm on my back, and I doze off.

Sometime later I wake up, feeling nicely refreshed from my nap, and it's with no great surprise that I realize he's still talking.

"See this scar right here?" Beckwourth points to his forehead. "You want to know how I got it?"

"No. Not really." I say this knowing it makes no difference.

"It was in '36." He scratches the white stubble on his chin, thinking. "No, it was '37. I remember because that was the year of all the floods, when the raft got away from us and Johnson disappeared down river and we never saw him again. Poor Johnson. He was quite the hand with a rifle, but he couldn't swim a lick." Beckwourth takes off his cap and bows his head for a moment.

Then it's straight back to talking.

"There were perhaps forty of us, counting women and children. We'd crossed the Hitchen River the day before and were making our way south when up ahead I spotted five hundred Indians coming toward us. When I saw they were Black Feet

85

Indians I knew our day was about to become troublesome. No one fancied white scalps like the Black Feet and they didn't care if they came from man, woman or child.

"I knew that if we could get back to the river there was a good spot we could make our stand and we'd hold them off even if there was a thousand of them. Placing the women and children in advance, I directed them to make all speed back to the river, while we menfolk formed a rearguard to hold the redskins in check. In this manner we commenced our retreat and it was a running fight the entire way. When they approached too near, we used our rifles to great effect, so that the way became littered with dead and dying Indians."

I look at him, wondering if he expects me to believe that forty men held off five hundred Indians. He looks very earnest and I consider telling him I don't believe him, but I give the idea up without trying. Let him talk. Sooner or later he has to get tired, right?

"In time when they found they couldn't break us the Indians began to hold back, doubtless thinking that sooner or later we'd have no run left in us and then they'd be able to kill us as they pleased.

"During our retreat this old gentleman, Travis his name was, suddenly went down, crying out, 'Oh god, I am wounded!' Quickly I reined my horse around and with no regard to my own safety I rode back and jumped down to help him. An arrow trembled in his back. I pulled it out and helped him back on his horse, saying, 'Ride fast, Travis! I'll see you to safety yet!' Before I could get back on my horse, two of the scoundrels caught up to me. One swung his tomahawk at my head but I ducked and stabbed him with my knife. He fell back and I struck the other a mighty blow with the butt of my rifle, killing him on the spot.

"Then I leapt back on my horse and raced to catch up with my companions, who had formed a line fifty yards ahead and were firing as fast as they could. I gained the safety of the line and together we laid out another dozen or so of the rascals, then rode off after the women and children again.

"After hard hours of this we made it back to the river. There was a big horseshoe bend in the river at that spot and I knew that we could hold the neck of that bend against a thousand of the devils while the women and children would be safe in the rear. Since the river was too swift to cross we didn't have to concern ourselves with the possibility that they would come up on us from behind.

"If our ammunition had held out, that is how it would have gone too, but all too soon it began to run low. Seeing that we must soon succumb to the red devils…"

Here Beckwourth stops his story and pats me on the arm. "Please, take no offense at my descriptions. I don't wish to imply that all Indians are devils. But you may trust me that the Black Feet are."

I shrug. I've heard worse.

"As I was saying, seeing that we must soon succumb to them, I rose up in front of my valiant companions and said, 'If we are to die, let us go to the bosom of the grave protecting the defenseless. Let us charge them with no regard for ourselves, that the women and children we protect will see and honor the memory of our sacrifice!'"

I try to imagine someone standing up in the middle of a fight and talking such foolishness but I can't. Does anyone actually talk that way? And how long would the women and children have to honor their memory if they all were going to die soon after as well?

Beckwourth continues on. "As you can imagine, the men cheered my words."

Sure they did. They're all about to die and you jump up and spout off with just about the worst nonsense imaginable and they cheer. Isn't that what anyone would do?

"Accordingly, sixteen of us mounted our steeds and, leaving the rest to fight until the bitter end, we charged into the midst of our enemy. Our foe, surprised by this sudden feat of bravery, fell back in confusion and for a time it appeared we would break them and win the day.

"But it was at this point that I was struck in the head by an arrow and fell from my horse. Seeing their leader go down, my companions faltered and the Black Feet, encouraged by the loss of one they had begun to believe they could not kill, regrouped and charged, driving my companions back.

"Fortunately for those brave souls, I was not killed, only stunned. For a time I lay there senseless, covered in blood and appearing very much dead. I awakened to find one of their braves pulling on my hair, preparatory to claiming my scalp. Instantly regaining my senses, I leapt up and stabbed the brute in the heart. At the same time I gave forth a mighty, bloodcurdling cry that struck fear in the hearts of all my enemies and they fell back from me, doubtless thinking me an avenging angel come to make them answer for their sins.

"I slew all those about me in that first sudden burst of righteous rage, then, snatching up my trusty rifle, I ran back to my companions, who were all overjoyed at the sight of me returned to them, safe and sound."

Does he expect me to believe this? I wonder. Does *he* believe it?

"Alas, our situation was still dire. My sudden return from the dead had bought us a brief respite but it had done nothing to address our fundamental problem, which was that soon we would be reduced to flinging stones at our attackers. It was mentioned then that a large body of trappers and soldiers were camped upriver of our position hardly more than twenty miles away. Maybe one of us could break through our besiegers and fetch help.

"'But who will go?' the others asked. 'Who among us possesses the bravery and the skill?'

"'I will go,' I told them, standing and wiping the blood from my eyes. 'For though I am wounded, it is merely a flesh wound and does not hamper me.'

"So saying, I mounted our fastest horse. 'God bless you!' the women cried when they saw what I meant to do. 'Truly you are our savior!'"

Okay, now this is too much. I have to say something. "That didn't really happen. You're spinning yarns out of whole cloth."

He gives he a horrified look, his eyes wide. "By my honor," he says in a quavering voice, filled with intensity, "every word I speak is true." He touches his heart as he says this. "Surely you cannot doubt me on this?"

He looks so pained that I give it up. "Sure. I believe you."

He goes right back to his story. "With the reins in my teeth and a pistol in each hand, I charged once again into the midst of my enemies, raining death upon them. I slew a great many of them before I broke free of them. They chased me for some time but they had no chance of catching me.

"I urged my stallion to ever greater speed and to his credit the beast seemed to know my urgency, for he gave me all his worth and ran like the wind. Sadly, his great strength gave out miles short of my goal and finally he fell and died, so that I had to continue on foot. But I am not exaggerating when I tell you that my speed on foot was hardly less than on horseback, so great was my concern for my companions and the innocents they protected.

"At length I reached the other camp and quickly explained to them the direness of our straits. Once again mounted, I led them at speed back the way I'd come, praying as we went that we would not be too late but vowing that if we were, I would have my revenge on the savages, killing ten of them for every one of my friends they had killed."

"Let me guess," I say. "You arrived just in time."

He nods somberly. "In the very nick of time. As we came into sight the defenders fired their last shots and were standing bravely awaiting the savages' charge, every one of them determined to sell his life dearly in the defense of the innocent.

"We fell on them from the rear as they began their charge, taking them completely by surprise. In no time we had routed them completely, killing them by the hundreds, so many that each of us ended the day with more scalps than we could carry."

I can only look at him and shake my head.

24

The next day we ride into this small town on the banks of the Arkansas River. "There is a trading post here," Beckwourth says, "where I will soon dispose of these pelts and you shall have your money."

Except that there isn't a trading post. We ride through town twice to make sure. There's a livery, a general store, a church, even a barber shop, but no trading post. At the livery, a man is sitting on the fence, watching us as we ride back and forth. Beckwourth rides over to him.

"There used to be a trading post in this town. Whatever became of it?"

The man looks at him from under the brim of his hat. "Burned down." He digs around in his ear with a dirty fingernail. "Ten years ago I reckon."

Beckwourth looks at me. "Apparently it has been longer than I thought since I was last here. We'll go to the general store, then. They will surely be able to oblige us," he says and heads that way.

He takes the bale of beaver skins off his horse, slings it on his shoulder and heads inside. I follow. The storekeeper is a little fellow with round spectacles and a bald head that's shiny enough a man could use it as a shaving mirror. He puts his hands on the counter and looks us up and down.

"What can I do you for?" he drawls.

Beckwourth slaps his beaver pelts down on the counter and gives the little man a big smile. "I have here three dozen of the finest quality beaver pelts, my good sir."

Wrinkling his nose, the shopkeeper picks up a pencil and pokes the pelts. "Beaver, you say?"

Beckwourth nods vigorously. "The finest quality."

The shopkeeper gives Beckwourth a look and one eyebrow rises. "You're a bit late."

Beckwourth frowns. "For what?"

"No one buys beaver pelts anymore."

"What? When did this happen?"

The shopkeeper shrugs. "Ten, twenty years ago?"

All the air seems to rush out of Beckwourth at once. "That is…most regrettable," he says in a choked voice. "So the European demand for beaver pelts has diminished."

"Nope. It died completely. One day the men in Europe got up and decided wearing a dead beaver on their heads looked foolish, I reckon. They up and quit buying them."

Beckwourth drums his fingers on the counter, thinking. "You don't say. But you'll still buy them, right? At a reduced price naturally."

"Why in tarnation would I go and do that?"

"They're fine pelts. They can be used for all manner of things."

"Like?"

"Like gloves, for one. Waterproof gloves. That's a fine thing to have in a cold winter."

The shopkeeper squints at him. "I never seen anyone wearing beaver skin gloves."

"It's only a matter of time," Beckwourth assures him. "They make fine socks too. Just the thing for warm toes on a cold winter's day."

The shopkeeper shakes his head. "I can't see that either."

"That's because you have no imagination."

The shopkeeper frowns at him. "I got plenty of imagination. Why, right now I can imagine you taking your pile of stinking hides and whisking yourself right out of my store. How's that for imagination?"

"I don't believe I like your tone, sir. It's no way to treat a customer."

"Oh you're a customer, are you? Because I thought you were trying to sell *me* something."

"I can't very well be a customer if you don't buy my pelts now, can I?" Beckwourth says this smugly, like he's made a key point and won the argument.

The shopkeeper takes a shotgun from under the counter and lays it down before him. "Now I'm imagining filling your backside with rock salt while you run for the door. What about you? Can you imagine that too?"

"I'll take my business elsewhere," Beckwourth warns.

"I sure as hell hope so."

We leave the store and Beckwourth turns to me. "Can you believe that man?"

"How do you plan to get my hundred dollars now?" I ask him.

"Oh, that." He pats me on the shoulder. "It's nothing but a trifle."

"Not to me it's not."

"Do not fret, my friend. I gave my word, didn't I? I have a plan."

"And does your plan include selling beaver pelts?"

"No," he says sadly.

"What is your plan?"

"I have a friend. When last I heard from him he told me he had become quite wealthy, that he struck a rich vein of gold ore. He lives in a town not two days' ride from here, and on the way to our destination, I might add. He owes me money from the old days. I'm quite certain he will be good for it. He was always a straight shooter."

"This friend of yours, are you sure he's still living there?"

"Of course he is. Why would you doubt me?"

"The trading post? The beaver skins no one wants?"

He waves his hand as if those things mean nothing. "Minor setbacks. Trust me, Ace. You'll look back one day and see that partnering with me was the best decision of your young life." He reaches into his pocket and pulls out a bill. "It is not the agreed-upon sum, I know, but it will hopefully prove to you that I am in earnest."

It's twenty dollars. I shouldn't take it. I can still cut out.

But Beckwourth is giving me this look that makes me feel sorry for the old guy and I'm almost out of ammunition.

"Two days, you said?"

He nods.

I take the money and go back into the store. The storekeeper looks me over to make sure I'm not carrying any beaver skins, then says, "He your friend?"

"That's kind of a complicated question."

"He seems a mite tetched in the head."

"I've had that thought myself."

I buy my ammo and go back outside. We mount up and ride out of town.

"Did I ever tell you about the time I lived for a winter with a pack of wolves?" Beckwourth asks me, pulling out his pipe. He doesn't wait for my answer, but goes straight into it.

"I was trapping beavers up in Montana…"

25

Later that day we're following this stream up the bottom of a small valley, when we come on this lonesome homestead. It's nothing special, a log cabin with a small barn nearby, a big woodpile. a few acres of plowed lands, some cows and chickens scratching around.

We probably would have ridden straight on by except that there's an awful ruckus coming from the cabin, some woman howling to wake the dead. When Beckwourth hears that his ears perk right up.

"I believe we may have someone in distress yonder," he says, and turns his horse down the wagon track that leads to the place.

"It's been my experience that people don't want others in their business unless they ask for it," I say, but it doesn't slow him down any.

"It can't hurt to look in," he says over his shoulder.

It can if they decide to start shooting, I think, but I keep it to myself. Like most people who talk a lot, Beckwourth isn't all that fond of listening.

Beckwourth dismounts by the front door and gives it a smart rap with his knuckles. I hang back a little and stay on Coyote. We might need to make a fast getaway.

After a bit the door opens and there's a woman standing there wearing an apron over a gingham dress. Most of her hair has come loose from the bun she tied it up in and her face is red, whether from crying or anger I can't tell.

"What is it?" she hollers.

It's anger. I don't know what's going on, but I know we don't want any part of it. Time to go.

But apparently Beckwourth comes to a different conclusion than I do because he touches his cap and says, "Excuse me, ma'am, but my companion and I were passing by and we couldn't help but hear your discomfort. Is there some problem that we could assist you with?"

Her eyes narrow and she looks Beckwourth up and down like she's figuring out which piece to bite off first. Any normal man who valued his hide would be heading for the hills right about now, but clearly Beckwourth doesn't fit that description because he stands there calmly with a little smile on his face. I brace for the explosion.

But the woman surprises me. She pushes hair out of her eyes and says, "Maybe you *can* help."

"Name it," Beckwourth says, "and if it is in our power we will speedily set to."

"Redskins," she says. "They took my daughter. I been trying to get the worthless lump of husband I have the misfortune of being married to—" She turns and kind of shouts the last part back inside. "—to get out and chase after her, but he's being contrary like usual."

The look on Beckwourth's face when she says this is something to behold. He plain lights up like this is the best news he ever heard. "That's terrible news!" he cries, though the expression on his face says something else altogether. "It's no wonder we find you in such a state, your precious daughter hauled bodily from the safety of her home and into the bosom of the wilderness. But you are in luck. I am James P. Beckwourth, noted mountaineer, scout, pioneer and chief of the Crow Nation, and I am at your service. You may be certain that my assistant and I will bring your stolen child back forthwith."

When he's done talking the woman gives him a gimlet eye. "Who talks like that? You a lawyer or something?"

Beckwourth draws himself up. "While I have studied the law somewhat, I would not be so bold as to presume—"

"Stow it," she snaps. "I can't stand here all day listening to you. A couple more minutes of that and I'd brain you with a spade."

"No doubt your concern for your daughter has made you ill-tempered," he says.

"No, it's menfolk that makes me ill-tempered and you should know right now you ain't seen nothing. My temper can get a whole lot worse."

"Ain't that the god's truth," a voice says from inside the cabin.

She turns. "You shut up, Harry! I wasn't talking to you!" She turns back to Beckwourth. His smile has slipped a bit, but he's doing his best to hang onto it. "I don't suppose I have any choice," she says bitterly, "since her own father won't do nothing. But that don't mean I got to listen to you jabber on."

A man emerges from the cabin. He's wearing a plaid shirt and suspenders. His boots are mud-caked and he has the gnarled look of someone who's worked hard for a lot of years. He gives his wife a hard look.

"I can't do it, Melba, I told you. It's my bum knee. Five minutes in the saddle and it'll give out altogether. And the horse fetched up lame yesterday, I already told you that too."

"I swear, Harry, you got more excuses than a hound dog's got ticks. Why, if excuses was pennies, we'd be rich as Rockefeller by now."

"By god, woman, I wish the Injuns had taken you instead. 'Spect they got more sense than that, though. No doubt you'd wear their ears out in the first hour and they'd be right back here looking to unload you."

He looks at Beckwourth. "I'm mighty obliged to you for doing this, mister. Be a mercy to hear the end of this."

"Is that all you have to say about it?" Melba screeches. "With your poor daughter out there in the hands of those savages? That innocent child is maybe even now being deflowered by those monsters and you don't even care!"

"Oh, I care all right," he snaps at her. "Least I would if you'd quit squawking long enough for me to line up two thoughts one after the other."

That sets her off again and she chews him up one side and down the other so hard I'm surprised there's anything left of him but scraps of leather when she finally stops to draw breath.

"Hold on," I say when I see my opening. "How do you know Indians took her? How do you know it wasn't someone else?" I know I sound peevish, but that's because I get tired of hearing everything bad that ever happens blamed on Indians. I've seen enough cruel, terrible things done by people of every color to know Indians don't have sole claim to being savages.

"Of course it's Injuns!" she shouts. "What else would it be?"

"Outlaws. A bear maybe."

96

THE BLACK PEARL TREASURE

She gives me a suspicious look, but with my hat pulled low and the sun at my back she can't get a good look at my face. "There's evidence. That's how I know it was Injuns. You'll see when you get over to the barn. Show 'em, Harry. If your bum knee will hold up that long."

"It'll hold up long enough to give you a good kick in the fanny, you old biddy," he says.

"Pshaw," she says contemptuously, "you ain't got it in you. You're all talk and no gumption."

Beckwourth cuts in before Harry can reply. "Perhaps I could point out that while we stand here arguing, your daughter is getting further away."

At first it seems like his words won't make any difference. The way Harry and Melba are glaring at each other puts me in mind of a pair of wolves circling, looking for an opening. Then Melba surprises me by backing down. The hard anger she wraps around her slips a bit and something softer shows through.

"I just want to know my daughter's safe," she says, dabbing at the corner of her eye with her apron. "It's all any mother could ask. She's all I got."

"Come on," Harry growls. "I'll show you what we found."

He leads us off toward the barn. "Last we saw Jenny was this morning, before sunup," he says. "When she came out to do the milking. I was out in the fields and didn't notice. It was Melba saw she was gone."

Outside the barn is a milking stool turned on its side. On the ground nearby are a couple of turkey feathers. I get down off Coyote and look over the tracks. "It looks to me like one person rode up on a horse. She walked over and he helped her on. No sign of a struggle. And I don't think it was an Indian she left with either. Look at this." I point at the horse tracks. "This horse was wearing shoes. Most Indians don't have shoes on their horses."

That clearly angers Harry. He scowls at me. "Of course you would say that."

"Meaning?"

"You a half-breed and all."

Beckwourth cuts in before I can tell Harry how I feel about his words. "I assure you that my companion is a man of the highest morals. If he says he doesn't think it was Indians, then likely it was not."

Harry swings to scowl at him. "Of course it was an Indian what kidnapped her. How do you explain the milking stool being tipped over? And those feathers over there on the ground? She put up a fight. Jenny allus was a fighter. In the struggle she kicked over the milking stool and tore some feathers out of her kidnapper's hair."

"Not only Indians wear feathers, you know," I say. "Turkeys do too. Which explains the turkey tracks."

"There's turkey tracks?"

I point. "Right there."

"That still don't explain the milk stool."

I stand up the stool. It immediately falls over again. "Maybe it fell over because one leg is too short."

"Is you fellers going to help or not? You said you would."

"Of course we will help," Beckwourth says stoutly.

"I'd come with you," Harry says. "If it wasn't for this bum knee."

"No need," Beckwourth says. "The two of us are sufficient. We'll find your daughter."

"I still don't think she was kidnapped," I say.

The huff goes out of Harry suddenly. He looks over his shoulder at the house. Melba is standing there watching us. "Jenny's gone. What else could it be but a kidnapping?"

"What does Jenny look like?" Beckwourth asks. "How old is she?"

"She's eighteen, about this tall." He holds his hand up about chin high. "She has brown hair."

Beckwourth gets on his horse. "You may rely on us. Let's go, Ace. Let's find Jenny."

I mount up and follow him away from the homestead.

26

We ride out of there and Beckwourth is actually rubbing his hands together he's so excited. "What fine luck this is," he says.

"You're still planning on going after her? I'm telling you, she wasn't kidnapped."

"Are you sure about that? Absolutely sure?"

I have to admit I'm not absolutely sure.

"We *have* to go after her. I gave my word to her mother and I always keep my word."

"It's that book of yours, isn't it?"

"What do you mean?"

"You're looking for adventures to put in that book. That's why you're so hot to chase that girl."

"While that may factor into my decision—" he starts.

"Save it. I don't want to hear it. Let's just get this over with."

The trail is easy to follow. Whoever it was, he didn't bother to hide his tracks. They lead up into the forest, over a high ridge, and down the other side. Tucked in a little hollow is an abandoned log cabin, half the roof fallen in from where a tree fell on it.

From the cabin is coming a terrible caterwauling, like someone's slaughtering chickens. Beckwourth and I exchange looks.

"It sounds like he's scalping her. We got here just in time," he says. He draws his pistol and claps his heels to his horse. I race after him. Could I really have been that wrong?

We jump down off our horses and run up to the front door. It's closed but it doesn't look too sturdy. We take up positions on either side of it.

"On my mark," he says. "One, two, three!"

He kicks the door open and we burst in, guns sweeping the room...

Oh no.

They're lying on an old blanket on the floor. He has his pants down around his ankles. She sees us over his shoulder and screams.

He rolls off her and tries to jump to his feet while pulling up his pants at the same time. Which doesn't work out too well for him. He trips and falls down.

Beckwourth and I are crowding the door, both of us trying to get out at the same time. About that time she lays hold of his pistol which is lying on the ground. She snatches it up and starts spraying lead everywhere, screaming curses at us.

Somehow we make it outside without getting shot. Bullets are still flying out the door and we press up against the side of the cabin.

"I told you she didn't need rescuing," I say. "Now we're the ones that need it."

Beckwourth looks shocked, like he can't imagine that his little adventure could turn to this.

There's a series of clicks as she runs out of bullets. Beckwourth puts his pistol away and steps back into the doorway, holding his hands up.

"Please accept our deepest apologies, ma'am." He ducks as she throws the empty gun at him. "Oh, shit," he says and starts backing up.

She comes flying out the door, scratching and clawing. Beckwourth tries to grab her wrists but she twists away and puts a fine scratch down his cheek.

"I could use some help," he yells, but I shake my head.

"You brought this on yourself."

Finally, he gets a good grip on her wrists and stops her. By then the young man she's with is poking his head out the door, looking sheepish. Looks like he managed to pull his pants up.

"Your mother sent us," Beckwourth says, but that only sets her off again. Since she can't get her hands free, she settles for kicking him. From Beckwourth's expression, I'd say a couple of them land. Good for her. Maybe next time he'll listen to me.

"Young lady, please!" Beckwourth cries.

She gets lucky and one of her kicks lands in the worst possible spot for Beckwourth. He lets go of her and staggers back, holding his crotch. His mouth works but nothing comes out.

THE BLACK PEARL TREASURE

That seems to calm her down. She brushes her hair back out of her eyes. She's pretty in a way, with good skin and a fine chin, but there's something in her eyes that makes me nervous. I've seen eyes like that before, when I was punching cows. Cows with eyes like that, you have to be real careful around them. You don't know what they're going to do. Cows like that can hurt you.

"You're not taking me back to my mother," she says in a calm voice.

Beckwourth gulps some air and manages to straighten up, though his color still doesn't look right. "I'm afraid we can't—"

"What?" she cuts in. I swear I see her eyes roll a little in her head, same as those crazy cows. I'm starting to think this would have been easier if she had been kidnapped by Indians.

"It wouldn't be proper, leaving a young maiden out here all alone with a man who clearly isn't her husband," Beckwourth says.

"I ain't no maiden. Not anymore. Besides, I'm full grown. I can make my own decisions, thank you very much."

"I promised your mother…"

"I don't give a fig for your promises. They don't mean nothing to me."

I can see the fix Beckwourth has gotten himself into, caught between his word and her refusal. I think I'm starting to enjoy this.

"I cannot leave you here," he says.

She gives him a hard look. "Are you saying you're fixing to kidnap me? Is that what you're saying?"

Beckwourth takes a little step back, getting himself out of her range. He looks skittish as a new colt and I don't blame him. "I'd rather it did not come to that."

"Leroy," she says, turning on the young feller who's still standing in the doorway. "Kindly get that gun of yours and reload it so I can shoot this man."

Leroy gulps. He's got a turkey neck and a real big Adam's apple so when he does that it's a lot like an actual turkey swallowing a large apple.

"I'm not sure that's such a good idea, sweetness," he says.

"I didn't ask you what you *thought*, Leroy," she says in a low, dangerous voice. "I asked you to *do*."

Leroy freezes like a mouse finally caught by the cat, but Beckwourth rescues him.

"If I may, I believe I have the solution," he says, holding up one finger. "Among other things," he continues, "I am an ordained minister, of the Calvinist persuasion."

"A what?" Jenny says, wrinkling her nose.

"A minister. That means I can get you two hitched."

"You don't say…" Jenny's thinking about it and it looks to me like the idea appeals to her. At least she doesn't look so much like a cougar about to attack.

"Once you are properly husband and wife, then there is nothing untoward about…whatever it is you choose to do."

"You could do that, right here and now?" she asks.

"Well, it is a bit irregular. Usually it's best if your parents—"

"The devil take my parents!" she snaps. "I want you to do this here and now."

"But who will give away the bride?"

She points at me. "I reckon he'll do."

Beckwourth nods. "Okay. It's not usual, but since you are both adults, I consent."

"Well, that's just peachy," she says. "Leroy, get over here!"

But it's too late. While all this went on, Leroy's been moving. He's already at the edge of the cabin and when she turns he takes off running, skinny arms pumping. He hits the trees and in about five seconds he's out of sight.

"Well, damn," Jenny says.

27

About the time Jenny starts rustling around looking for that pistol she threw, Beckwourth and I decide it's time to go. We run for our horses, swing into the leather and high-tail it out of there.

"Don't you run off on me, Leroy!" she screams.

She starts cussin' up a blue streak and then a couple of shots go off. I wonder where she found the bullets, but I'm not about to turn back and ask.

We don't slow down until we've put a couple of miles behind us, then Beckwourth says, "I believe that worked out fine in the end, don't you think?"

"How do you figure? What part of that worked out fine?"

"We found their daughter."

"Who didn't want to be found. We almost got shot. How is that fine?"

"The child is safe. That is what matters. Now we can continue on without worrying about her."

"Which I wasn't planning on doing."

"Come, come, Ace. Where is your sense of adventure?"

"You really enjoyed that, didn't you?"

He rubs his hands together. "It was exhilarating. Surely even you can admit that."

"And the part where you got kicked in the balls? Was that exhilarating too?"

He gets a pained look on his face. "Not so much," he admits. "I may be sore for some days. Still, all in all a good trade."

I pull up and look at him. "You can read sign too. You knew all along that girl hadn't been kidnapped."

"I couldn't be sure."

"That's bullshit and we both know it. You *knew* she hadn't been kidnapped and yet still you insisted on chasing her. You almost got us killed."

"The key word there is 'almost'," he says triumphantly, as if he found the hole in my argument and won something.

I start riding away. "I'm done with you, Beckwourth. I didn't sign on to get shot for no reason. Good luck finding your treasure ship."

He spurs his horse and catches up to me. "Ace, wait! You can't quit."

"I already did."

"But…" He searches for something, some way to make me change my mind. What he settles on is "You already spent the money I gave you."

That's irritating. I forgot about that. "I took you part way. You gave me part of the money. That makes us even."

He gets a very stern look on his face. "You gave me your word, Ace. We *shook* on it. Out here in the West, a man's word is everything. I find it hard to believe you would throw your honor away like that."

That's beyond irritating. That cuts to the bone. I stop and face him.

"But your part of the bargain was to pay me the whole hundred dollars up front. Which you didn't do. You broke your word first." There. That should shut him up.

But he won't be stopped so easily. "I would have too, if the man at the trading post would have bought my beaver pelts."

"General store. The trading post burned down ten years ago. Remember?"

His voice gets sad. "I really loved that place."

"And why didn't the man at the general store buy the pelts?" I already know the answer, but I'm feeling a mite peeved. I want to hear him say it out loud.

Beckwourth hangs his head. "It seems people in Europe aren't wearing beaver skin hats anymore."

"And this didn't just happen!" I know I'm practically yelling, but I can't seem to help it. "He said it had been ten or twenty *years* since the beaver trade died!"

"He might have exaggerated a bit."

"No, he didn't. I'm only a poor half-breed from nowhere and even *I* knew there was no trade in beaver pelts anymore. I thought you were this great explorer and pioneer. How could you *not* know that?"

"I've been busy with other things."

"Like what?"

"Like writing my book. It's a lot harder than you realize. Commas give me a lot of trouble. They don't seem to make any sense."

"*You* don't make any sense."

"I think we're getting off track here. The vicissitudes of fashion are not relevant to us right now. What *is* relevant is the deal you made with me. You shook on it remember?"

Dammit. He's right. I did.

But I'm not done yet. "Before I go one more step with you, I want the truth. Why are you doing this?"

"I told you. It's for the book."

I shake my head. "I'm not buying the nag you're selling, Beckwourth. I've heard your stories. If half of them are in that book, you've got more than enough. You're *looking* for trouble to get into. Trouble that could get both of us killed. If you're going to get me killed, I want to know why."

He thinks about this, then nods. "Fair enough." He sighs. "When you're young, you feel like you have all the time in the world. There's plenty of time to do whatever you want. But somehow the years pass and before you're aware of it, old age creeps up on you. Suddenly you realize you don't have that much time. Sadly, by the time that realization comes, most of us are too old and too sick to do anything about it. Then all that's left is the past. You sit there and dream about the past until it becomes more real than the present."

There is a sadness on him that I've never seen before. It's a little shocking. I'd come to see him as always cheerful, always energetic. I'd never expected to find this.

He reaches into his saddlebags and pulls out the little brown bottle I've seen him drinking off of. "This is laudanum," he says. "I take it for the pain." He taps his chest. "I'm sick, Ace. No, more than that. I'm dying. There's something growing in my chest. The doctor says I don't have long."

It bothers me, seeing him like this. He looks old suddenly. "Doctors are wrong all the time," I say.

He gives me a sad smile. "That they are. But not this time. I can feel it. It's larger every day. I expect soon it will be hard to breathe. Soon the laudanum won't be enough." He puts the bottle away.

"I was in the hospital in St. Louis. Not really a hospital, I guess, more of a home for people who are dying. There was a man in there we called Old Joe. He was probably ninety. He claimed he traveled with Lewis and Clark on their great expedition when he was little more than a boy.

"I watched him die, slipping more and more each day. Like most old people, he talked about his youth and the things he'd done. But what he talked about most was the thing he'd never done. See, he's the one who first told me about the black pearl treasure. He said on his last trip out west he met a man who'd seen it in person. The man was willing to tell him how to find it, but Old Joe turned him down. He said he thought about it, but decided he was too old. It was too risky. Instead he went back to St. Louis. Where he ended up in the hospital, laying on a bed and waiting to die.

"Old Joe's only regret was he didn't go after that treasure himself. He told me over and over how much he'd rather have died searching for it than lying in a bed crapping himself." Beckwourth's voice gets husky. "Old Joe died late one night. I was sitting by his bed when it happened, when he closed his eyes for the last time.

"The next morning I got up early and walked out the door." He looks up and fixes his sad eyes on me. "I'm not dying in a bed surrounded by other people who are dying, Ace. I want to die like I lived. That's why I'm here. I'm looking for one last, great adventure."

His words hit me pretty hard. There's a lot to take in there and I reckon it will take me a while to sort through it all. But one thing I can figure out right away. One thing, above everything else, is clear, and that's how much he needs this.

"I'll get you there, Beckwourth. If that ship can be found, we'll find it. You have my word on that."

A smile comes over Beckwourth's face and tears start in his eyes. He leans over and clasps my hand. "Thank you, Ace. That means more to me than you realize."

28

We hit the town where Beckwourth's friend is supposed to live late in the afternoon. It's not much of a town, even as Western towns go, nothing but a handful of warped, unpainted wooden buildings huddled in the bottom of a gulch like old dogs too tired to wander off and die. The hillside above the town is dotted with wooden mine structures and tailings piles but none of the mines look active.

Which doesn't make me feel too hopeful about that loan Beckwourth was talking about. Still, I suppose as long as we're here we might as well look his friend up.

A little fellow in a suit so old and worn that it's gone shiny comes trotting out of one of the buildings when we ride in.

"Welcome to Bloody Gulch!" he hollers. "I'm Al, which isn't short for anything and doesn't need to be, on account of how short I am." He pauses to chuckle at his joke. "If you gents are looking for anything, anything at all, I'm your man." He pats himself on the chest and gives us a big, shiny smile.

"Perhaps you can help us. We're looking for a friend of mine," Beckwourth says.

"That's fine," Al says. "Bloody Gulch is a fine place to find a friend, our harsh moniker notwithstanding. Say, would either of you gents be looking for a bank by any chance? I happen to run the safest bank in town."

He sweeps his arm at the building he came out of. It's a particularly dilapidated building. Part of the roof has blown off and the only thing keeping it from falling over on its side is a couple of timbers propping it up.

"That's a bank?" I say.

"Don't let the outside fool you," he says. "Your money is as safe with me as if it was in the hands of the Lord."

I can see through gaps in the front wall and it doesn't look like there's any furniture in there. No safe either. "I don't see a safe."

"A minor detail, I assure you."

"Doesn't seem so minor to me."

He gets a little peevish then. "Gol-darn it! Safes are expensive! It ain't like they're lying around to be had." He makes an effort to get a hold of himself and picks up his smile again. "Look at it this way. I save money by not having a safe. That means I can pass that savings on to you."

"How do you keep people from stealing the money?"

He looks up and down the street and lowers his voice. "It's hidden. Only I know where it is."

A man comes out of the next building over and shouts, "Leave off, Al! Go on before I take a switch to you!"

"It's a free country, I guess! 'Sides, I ain't hurtin' nobody!" Al yells back.

But when the man starts for him Al kind of yelps and darts back into the falling-down building, slamming the door behind him. Whereupon the door falls off.

The man who ran Al off comes up to us. He's wearing overalls and chewing on a twig. "Don't mind Al. He's harmless, but he ain't right in the head. Ever since he took that old suit from the banker after he died, he thinks *he's* a banker. So long as you don't give him any money, you won't have any problem with him."

"Not much chance of that," I say.

"I'm looking for an old friend of mine," Beckwourth says. "His name is Willard Easton. Do you know where I could find him?"

The man shakes his head. "Can't say I know anybody by that name. You sure he's still here?"

"He's an older gentleman, a bit on the short side. He walks with a limp." Beckwourth points to his temple. "He has somewhat of a dent in his skull right about here, from where a buffalo kicked him years ago."

The man's eyes light up. "Oh, you mean Drunk Willy! Shoot, I know him. Everybody knows Drunk Willy. Don't believe I've ever heard anyone call him Willard though."

"Maybe it's not the same man," Beckwourth says.

"How many fellers have a dent in their head?"

"You have a point," Beckwourth concedes. "Where would I find him?"

"I don't rightly know. You can check the trough down at the livery. Drunk Willy likes to sleep it off behind there sometimes. But most times you'll find him under the front porch of the saloon. That way he doesn't have to go too far for his next bottle. Either way, once the sun goes down you'll find him in the saloon." The man gives us a speculative look. "What do you want with the old souse anyhow?"

"We were trappers together, back in the old days," Beckwourth says.

"No kidding?" the man says. "So Willy was telling the truth about that anyway. I always figured he'd made that up too."

"He was quite the frontiersman, you can be assured of that," Beckwourth says.

"Whatever he was, he ain't no more. Don't expect much and you won't be disappointed much, that's what I always say, though I reckon it applies here more than about anywhere." The man leaves and goes back inside.

"Drunk Willy?" I say. "That doesn't sound too promising."

"Doubtless he's exaggerating," Beckwourth says. "As people out here in the West are prone to do with newcomers. Willard enjoyed a drink as much as anyone, but I refuse to believe he has sunk so low as to be sleeping under porches."

"You seem awfully sure about that."

"When you've ridden as many trails with a man as I did with Willard you come to know him."

"One way to find out." We ride on over to the saloon and I climb down out of the saddle. I kneel down and peer under the porch. Sure enough, there's someone under there. He's awake too. I can see his eyes reflecting the light.

"You've got visitors, Willy," I say.

"I'm not home" is his muffled reply.

"You look home."

"I'm busy."

"Too busy to see an old friend?" Beckwourth asks, kneeling down beside me.

The eyes shift over to him. "Do I know you? Because I sure as hell don't know him."

"It's Samuel P. Beckwourth. You remember me, don't you?"

"Beckwourth?"

"One and the same."

"We'll see about that. Give me a moment to tidy up and I'll be right out."

Beckwourth and I stand up. "I don't think he's going to have your money," I say.

Beckwourth pats me on the shoulder. "There are more important things than money, Ace."

"True, but most of them can't be traded for supplies. I'd like to eat something other than beans now and then."

"Why, I spent an entire winter on the upper reaches of the Powder River living on nothing but moss and the occasional squirrel. It didn't start out that way, of course, but I lost all my supplies…"

His words taper off as we both hear a sound coming from underneath the porch. It's the sound of Willy peeing. We're not the only ones who hear it either, because a moment later the bartender comes storming out of the saloon with a broom in his hand. He starts banging on the floor boards with the handle.

"Dammit, Willy! I told you you could sleep under the porch but if you used it as an outhouse I'd run you off!"

"It's not me," Willy protests.

"The hell it's not!" More banging with the broom. "You get out from under there right now or I swear I'll go back inside and get my scatter gun."

Amidst much grumbling, Willy drags himself out from under the porch. "You happy, Mel?" he asks the bartender. "You interrupted me and now I've gone and soiled myself."

There's a wet patch on his trousers but it's hardly noticeable what with the general state of disrepair his clothes are in. Whatever color his clothes once were is lost under layers of dirt and grease. There are holes everywhere and several of the seams have sprung.

Mel curses him a few more times then goes back inside. Willy turns to us. He smells like something crawled into his shirt and died. There's leaves and twigs stuck in his matted hair. His eyes are badly bloodshot. He leans in and peers at Beckwourth.

"Well, so it is Beckwourth," Willy says. "You wouldn't happen to have a snort on you, would you?"

"I'm afraid I don't."

Willy scowls at him. "Then why'd you go and call me out then? You interrupted my nap. Now I'll be cranky as a bear with a sore tooth all night."

If his hostility bothers Beckwourth it doesn't show. He still looks just as cheerful. "I apologize for that, Willard. I will surely keep it in mind for the next time."

"How do you like that," Willy grumbles. "It's getting so a man can't even have a proper sleep without someone disturbing him. And then he don't even have a snort to share with old Willy." Willy gets down on his knees and makes like he's going to crawl back under the porch.

"Hold on, Willard," Beckwourth says, taking hold of his shoulder.

"What is it now?" Willy mutters. "Make it snappy too. I'm a busy man."

"I've come to see you about the money you owe me."

Willy glares up at him. "The hell you say."

"Come, Willard. Surely you remember. You borrowed one hundred dollars from me, I believe it was the summer of '38."

Willy makes it back to his feet and turns on Beckwourth. "That's a damn lie. I never borrowed money from you. I..." He gets a puzzled look on his face and frowns. "What do you know, I think I do remember. It was at that trading post on the Snake River, right?"

"That's it."

"But it was '36, not '38."

"No, sir. It was '38," Beckwourth says.

"I'm certain it was '36. It was the year of the floods."

"You're thinking of '33."

"No, '33 was the year the Kiowa went on the warpath."

"Stop," I say. "What difference does it make?"

"It's best to know for sure," Beckwourth says. Willy nods in agreement.

"I don't want to hear any more about it." I turn to Willy. "Do you have *any* of the money you owe him?"

Willy shakes his head sadly. "Not a dime."

I look at Beckwourth. "We're done here, right?"

"Wait!" Willy says. "The reason I don't have your money is I was robbed."

111

I don't believe that for a second, but it's clear Beckwourth does. "What happened?" He lays his hand on his gun. "Only point out the scoundrel and you may be sure that my friend Ace and I will put it right."

Great. Here we go again. Beckwourth has found himself another adventure. I expect someone will be shooting at us soon.

"I kin do better than that," Willy says. "I kin lead you right to him." He chuckles and rubs his hands together. "Get ready for it, Leo. The hand of justice is coming for you at last."

I'm liking this less and less. "If you were robbed, why didn't you go to the sheriff?" I ask Willy.

"Because there ain't no damned sheriff in Bloody Gulch. Hasn't been for over a year. That's why bartenders can threaten innocent citizens and get away with it!" He yells this last part into the saloon.

"I ain't even started threatening you yet!" Mel shouts back. "You'll know when I do!"

"See what I mean?" Willy says. "This is no place for a man in his golden years, no place at all."

"Why don't you tell us what happened?" Beckwourth asks.

"What happened is I hit it rich. A fat vein of gold, as wide as your finger." Willy's holding his fingers about an inch apart, showing us how wide the vein was. His eyes are wide with outrage. "But a back-stabbin' dry-gulcher jumped my claim and now I have nothing!" Tears well up in his rheumy old eyes.

"Don't fret," Beckwourth says, patting Willy on the back. "Ace here is quite the hand with a gun. He'll set that rascal straight."

"Downright generous of you to volunteer me like that," I say. "Some folks would ask first."

"But I don't need to ask, do I?" Beckwourth leaves off patting Willy on the back and commences to patting me on the back. I've never seen anyone who likes patting people like he does. "You'll help Willy for the same reason you're helping me. Because it's the right thing to do and you're a man who does the right thing."

"You can leave off patting me now. I'm not a horse."

Beckwourth gives me one more good pat and stops. "You're a good man, Ace. One of the best."

"Let's get this over with," I say. I look at Willy. "Where's the claim?"

29

"It's right up the hill." Willy's tongue pushes out between his brown teeth a couple of times and he darts a couple looks at the saloon. "But we oughtn't rush off too hasty. I think a drink or two first would be wise. It's best to make sure we're properly fortified."

"I suppose one drink couldn't hurt…" Beckwourth starts.

"No." Willy's already heading for the door of the saloon and I grab his arm.

"I'm powerful thirsty," Willy says, trying to pull his arm away.

"And I'm impatient."

"That's really more your problem than mine, don't you think?"

I pull my duster back so he can see my pistols. "Are you sure about that?"

He looks at the guns. "That's a good argument," he admits.

"Where's the claim?"

"It's up there." He waves vaguely at the hillside. "Not safe climbing it in the dark though."

I point at the sun, still visible above the horizon.

"Darkness falls fast, here in the mountains," he says, nodding like this is something he has figured out and is sharing with me out of a sincere desire for my welfare.

I lean in close and stare into his bloodshot eyes. "*Now.*"

"I know," he says, suddenly cheerful. "Let's go now. That way we can be back in plenty of time before the saloon closes."

We follow Willy up the hillside. The trail is bad, with plenty of loose rocks and exposed tree roots to trip over. We haven't gone twenty yards before Willy is bent over with his hands on his knees.

"This hill gets steeper ever' year," he wheezes.

"You may need to carry him," Beckwourth tells me in a loud whisper. "He's quite old, you know."

"I'm not carrying him," I say.

"You try to pick me up and I'll bite you!" Willy hollers. "I don't need to be carried. I only stopped because I got something in my eye."

"It's not easy, getting old," Beckwourth says, patting Willy on the back.

"I'm not old! Stop calling me old, you old coot."

"How much further is it?" I ask.

"Up yonder a ways," Willy says, waving his arm. "We'll be there shortly."

It takes an hour. We're on something of a ledge by then. About thirty yards away is the mouth of a mine shaft. The tailings pile spreads down the hill from it. There's a fire pit with a little smoke coming off it and a pile of rusted tin cans and old rags. The sun is nearly down.

"I told you we shoulda waited," Willy says, all but collapsing. He's wheezing so hard he can barely get the words out, but he's not about to give up on what he has to say. "Now it'll be dark when we head down and if I twist my ankle it'll be on your head."

"If you'd carried him…" Beckwourth says.

"I'm not carrying a grown man who's still got both his legs," I say.

That's when I see the gun barrel poke out of the mine shaft.

"Get down!" I shove Willy sideways and grab Beckwourth and yank him down behind a pile of dirt. A heartbeat later there's a gunshot. The bullet whines over our heads.

"Don't you shoot at me, Leo!" Willy yells. When he tries to stand back up I kick his feet out from under him and he falls back down. He glares at me. "Whatcha do that fer?"

"Trying to keep you alive, though right now I can't think why. Stay down unless you want to get your fool head shot off." Another shot and the bullet pings off a rock.

"We just want to talk!" I yell up at the mine. "There's no need for shooting!"

"Ain't interested in talking. Head on back the way you come or I send you out of here packing a bit of extra lead weight!" he yells back.

Willy has crawled over to take cover with us. "Ol' Leo always was a pig-headed cuss. I guess you're gonna have to shoot 'im."

"I'm not shooting anybody unless I have to," I reply.

"Give me one of them fancy guns, then. I'll shoot him all right."

"You're not getting one of my guns."

"All right then. No need to pitch a fit." Willy looks away. A second later I see one of his hands creeping toward my pistol.

In a heartbeat I have it out, the barrel pressed to his nose. "Is this the gun you were reaching for?" I ask him in a hard voice.

"I was only stretching. What's got you so twitchy?"

"Being shot at for one thing." I put the pistol away. "You done trying for my guns?"

"I reckon," he says sullenly.

"Good. Next time you might get shot."

I look up in time to see that Beckwourth has stood up. He's holding his hands over his head. "We don't want any trouble!" he yells.

I grab him and jerk him back down right before another shot rings out. "Not going to be much of an adventure if you get killed straightaway," I tell him.

"I thought he would see reason."

"You let me do the reasoning, okay?" I inch up the mound of dirt to where I can see the mine opening. The barrel of his rifle is visible, but Leo isn't. "I don't want to shoot you, Leo!" I call out.

A bullet whizzes by me.

"You're not making this easy, Leo."

Another bullet.

Now I'm getting annoyed. I don't like people shooting at me when I'm being reasonable. "Let me put this in a way you can understand. You're in a bad position. That's on account of you being in a mine shaft. You see, all that packed dirt and rock is perfect for ricochets. You get what I'm saying?"

There's a pause. Then he says, "Them bullets is gonna bounce." The rifle barrel lowers.

"That's right. Now how about you lower that rifle and come on out. We're not here to shoot you. We only want to talk."

"*I* want to shoot him!" Willy yells.

The barrel comes back up.

"Don't listen to him, Leo!" I yell. "He doesn't have a gun. If he tries anything, I'll knock him out myself."

THE BLACK PEARL TREASURE

I look at Willy. "I'll do it too."

"You'd hit an old man?" he cries.

"You want to find out?"

He looks away. "I believe you would."

I turn back to the mine. "What do you say, Leo?"

"All right," comes the angry reply. "I'm outta bullets anyhow." He steps out of the mine shaft carrying a shovel. "But I still got this shovel. Try anything and I'll brain you."

I holster my gun and stand up. Beckwourth helps Willy up and we approach the mine.

"If he tries anything," I tell Leo. "You have my permission to beat him to death."

Leo gives me a wicked smile when I say this. If anything, he is even dirtier and more disreputable than Willy is. He looks to be mostly dirt. His beard is huge and bushy as is his hair. He's got no teeth at all and he's barefoot. What he doesn't look is feeble. The way he's holding that shovel says he can still use it. I stop outside his range.

"You shouldn't have brought that snake up here," Leo hisses.

"I admit to having that feeling myself," I say. "But now that we're here."

"Don't listen to his lies!" Willy shouts. "He ain't nothing but a low down skunk!"

Just like that he charges Leo. Leo raises his shovel and charges his. His first swing misses, which is good for Willy as it likely would have brained him. The two men go into a clinch, growling and flailing at each other.

I've a mind to let them go at each other for a while. Let them work it out of their systems a bit. Besides, they're not actually harming each other that I can see.

"Ace," Beckwourth says, "if you would break them up, please?"

"Doesn't this count as part of the adventure?"

"They're quite old. I don't want to see them hurt each other."

So I head over, grab them each by the scruff of the neck, and pull them apart. It's easier than I thought it would be. Neither one weighs much more than a sack of straw. I give them both a good shake. "Stop it!"

By and by they leave off with the snarling and settle for bared teeth. I let go of them but I keep a close eye. Pretty soon I reckon they'll be at it again. "We ought to put them in the mine and seal it off," I tell Beckwourth. "Let them eat each other if that's what they want."

"Perhaps something less drastic first," Beckwourth replies. "Now, Leo, Willy here says you jumped his claim. What do you have to say to that?"

"It's a damn lie!" Leo shouts.

Before he can throw himself at Willy I put a hand in his chest and push him back. "Try something a little more civilized."

"He lost the mine to me in a poker game," Leo says.

"The hell I did!" Willy shouts and tries to throw himself at Leo. I shove him back hard enough that he trips and falls down. He looks up at me, surprised. "Hey, that hurt."

"Good. Why don't you stay there for a bit?"

"Do you have any proof?" Beckwourth asks Leo.

"I shore do." Leo hustles off into the mine. I can see a bedroll in there and a stub of candle on an old wooden box. None of the piled dirt out here looks fresh. I'm thinking he's doing more living here than mining.

"He better not come out of there and shoot me," Willy grumbles. "You should give me one of your guns, just to be safe."

I ignore him. Leo comes out a bit later with a folded piece of paper in his hand. "Here it is," he says, and unfolds it.

The paper is nearly black with dirt and hard to read. Beckwourth takes it and looks it over. "It seems to be in order," he says.

"What in tarnation?" Willy squawks. "Now you're taking his side too? Lemme see that." He struggles to his feet and snatches at the paper, which Beckwourth pulls away.

"You don't need to hold onto it to look at it."

"See?" Leo crows, pointing at the bottom of the sheet. "There's your X right there, Willy. I told you I didn't jump your claim."

"That ain't my X," Willy says, peering at it. "I make my X's skinny like. Not fat like that one." But he doesn't have much conviction in his voice.

"Are you sure that's not yours?" Beckwourth asks him.

"Well…" Willy wavers. "It might be. But I don't remember it."

"Maybe you were drunk," Beckwourth says.

Willy scratches his dirty neck. "It happens," he admits. "I still say I've been cheated."

"Why you filthy polecat," Leo growls.

"Hold on, you two," Beckwourth says calmly. "Let me ask you a question, Leo. How much gold would you say you take out of here every week? On average?"

Leo looks at the ground and mumbles something.

"What was that?"

"On average?" he asks.

"On average."

"About nothing. The durned vein played out a year ago, about the time I won this thing off Willy. Ain't nothing left."

"Why do you stay here?" Beckwourth asks him.

He kicks at the ground. "Got nowhere else to go."

Beckwourth turns to Willy. "It could be a judge would find in your favor, Willy, if you wanted to fight this. Then I suppose you could live up here."

I see where Beckwourth is going with this and I have to hand it to him. It's pretty smart.

Willy gets an alarmed look. "Way up here?" he asks. "But it's so *far* to the saloon!"

"So if the mine is played out, and you don't want to live here, then are you sure you still want this claim?"

Willy doesn't take long to ponder it. "Nossir," he says. "I almost died getting up here this once. If I had to do it every day I wouldn't last a week."

30

We leave Willy off in town. He sulks when he sees Beckwourth isn't going to buy him any whiskey. He turns to me but I give him a look dark enough that he shuts his mouth with a snap and stomps into the saloon.

It's dark when we hit the road again. We ride for about an hour, following a wagon road that leads west, before we come on a decent clearing beside the road that other travelers have clearly camped at.

I build a fire and we sit around it, chewing on some leftover beans and jerked meat. Now and then I sneak a look at Beckwourth. He has me worried. He hasn't tried to tell me a single story since we left Bloody Gulch.

"You think maybe we could hold off on having adventures for a spell?" I ask him. "I'm tired of being shot at. Might be nice to have things quiet for a bit." Mostly I'm trying to get some kind of rise out of him. I've never seen him low like this.

"I never thought I'd see Willard sink to such a state," he says quietly. "He was always a steady hand, a man you could ride the river with."

"It was the drink got him. I've seen it happen to others. Some men climb into the bottle and they can't ever climb back out."

"It seems silly now, how much I was looking forward to seeing Willard." He says it with this sad kind of smile on his face. "I was hoping we could chew over the old days for a bit. It's a weakness peculiar to the old. I don't expect you to understand. Every year that passes there are fewer and fewer who remember how the world was."

Beckwourth gets out his pipe but doesn't load it, only sits looking at it like he can't remember what it's for. "Now I expect I'll never see him again. One more who remembered, gone forever. Gone like the buffalo, like most of the Indians."

I wish I knew what to say. I latch onto the first thing that comes to mind. "You think sleeping under a saloon porch beats sleeping in a hospital?" I ask.

He looks at me, a little surprised by the question. "I don't know. For me, I'd like to have some other choices on the table."

"Seems to me, that's what you're doing. Making other choices."

He nods. "It's silly, clinging to the past. It's gone and I have to let it go." He puts the pipe in his pocket, digs around in his saddlebags and comes out with the brown bottle.

"How's the pain today?" I ask him. I've seen him wincing a few times during the day. It's not something I've ever noticed before, though to be honest I was never watching for it either.

He takes a sip and puts the bottle away. "I've had better days. I've had worse too."

"Maybe we should have stayed in Bloody Gulch. The hotel looked like it's not planning on falling down for a few days yet."

"I don't know a bed would've made me rest any easier. And we're low on funds. I don't consider starving to death to be the sort of adventure I'm looking for." He manages a bit of a smile there at the end.

He packs tobacco in his pipe. I put some more wood on the fire. It's bigger than I usually make fires, but somehow tonight seems to need it.

After a bit I ask, "This man we're going to see. Where does he live?"

"According to Old Joe, he lives in the hills outside Durango. Knuze is his name."

"I never heard that name before."

"Nor have I."

"You think he really knows where the treasure ship is?"

"Old Joe believed it and my impression of him is that he was not a gullible man."

"Seems strange…"

"What does?"

"A ship sitting out in the desert. You'd think people would notice a thing like that. I understand how something can be lost in the mountains," I say, thinking about the temple of Totec, "but I don't see how it can be lost out in the open."

"I've wondered that too, Ace. Maybe Knuze can shed some light on it for us."

I'm about to answer when I hear the sound of a wagon approaching.

31

It's a black wagon, built tall and enclosed, like a box on wheels. A pair of dappled gray mares are pulling it. On the seat is a man dressed in a black suit. He pulls up next to the fire and comes to a stop, leaning over to set the brake. He's wearing a top hat and he tips it to us.

"Good evening, gentlemen," he says. He speaks softly, yet his words carry well in the still mountain air. "May I ask if there is room at your fire for a weary traveler such as myself?"

"There is," Beckwourth says quickly. "Stay and be welcome."

"Much obliged," the stranger says. The springs creak when he climbs down. He's very tall and very lean, with a hawk nose, thin lips and deep set eyes that look black in the firelight. His hair is straight and gray and falls to his shoulders. "I am weary and my joy at not having to gather firewood in the dark knows no bounds." He smiles as he says this, but his smile is mostly long, yellow teeth. Right away I don't trust him.

Beckwourth stands up and holds out his hand. "I'm James P Beckwourth, mountaineer, pioneer, scout and chief of the Crow Indian tribe and this is my good friend, Ace Lone Wolf."

"Ah, Beckwourth and Ace," he says, dragging out the end of my name so it sounds like a hiss. "It is my great pleasure to make your acquaintance. I am Dr. Charles Hamlin and I am at your service." He gives a slight bow.

His accent sounds funny and I can't place it. He sounds a little bit like a Dutchman, but there's something else there. I notice that he does not take Beckwourth's hand. It is almost as if he doesn't see it. After a moment, Beckwourth lowers his hand, a puzzled look on his face.

"We don't have much food to share, but what we have you're welcome to," Beckwourth says.

"Thank you, but no. I find I no longer need to eat much. I sometimes go for days at a time without sustenance."

"Really?" Beckwourth says. "If you don't mind my saying, that's odd. How do you manage this?" His ears have perked up and I have a feeling Dr. Hamlin will end up in Beckwourth's book if he's not careful.

"It is nothing. A little trick I learned while in India, some years back. Merely a matter of controlling one's breath through certain esoteric exercises."

"You've been to India?" Beckwourth asks, his eyes shining.

"Among other places. I spent two years there before moving on to the Orient."

"Fascinating, simply fascinating. I've read books, but of course that's nothing like actually going there."

"There is much to be learned from our foreign brothers," Hamlin says. From under the seat of his wagon he takes a wooden box, which he sets by the fire and sits down on. "As fascinating as those two places were though, they did not hold a candle to the mysteries of the African jungles."

Beckwourth is fairly glowing with excitement now. His earlier dark mood has completely gone. He's sitting forward, watching Hamlin closely. As for me, there's something I don't like about this man. He puts me in mind of a vulture, perched there on his box.

"You've been to the jungles of Africa," Beckwourth says with a sigh. "I can only imagine."

"I'm afraid, my dear fellow, that you cannot. The mysteries of this world must be experienced directly. All else is but a pale shadow."

Well, that sounds like an insult to me, but when I look at Beckwourth it's clear he didn't take it that way. "You must tell me more," he says.

On the side of the wagon, in gold letters, it says, "Dr. Hamlin's Patented Miracle Cure" and under that, "Cabinet of Curiosities."

"I know what patent medicines are," I say, wanting to cut in on this, "but I don't know what a cabinet of curiosities is." I once watched a man wearing a top hat very similar to Hamlin's spend an hour telling a crowd of people all about the wondrous healing properties of the medicine he was selling. It seemed to me he thought that medicine could heal everything but being born.

Judging by how many people bought the medicine, a lot of people believed him.

"And there is no reason that you should," Hamlin says. "Not in this remote corner of the world." He stands up and walks over to the side of the wagon, laying his hand on it and caressing the gold letters.

"A cabinet of curiosities is a window into another world, my friend. A veritable cornucopia of wonders."

I don't know what a cornucopia is, but from his tone I'm guessing it's a lot.

Hamlin looks at each one of us in turn. "It is against my general principles, gentlemen, but as a measure of my gratitude for your generosity, I am prepared to break new ground."

"And that means what?" I ask him irritably. I feel like he is talking down to us and I don't like it.

"It means that I will allow you to gaze upon the wonders contained herein, without charging you one red cent," he replies.

"You're too kind," Beckwourth says.

"It is the least I can do, after the hospitality you and your red-skinned friend have shown me."

Okay, now I'm mad. I get tired of that description, you know? As far as I can see, my skin is no more red than anyone else's. I've seen plenty of white men turn red in the sun, but I guess that doesn't count.

"What you gentlemen are about to see rivals the seven wonders of the world. Wonders that will stagger your mind. Curiosities to unsettle your very perception of reality." He holds up one finger. His fingers are unnaturally long. "But I warn you. After you look upon this, you will never see the world in the same way again. You will be changed forever."

I'm tired of listening to him. He's not the only person who's been places and seen things. "You got an Aztec god in there, Hamlin?" I ask.

His eyes flash with sudden anger, but a moment later it's gone. "Behold!" he says, and presses something on the side of the wagon. The side of the wagon drops down, revealing rows of cubbyholes.

It's a pretty strange collection, I'll give him that. A lot of it is in jars, floating in some greenish liquid. One jar holds a snake that looks like it has two heads, though it's hard to tell because the liquid is so murky. Another holds some kind of creature with a whole bunch of tentacles. In one jar is a spider bigger than my hand, with long, hairy legs.

"What's that?" Beckwourth asks, pointing at what looks like a very small human head. It's not in a jar. The head has long, black hair and the eyes and mouth are sewed shut.

"It is the shrunken head of a witch doctor from the jungles of Borneo," Hamlin says, taking it out of its cubbyhole. "Powerful magic went into making this."

"A shrunken head?" Beckwourth cries. "That's incredible. May I touch it?"

Hamlin shakes his head. "Not unless you want nightmares to plague you for the rest of your life."

"But you're touching it," I point out.

"Only after years of the strictest mental preparations. I trained in India, learning the ways of the great swamis. My mind is a fortress. That is why I can touch it. But yours..." He hesitates ominously. "Your mind would crumple like tissue paper."

Beckwourth draws his hand back like the head is a snake. "Why are the eyes and mouth sewn shut?"

"Because the witch doctor's spirit is still trapped in there, waiting for its chance to be free. If those stitches were to fail and his eyes and mouth were to open..." Hamlin shudders.

"What would happen?" Beckwourth asks, his mouth open.

"He would be able to once again cast spells. Powerful spells. He would burn us all on the spot." As he says this he thrusts the head towards us.

I don't believe a word of it, but I take a step back anyway, same as Beckwourth. You never know.

"And that?" Beckwourth asks, pointing to a wooden mask on the top shelf. Its mouth is a gaping snarl of jagged teeth and the eyes are tilted upwards, flames painted around them.

Hamlin puts the shrunken head back on its shelf and takes down the mask. "The Mask of Eternal Horror," he says. "Brought from deepest Congo at great personal risk."

"You've been to the Congo?"

"Twice. I had to return to have the curse removed after the first expedition. The tribe I acquired the mask from cursed me and the only cure was to be found in the waters of the lake they lived on."

"What was the curse?"

"Blood wept from my eyes every day. That was only the first part of the curse, though. Other, more horrible things would have followed, had I not partaken of the cure."

"It's all very impressive," Beckwourth said as Hamlin closes the side of the wagon. "Don't you think so, Ace?"

"It was okay," I say.

Hamlin gives me a dark look. It's nice to see I can get under his skin. Maybe if I anger him enough he'll climb back on that wagon and roll out of here.

Hamlin opens the box he's been sitting on. It's filled with brown bottles. He takes one out.

"As fascinating as those curiosities are, they were not the real reason for my journeys. This is the real reason," Hamlin says, holding up the bottle. "Dr. Hamlin's Guaranteed Miracle Cure" it says on the label over a small picture of a woman who is either smiling or grimacing. It's hard to tell which.

"It took twenty years of my life to learn how to make my guaranteed miracle cure. Twenty years of traipsing dangerous jungles and scaling forbidding mountains, all to bring you what waits in this simple bottle."

"What's it good for?" Beckwourth asks.

"Far easier to tell you what it isn't good for, my friend. Do you suffer from rheumatism, gout, lumbago? It cures all of them. It cures boils. It cures the pox, the drips and whooping cough." His voice has a kind of singsong quality to it. "It cures impotency and incontinence. It even cures baldness as you will witness." He points to his own hair.

Beckwourth says, "It sounds incredible, Dr. Hamlin. I commend you on your work. However, I have no need of your elixir. I'm in excellent health."

"Is that so?" Hamlin says.

"Indeed it is."

"Good health is a wondrous blessing," Hamlin says. He glances at me.

"Don't look at me," I say. "I never get sick."

Hamlin looks back at Beckwourth. "Perhaps one bottle against the uncertainties of the future? You never know what might happen tomorrow."

"Thank you, but no." Beckwourth grimaces. "Frankly, my current finances are such that I would be hard pressed to purchase a sack of beans, much less medicine that I don't need right now."

"Very well," Hamlin says. He puts the bottle back in the box, then walks around to the far side of the wagon.

"I don't trust this guy," I say to Beckwourth in a low voice. "He's shifty."

"You're seeing things that aren't there, Ace. He is merely a salesman, and a very good one at that. I imagine he does very well."

"Whatever you say. I'd be happier if he moved on, though."

Hamlin comes back carrying a different bottle. "I must apologize to you gentlemen," he says softly. "You have welcomed me to your fire and I repaid your hospitality by trying to sell you something. I'm afraid it is one of the hazards of my trade, a habit so deeply ingrained that it is difficult to switch it off."

"That's quite all right," Beckwourth says. "A man has to make a living, doesn't he?"

"Indeed he does," Hamlin replies. "But to salve my conscience I would like to share some of this fine brandy with you." He holds the bottle up. "It is imported from France and it is the highest quality."

"Brandy, you say?" Beckwourth says, perking up. "I haven't had brandy in a coon's age. What about you, Ace? Do you like brandy?"

I've only had it once, but I remember liking it. "I wouldn't say no to some."

"Excellent," Hamlin says. We dig out our cups and he pours us each a good dose, then pours himself some.

I take a sip. It's a whole lot better than the rotgut I'm used to drinking, that's for sure. It burns, but not in the eat-a-hole-in-your-gut way. I take another sip. Maybe I've been too hard on Hamlin.

"This brandy is very tasty," Beckwourth says, smacking his lips. "I've forgotten how much I like the stuff." He frowns a little.

"There's something else in here, a hint of a flavor I can't quite place."

"No doubt due to the region where it was produced," Hamlin says. "I tried to find out what it was, but the makers of it keep their secrets close. Drink up, my friends." He raises his cup.

We toast him and I finish what is in my cup.

"Would you like more, Ace?" Hamlin asks. I look up from my cup to see him staring intently at me. Is it my imagination, or are his eyes brighter? They're practically glittering in the firelight.

"Sure." He pours me some more and I take a drink. I could really develop a taste for this stuff.

"What do you think?" Hamlin asks me.

There's this amazing warmth spreading throughout my body. My fingers are tingling. I feel pleasantly sleepy. "It's good. Really, really good."

"Indeed." He tilts his head to the side. "If I may be so bold, what tribe are you from?"

I take another sip off the bottle. I feel sort of warm and fuzzy all over. I decide I like this feeling. Then I remember that Hamlin asked me a question. What was it?

"Your tribe, Ace?"

"Oh, sure. My mother is Apache." I wonder why I ever mistrusted this man. I feel a great wave of affection for him. "My grandfather was the great chief Cochise, you know."

"Perfect," he says. "Absolutely perfect. You have such long, beautiful hair."

That seems a little odd to me. I've never had a man tell me I have beautiful hair before. But I decide it makes no difference. "I got it from my mother," I say. "I've never cut it. People told me I should. They said I'd fit in better with the white man, but I said no."

It seems important for some reason that Hamlin understands how strongly I feel about this. Cutting my hair short would be losing some vital part of myself. But when I try to tell him my tongue feels very thick and I can't find the words. It doesn't matter, though. I can tell by Hamlin's eyes that he understands.

His eyes are definitely shining now. It's the most amazing thing I've ever seen.

I turn to tell Beckwourth about it and I'm surprised to see him lying on his side. It looks like he's sleeping. When did that happen?

When I turn back to Hamlin I topple over on my side. I lie there on the ground, thinking how wonderful it feels. It's so much softer than I remember.

A voice says, "Sleep now," and I close my eyes and drift away.

32

I'm brought out of sleep by a sharp pain on my forehead. I jerk back and try to push whatever is causing it away.

But I can't.

It takes a moment for my fogged brain to register that my hands are tied behind my back. My feet are bound as well. I blink a few times, trying to get my eyes to focus.

"There, there. Hold still. It will all be over soon."

It's Hamlin. He's bent over me, holding a straight razor in his hand. I feel blood running from the cut he made on my forehead, just below the hairline.

"What's happening?" My words sound funny.

"I'm scalping you," he says calmly. "Trying to anyway." He looks at the razor disgustedly. "But it seems I have allowed my razor to grow shockingly dull." He stands up and walks away.

I fight the ropes, but get nowhere. I roll onto my side and see Beckwourth lying across the fire, also tied up. His eyes are closed and he's not moving.

"I'm surprised you woke up," Hamlin says, coming back. He's holding a strop and is sharpening the razor on it. "With the quantity you drank, I expected you to be out much longer."

I struggle to make sense of his words. Gradually they sink in. "You drugged me."

He nods. "Opium is a powerful substance."

I consider this. There's something that doesn't fit, if only I could figure out what it was. Then I get it. "But you drank some too. I saw you."

He smiles, showing his long, yellow teeth. "Not really. It only appeared that I did."

He kneels down beside me and takes hold of one of my eyelids, pulling it back to look at my eye. "I find the fact that you are awake most surprising. You're not a regular user, are you? No, I suppose not. Just one of those things, I guess. Too bad for you, though. This would have been much more pleasant for you if you could have slept through it. Now you'll have to be awake to feel the pain. I could kill you first, of course, but I've found it's much easier to take a clean scalp from one who is still living. And above all else I don't want to damage yours."

"Why do you want my scalp?" It's still hard to talk, with my tongue as swollen as it is. My brain feels swollen too.

"Because it's perfect. And terribly authentic. I'm traveling to San Francisco, you see. Imagine how the audience will gasp when they see, not just an Indian scalp in my cabinet of curiosities, but an *Apache* scalp. Cochise's grandson, no less. Your scalp is going to make me quite a lot of money, you know."

He takes hold of my hair, pulls on it and readies the razor.

Desperately, I say, "If you take my scalp, you'll regret it."

He glances down at me. "How is that?"

"I'll put an Apache death curse on you." What the hell, it worked before, didn't it? Sort of. "My spirit will follow you and take revenge on you."

"That's brilliant," he says. "I must remember that. I'll have to work that into my spiel. The rubes will love it."

"It's true!" I say, trying to twist away. I really want to keep my scalp.

"Of course it is," he says. "Sadly, it's not true enough to help you, Now hold still. I don't want to damage your scalp in the process." He lifts the razor once again.

I fight as hard as I can, but I'm still weak from the drug and all I manage to do is hit the back of my head on a rock.

He lowers the razor to my forehead. I feel the blade slicing my skin. "Easy does it," he murmurs.

Is this really how it ends for me? After all I've been through? I rack my brain, trying to think of something, anything, but it's so hard to think.

He cuts deeper. It hurts, though not as much as it should. The pain feels distant, unreal somehow. Part of me is wondering why I bother to struggle. Wouldn't it be so much easier to simply go back to sleep?

All of a sudden Hamlin gets a peculiar look on his face, like something he'd never considered just occurred to him.

"Oh," he says. Blood starts leaking from his mouth. He tries to turn but collapses across me.

I look up and see Beckwourth standing there, a bloody knife in his hand and a smile on his face.

"That was something, wasn't it?" he says brightly.

"Don't say it," I warn him.

"Say what?"

"That it was an adventure."

His smile fades somewhat. "Even if it was?"

"You didn't almost get scalped."

He nods. "True enough."

"Would you get him off me already?"

"Gladly." He sets the knife down and pulls Hamlin's body off of me. Then he cuts my bonds and helps me sit up. He goes through Hamlin's pockets and finds a handkerchief, which he hands me. "Press this against the cut on your forehead. It doesn't look too deep."

I'm still having trouble getting past the effects of the opium. It's like my brain is stuck in quicksand. "What…how did you get free?"

"It was nothing, really." He sits down and takes out his pipe, starts packing it with tobacco. I groan a little. I know what this means. He's going to turn this into a story.

"How about the short version?" I ask him.

"The short version it is," he says agreeably. He takes a twig out of the fire and lights his pipe. "By the time I was on my second cup I realized what that other flavor was. It was opium, a drug I had a few times in the hospital."

"And you didn't think it was a good idea to tell me?"

He gives me an apologetic look. "By then it was already too late. You'd already finished your second cup and the first signs of the drug were showing. I could see that you were only minutes from unconsciousness."

"I could have shot him. That only takes a few seconds."

"Had I shouted a warning, which was my first thought, mind you," he says, puffing on the pipe contentedly, "most likely Hamlin, being in command of his faculties, would have disarmed you easily. And, most importantly, I would have lost the element of surprise. He would have known that I knew what was happening. Who knows what steps he might have taken then?

"As it was, I was able to feign unconsciousness. Doubtless he did not think me much of a threat and so took no great pains to secure me well or even to eliminate me completely. While he was binding me, I called upon something I learned long ago, something that saved me once from the bloodthirsty Snake Indians. It was when I was trapping up an unexplored fork of the Poudre River. I'd been on my own for some weeks and I'd foolishly let my guard down when—"

"You promised me the short version."

He looks startled. "So I did." He takes another stick out of the fire and relights his pipe.

"It's simple, really, and something which may aid you someday. When someone is binding you, flex your muscles. Not so much that they discover what you are doing, but enough to create some space. Then, when they move away, you have some slack to work with. It makes freeing yourself much easier, as it did when the Snake Indians—"

I cut in before he can get rolling. "It was close. Another minute and he would've had my hair."

He nods. "It took me somewhat longer than I expected to get free. It seems age has diminished my skills."

"Thank you. I owe you."

"Don't mention it. I'm quite certain you would have done the same for me." He looks at Hamlin's body. "I suppose we should bury him."

"I don't see why. Let the coyotes eat him, I say."

"It's the Christian thing to do."

"Which I'm not."

"What shall we do with his wagon?"

"Burn it."

"What about his next of kin?"

"How are we going to find them?"

"You have a point," Beckwourth says. "We should at least go back to Bloody Gulch tomorrow and inform the sheriff."

"They don't have a sheriff, remember?"

"True. Still, burning it seems a bit…wasteful?"

"Look at it this way. If anyone was to come along and see this, they'd think we murdered him. Then they'd go to the sheriff and we'd end up on wanted posters. I don't need to be on any more of them. What we need to do is hide his body and get rid of the wagon. That's the only way to be sure."

"You raise some good points."

I roll Hamlin over and start going through his pockets. "I hope the sonofabitch has a lot of money. Be nice to get something for my troubles, after he almost scalped me and all."

33

Turns out Hamlin only has a couple of dollars. At least that we can find. There's a lot of little compartments in his wagon, so maybe there's some hidden ones we can't find. I was hoping for more, but it's better than nothing.

In the end we put Hamlin up on the seat of his wagon and douse the whole thing with his patent medicine, which has a lot of alcohol in it and lights right up when we put a match to it. Once it catches fire we push it over the edge down into this steep-sided gorge about a mile from camp. We turn the horses loose. I'm tempted to take them into town and sell them, but horse stealing will get you hanged faster than just about anything else in these parts. As I know from direct experience.

We head out for Durango. After a couple of days we're getting close when late one afternoon we come upon an old Indian man riding along on an old swaybacked mare with only a tattered blanket for a saddle. His hair is gray and tied into twin braids that hang down over his chest. He has an eagle feather tied in his hair. He pulls up when he sees us coming and watches us approach, his face showing no expression.

"Hello!" Beckwourth calls out when we get close. The old man makes no reply.

"We're looking for a man who's supposed to live around here. His name is Knuze. Do you know him?"

The old Indian nods.

"Can you tell us where he is?"

The old man looks at the sun. It's close to the horizon. "Be dark soon. Best to wait until tomorrow."

"Why?" Beckwourth asks. "Is it far?"

"Not far."

"Then why wait?"

"My people know this man you seek. We stay away from him. Dark spirits walk in his shadow."

I wish he wouldn't have said that. I don't like the way that sounds at all.

Beckwourth looks at me and smiles. I can see that he's now more interested than ever. "What do you mean by that?" he asks the old man.

"He talks with ghosts. Bad medicine."

"Where do we find him?"

The old man shrugs, but not because he doesn't know where to find Knuze. He shrugs because he doesn't understand our foolishness and probably because he doesn't care. He warned us of the danger. If we're going to rush headlong into it anyway, it's our problem.

He points. "The next valley. High up there is a cave. Spirit man is there." He kicks his horse and rides past us without looking at us.

"That was a stroke of luck, don't you think, Ace?"

"Bad luck or good luck?"

"Good luck," he says. "Now we don't have to ride all the way into Durango and then clear back out here." He turns his horse and starts riding in the direction the man pointed. I tap Coyote with my heels and catch up to him.

"You don't want to wait until morning?"

"You're not worried about what that old Indian said are you?"

"I'm not pretending he didn't say it like you are."

"He's just superstitious. I don't put any stock in it."

"You're sure about that?"

"Sure enough."

I don't say anything more after that. I wish I felt as sure as Beckwourth, but something about the way the old man said it makes me uncomfortable.

It's dark by the time we find him. He lives in a shallow cave high up on the side of a long ridge, overlooking a wide valley below. The only reason we find him is his fire is visible from a long way off.

Knuze is sitting hunched over by the fire, wrapped in a threadbare old blanket. His white hair is long and wild, hanging loose, shielding his face. On the wall of the cave behind him there are creatures painted in red. They have wild eyes and long teeth. I think the paint might be blood. There are a lot of them, nightmare images frozen in time.

We dismount and walk over to the fire. Beckwourth calls out a greeting, but Knuze doesn't answer, doesn't seem to have even heard us.

"Are you Knuze?" Beckwourth asks him.

Only then does he look up. One eye is milky. Even in the poor light it's clear he's painfully thin, his cheekbones standing out sharply. His beard is long and as wild as his hair. We're standing on the side where his milky eye is and I get the feeling he is studying us with it, though clearly he can't see through it.

"You're looking for the lost ship," he says. His voice sounds rusty, like he's almost forgotten how to use it.

"We are," Beckwourth says, crouching down. His expression is eager. "How did you know?"

Knuze ignores the question. His milky gaze is fixed on me. I have to fight the urge to back up. "You should know better," he says to me. "After all that you have seen."

I think of the Aztec temple in Mexico. Was it really a god I saw there? And if it wasn't, what was it? I've never been able to find any good answers.

"You've been there, haven't you?" Beckwourth says. He's practically whispering. I understand why. There is a feeling about this cave, like it belongs to a different world. A world where we are intruders.

Finally, Knuze looks at Beckwourth. "You don't care if you die."

Beckwourth pulls back a little, shocked by the bluntness of the words. He licks his lips. "Not really," he says at last.

"Which means you won't listen. You won't hear."

"Won't hear what?" I ask.

The milky eye swings back to me. "Don't go," he rasps. "Erase it from your mind."

A chill runs through me when he says it. I'm starting to see why the Indians around here leave him alone.

"Why?" Beckwourth asks.

"I spent thirty years looking for that ship," Knuze says. "I lost everything I ever cared about. If you go looking for it, you'll lose everything too."

"I don't have anything left to lose," Beckwourth says.

"And what about you?" Knuze asks me.

"I'm only the guide. It's his journey."

Knuze goes back to staring into the fire. He is quiet for a long time. I'm beginning to think he's said all he's going to say, when all at once he begins speaking again.

"The ship is cursed. Once you start toward it, the curse will attach to you. After that, it won't matter what you do. You'll never be free again."

Damn. I wish he wouldn't have said that. I've never had a curse and I don't feel like starting now.

But if his words make me want to ride the other direction as fast as I can, they have the opposite effect on Beckwourth. His eyes are wide and a little smile plays at the corner of his mouth. "What sort of curse?" he asks.

"I was like you," Knuze says like he didn't hear him. "I first heard of the lost ship of Juan de Iturbe when I was a young man in Mexico City. An old Catholic priest told me of it. He warned me of the curse, but I refused to listen. Now I'm dying, and it's the ghost ship that killed me."

A chill goes through me when he says that. Suddenly the cave and the other men are gone, replaced by the image of a ship, its masts bare except for the rags of sails. It's listing in the sand dunes, a full moon in the sky behind it.

I shake my head and the image vanishes.

"Did you say ghost ship?" Beckwourth asks. "How can a ship be a ghost? It's not possible."

"And yet it is." He looks at me. "He knows there are things which can't be and yet are. Ask him."

Beckwourth looks at me but I'm still reeling from what I have seen. "Tell me more," he says. "Why do you say it is a ghost ship?"

"Because it's not always there, that's why. Most of the time it's not."

"Where does it go?"

Knuze shrugs. "It goes where ghosts go. It only appears once a year, on the first full moon after the spring equinox. It stays for a few hours, then it's gone. Don't ask me how. I know what it is, but not how."

"I don't see how—"

"It doesn't matter what you see or don't see," Knuze cuts in. "It doesn't matter what you believe. It is what it is. Your belief doesn't change anything."

"I *want* to believe," Beckwourth says.

"It was four of us who found it," Knuze says. "We were there when the ship appeared, rising out of the sands." He's staring into the flames as if he can see it all there, happening once again. "We boarded her and we found the treasure, a whole chest filled with the black pearls."

"If it's a ghost ship, how did you—"

"Stop asking me how!" Knuze shouts suddenly. "How is for the world of men. The ghost ship belongs to another world and how has no part of it."

Beckwourth clearly has more questions he wants to ask, but Knuze's outburst has startled him and he keeps them to himself.

Knuze fumbles at a leather thong around his neck. On it is a small leather bag. He opens the bag and pours something into his hand. "Here," he rasps. "Here's your proof that what I say is true, damn you."

In his hand are three black pearls.

A shudder passes over me as I see the ship once again. I can hear the rotted masts creaking in the wind and I see a dark figure standing on the deck.

Beckwourth's eyes grow very large. "They're...beautiful," he sighs.

"Three pearls for three dead men," Knuze says grimly. "There should be four. I should be dead too.

"There were four of us who survived the desert and the Indians. When we found the chest filled with black pearls we knew our dreams of riches had come true. All we had endured, all we had sacrificed, it was all worth it." He closes his hand around the pearls and his face tightens with pain as if they are coals burning his flesh. But it is a pain he will not pull away from, a pain he feels he deserves. To my surprise he begins to cry. The tears run down his face and disappear into the depths of his beard.

"I killed them," he says. "They died on the ship and it's my fault."

The tears continue to fall. I begin to wish we hadn't come. This is a mistake.

After a time he looks up and stares out into the darkness outside the cave. "It won't be long now," he says. "I'll come and join you in death as I should have all those years ago. I should never have escaped. I know that now."

The wind picks that moment to gust. Sparks blow out of the fire and Knuze's hair blows around his face.

He smiles and looks at us once again. Something has changed in him. Both of us can feel it. Some burden he has carried is gone.

"It's finally here," he says, a ghastly smile on his face. "The death I escaped so long ago is finally coming."

Beckwourth swallows and wipes his mouth. Every muscle in my body is rigid. I want to flee right then. I can feel things swirling around me, things that make my mouth dry and fill me with ice.

"One pearl for each man who died. It's a high price to pay, don't you think? Especially for the dead. It was the captain who killed them," he says. "We were so fascinated by the pearls that we didn't see him. One moment we were celebrating and the next Rodriguez was dying. He turned pure white, his eyes bulging from his head. Before we understood what was going on, de Iturbe had hold of Ellis and Peters too. He killed them with a touch and sent their souls straight to hell. I saw the fires myself."

He looks at us. "I alone escaped. I don't know how I made it out of the desert alive. A terrible fever gripped me and I have only pieces of memory, of stumbling through the dunes, mad with heat and thirst. Finally I collapsed and would have died but someone found me. He took me to a town and put me up in his own home while I clawed my way back to life. I always knew it was only temporary. I always knew my death would come for me."

Knuze looks down at his hand. "When I came to, these were in my fist. It was a day before I could open my hand and see what they were. I still don't know how they got there.."

When he says this a cold wind blows through the cave. Knuze spreads his arms, welcoming it. "I'm coming, boys!" he cries. "After too long, I'm coming!"

He goes rigid then. Foam appears at the corner of his mouth. He falls over on his side, his eyes wide and staring. Beckwourth bends over him.

"What was the name of the town?" he asks.

Knuze's eyes flick to him. A grim smile pulls at his face. "Still you won't give up."

"I must know."

"Bedbug," he whispers, and dies.

34

Beckwourth looks at me. "Bedbug?"

"It's a town on the Colorado River."

"It's not a lot to go on."

"It's something."

We roll Knuze onto his back and close his eyes, then cover him with his blanket. "I guess we'll bury him in the morning," Beckwourth says.

"I think I'll sleep somewhere else, though," I say.

"What do you think about what he said? Do you believe him?" Beckwourth asks me.

"I wish I didn't."

"A ghost ship. A curse. It's a lot to swallow."

"Do you still want to go through with this?" I ask him.

"Nothing's changed there. I'd hoped for better directions. It's not spring yet, so at least we still have some time. Maybe someone in Bedbug will know something." He looks at me. "You don't have to do this, Ace. You don't owe me anything."

That sounds good to me. I'd like to mount up and ride out of here this minute. I believe everything Knuze said, about the ghost ship, about the curse, everything. Trouble like that I don't need in my life. I find plenty of trouble without going to look for it.

But I can't let Beckwourth do this alone. It's foolish, but I feel sort of responsible for him. Besides, I at least have some experience dealing with this sort of thing. He doesn't.

So I say, "Are you trying to cheat me out of my share of the treasure?" and give him a hard look.

Beckwourth grins and claps me on the shoulder. "I was hoping you'd say that. Thank you, Ace."

"I meant what I said, though," I say, standing up. "No way am I sleeping in this cave."

In the morning while we're digging the grave a raven flaps down and lands on a tree limb nearby. It croaks and stares at us with its yellow eyes. Beckwourth doesn't notice it, but the thing makes me uncomfortable. Raven isn't one of the friendly spirits. Is he here to tell me the curse has started?

Coyote comes walking up then, wondering what I'm doing grubbing around on the ground. With his muzzle he knocks my hat off.

"Knock it off, Coyote," I growl. "I'm busy."

He shakes his head and stamps his foot. I feel like he's trying to tell me something.

Then it comes to me. Raven is known for being malicious. His being here is a bad sign. But Coyote is a powerful spirit too. I think Coyote, the horse, is reminding me of this. He's letting me know I'm not alone.

Of course, Coyote is known as a trickster. He's unreliable, as likely to help as to make things worse.

Now I don't know whether I feel better or not.

Coyote sneezes right then and sprays me with snot. I think I have my answer.

The ground is hard and rocky. Without a shovel and a pick we can't dig the hole very deep, but it will have to do. We lay Knuze in his grave and pile rocks on him. Then we stand with our hats off while Beckwourth says a few words about this man we didn't know.

As we ride away I look back. The raven is perched on the grave, watching me.

We ride hard that day, both of us wanting to get as far from that place as possible. The Rocky Mountains recede into the distance behind us as the desert takes us into its stony grip. Red sandstone buttes rear up in the distance. The countryside is sandy with only tufts of yellow grass and clumps of sagebrush dotting the eroded hills.

Near dark we make camp at the base of a butte. A single cottonwood grows there and a small patch of yellowed grass. There's probably a seep that feeds the tree, but there's no water or even dampness on the surface. We'll have to make a dry camp.

"This is hard country," Beckwourth says. He stares off into the distance. There are no mountains to speak of. Only hills and sandy wastes. "How long will it take to cross it?"

"It depends."

"On what?"

"Mostly on water."

He turns to me. "Have you traveled through here before?"

"Once."

"And you remember where the water is?"

"Probably."

"You're not inspiring confidence, Ace."

"Let's just hope they got some winter rains down here."

We build a small fire with fallen pieces from the cottonwood tree. Darkness falls and the sky over us is huge and empty. The stars seem almost to press down on us. In the east is a faint glow of the moon getting ready to rise.

"Thank you again for coming with me, Ace. I couldn't do this without you."

I don't answer. The truth is I don't want to think about it. If I do, I'm afraid I'll realize how stupid this whole thing is. It's like slapping Old Mose. Sometimes it's best to act and not think.

Unless it gets you killed.

"We have nearly four weeks until the first full moon of spring," Beckwourth says. "That will be enough time to get there, won't it?"

"It is. If nothing goes wrong."

As if my words have summoned him—and maybe they do— a man calls out to us from the darkness.

35

"Ho there, at the fire. Can I come in?" he says.

I'm on my feet and my guns are in my hands, though I don't remember drawing them. Beckwourth scrambles to his feet as well.

"Come on in," I say. "Nice and slow, with your hands where I can see them."

He enters the circle of firelight. The first thing I notice is the raven feather stuck in his hat. Then I realize that I know him.

"Has-kay-bay-nez-ntayl," I say. It was what Dee-O-Det, the old shaman, always called him, the few times he came to Pa-Gotzin-Kay. It means brave and wild and will come to a mysterious end. "What do you want?"

"Ace," he replies. "It has been many moons." He wears a faded white hat. Bandoliers of ammunition cross his chest. A pistol hangs from one hip and a long knife from the other. A gold chain is around his neck. He is leading a gray horse.

"You two know each other?" Beckwourth asks.

Neither of us pay any attention to him. We're both focused on each other. I haven't put my guns away.

"Why are you here?" I ask, this time in Apache.

"To share your fire," he replies, also in Apache. Unusual for an Apache, his hair is cut short. His eyes are flat and very dark, his mouth thin and unsmiling. His eyes flick to my guns. "Do you fear me that much?"

"I don't fear you. I just don't trust you."

"What reason have I ever given you to mistrust me?"

"Besides hunting your own people?"

"Perhaps I do so because man is the only prey worth hunting." He watches me as he says this, looking for my reaction. I remember him this way, how he says things so that he can see how his foe will respond. Because for him, all other men are foes.

"You speak of the Apaches I tracked for the army," he continues. "They were not women and children. They were outlaws. Killers. Some killed Apaches."

146

"They were your own people and you chased them for money," I say.

"Were they? Who are my people, really? Tell me."

"We are. We took you into Pa-Gotzin-Kay when you needed refuge. You repaid us by killing Jemez. He was my friend."

"It was a fair fight. You saw that."

"You goaded him into it. You challenged his courage."

"And he proved himself brave."

"You were our guest and you left behind a mourning widow and two small children."

Beckwourth is watching us closely, but he wisely keeps his mouth shut.

"You speak of the Apache as my people," he says. For the first time he looks angry. His eyes narrow and he shows his teeth. "Tell me, where were my people when the Yuma Indians captured me? Did they ride and save me?" he hisses.

"No, they didn't. They abandoned me. It was the U.S. Cavalry who rescued me. And then, when I was an orphan trying to survive in the white man fort, where were my people then? Did they come and claim me?

"Who, exactly, are my people? Is it the Apaches who abandoned me? Or is it the white soldiers who raised me, but who have never trusted me, who have treated me like a dog? Answer me this, Ace, for I do not know."

I stare into his eyes, understanding for the first time some of the rage which drives him. "I don't know," I say simply, and holster my guns.

"Neither do I." His sudden anger is gone now and he is once again calm. "Maybe the answer is that I have no people. I am my own and only that. As a half-breed, you must understand some of what I speak of, trapped between two worlds as you are."

I nod. I know what it feels like, not to know where or if you belong anywhere.

He looks at Beckwourth. "Who is the dark-skinned one?"

"A friend."

"Strange companion." His eyes sweep our camp. "Where are you going?"

"South." I don't want him to know any more than that.

"I hear you were in a gun fight at the OK Corral."

147

"I stood with my friend Doc Holliday."

"I've heard of an Apache wanted in Colorado for killing a U.S. Marshall. They say he wears two guns."

"So?" I say.

"There is a reward."

"Is that why you're here?" I'm not looking at the hand that hangs near his gun, but at his eyes. When he decides to draw, that's where it will show first. I'm ready for him. I can beat him.

"I no longer hunt men, not for anyone."

"I should believe you?"

He shrugs. "Believe what you want, but it is true. I reach for something higher now. There is only one more step to take. Soon I will be free of all this."

"What does that mean?"

"You will see," he says mysteriously.

"What I'd like to see is you riding away."

He mounts up, then looks down at me. "We will meet again. You'll see what I mean then." He wheels his horse and rides away.

"Who the devil *was* that?" Beckwourth asks.

"That was the Apache Kid."

Beckwourth's eyes get round. "I've heard of him. He was a scout for the U. S. Cavalry. One of the best. Maybe even as good as Mickey Free. But there was some trouble. He got drunk and killed a man, then wounded some soldiers when they tried to arrest him."

"He's a dangerous man," I say. "We'll have to be extra careful. I'll stand watch tonight."

"You think he'll double back and come for us in our sleep?"

"I think there is no way of knowing what he might do. With the Kid you can't tell."

I keep watch all night, but there is no sign of the Apache Kid. I find myself puzzling over his strange words, wondering what they mean. I think of the raven feather he was wearing in his hat. I don't believe it was there by accident. Raven is involved in this and anything can happen.

I have a feeling of events building in the background. It's like the moments before a flash flood in the desert. Everything seems normal. The wash is utterly dry. But somewhere beyond rational thought there is a sense of imminent danger.

At any moment I'm going to look up and see the wall of water bearing down on me.

36

We get started early the next morning. The horses are thirsty and we need to find them water. For the next few hours we ride across slickrock. There isn't a tree in sight, no plants at all beyond a few clumps of dried grasses, patches of cactus and a few thorny bushes. The sky is blue, the sun surprisingly hot for so early in the year.

"I sure hope you know where you're going," Beckwourth says, wiping sweat from his face. "This looks like the surface of the moon."

"I hope so too," I reply.

Then, seemingly out of nowhere, a gash appears in the rock. It's a narrow canyon about a hundred feet deep and not much more than a few hundred yards across. The sides are mostly sheer cliffs. In the bottom is a creek, only a few inches deep. Willows and cottonwoods line the creek.

"That's a welcome sight," Beckwourth says. "How do we get down there?"

We turn right and follow along the edge of the canyon. After a bit we come to a spot where the side of the canyon has collapsed. There's a faint trail, leading down the scree slope. The horses can smell the water and they're eager to get at it. We reach the bottom. The horses drink deep and we refill our canteens. I splash water on my face and look down the canyon.

That's when I see the smoke.

"That's a lot of smoke for a cook fire," Beckwourth says when I point it out to him.

I swing into the saddle and pull out the Winchester. "That's what I was thinking. Come on, let's go see. Could be someone needs our help."

We ease our way down the canyon, watching for movement. The canyon is quiet, peaceful except for the ominous smoke rising in the distance. On the way I spot a possible way out the other side of the canyon and make a note of it. If we have to leave fast, the more exits the better. We round a couple of bends and find the source of the smoke. I hold up my hand for Beckwourth to stop.

It's a homestead. A small cabin and a barn. The fire never really caught and they are still mostly intact, only smoldering.

But it's the bodies that draw my attention.

"Wait here and cover me," I tell Beckwourth. "I'm going to take a look." I climb down off Coyote and approach on foot.

The first body is lying in a small field of corn growing beside the creek. It's a man. He's lying on his face. There's a bullet hole in his back and a hoe by his outstretched hand. He's been scalped. He has no gun.

I look around and see where the killer waited behind a fallen cottonwood. The man never even saw him.

The wife is lying by the barn, a bullet hole in her throat. She's also been scalped. There's a bucket of spilled milk beside her. She has a look of surprise on her face. From the way she's lying it looks like she started running toward her husband when she heard the first shot.

I hope that's it. I hope there's no children. I walk over to the cabin and that's when I see it, lying on the ground. I pick it up. A single raven feather.

The Apache Kid dropped it here. He meant for me to find it.

He wants me to know he did this.

I hear the crack of a gun and a bullet whizzes by me. I duck and take cover behind the corner of the cabin. I bring the Winchester up to my cheek to return fire, sighting up at the rim of the canyon, where the shots came from.

Damn.

It's the cavalry.

More bullets spatter around me but the range is long and I've got shelter behind the corner of the house. I don't shoot back. The last thing I need is for the U.S. Cavalry to think I killed these people.

A moment later I realize it doesn't matter what I do.

There are two dead settlers, both of them scalped, and an Apache standing over their bodies. It doesn't matter what I say. There's no way they'll believe me. Sure, Beckwourth will vouch for me, but they won't listen to him either.

There's nothing for it but to run.

Fortunately, there's no trail down into the canyon where the cavalry is, so that gives me a couple of minutes. I need to make my way back up the canyon to the exit I noted on the way down.

I duck into the trees behind the house and start circling around to where I left Beckwourth. Bullets patter around me but they have no clear target so they don't get very close. I hear an officer shouting and the shooting dies off.

"Where did *they* come from?" Beckwourth asks when I get back to him.

"Best guess, they were following the Apache Kid."

"You think he killed those people?"

"I'd bet on it." I leap onto Coyote's back and wheel him around. It's time to run. I don't want to be trapped down here. Beckwourth starts to follow but I stop him.

"You stay here. It's not you they want, it's me."

"I'm not leaving you," he says stoutly. "We're partners."

"That we are, but you'll slow me down. Your best bet is to lay low. With luck they'll be so busy chasing me they won't even see you. As soon as they're out of sight, head out. Go to Bedbug. Once I shake them I'll meet you there."

I lean over Coyote's neck. "Time to run now, brother."

37

Coyote and I make our way up the canyon, splashing through the creek, ducking under tree limbs. As we go I'm watching the canyon rim on my left, hoping I don't see a swarm of blue coats up there. With a little luck they're heading the other way looking for a way down and I'll gain a few precious minutes on them.

I get to the other exit I saw. It's steep with a lot of loose rock, more a trail for mountain goats than horses. Good place for a horse to pick up a broken leg.

"Go easy," I tell Coyote.

I don't need to worry. Almost like he's part mountain goat, Coyote goes right up the trail, picking his way with surefooted ease. The whole way I've got this itchy feeling between my shoulder blades. I can feel the rifle sights centered on my back, already hear the crack of the shot and feel the sudden pain. I want to twist around and look, but I don't want to upset Coyote's delicate balance. There's nothing for it but to grit my teeth and stay low in the saddle.

We make it to the top with no problems and I breathe a sigh of relief. I turn and look back and what I see chills me.

A single rider sits on his horse on the opposite rim, staring at me. He's wearing a gray cowboy hat, a long, brown coat, and the long gloves the cavalry favors. The wind gusts and his long hair blows around his face.

It's Mickey Free.

As good of a scout as the Apache Kid was for the army, Mickey Free's better. He's the manhunter no Indian wants to see on his backtrail. They say he can track a fly across glass. They say he has a sixth sense, that he knows what his prey will do before the prey knows it. Even Golthlay—who the white man calls Geronimo—fears him.

I've met Free before, when I was pretty young. He came to Pa-Gotzin-Kay a few times while chasing men. One time he was chasing Golthlay. He always frightened me for some reason.

There were times when I was sure he was staring at me, though I realize now that was probably my imagination.

Free has an unusual background. His mother was a Mexican maiden who was kidnapped by Pinal Apaches. She became pregnant by the warrior who stole her, then escaped and took up with a border-jumping adventurer named John Ward. Not long after that Free was kidnapped by the same Pinal Apaches. When he was eleven he escaped the Pinals and a pioneer family took him in and raised him. At twenty he joined the army scouts and he's spent most of his life since then helping them chase down renegade Apaches.

I pause there for a moment and we stare at each other. He could pull the rifle out of its boot and shoot at me. The distance isn't that great. He might even hit me.

But he doesn't and I think it's because he wants me to run. He wants to chase me.

He raises one hand and waves.

I wheel Coyote around and we head south in a fast lope. It's a pace Coyote can keep up for hours and it will eat up the miles. My thoughts are racing. On the way up the canyon my mind was already working on plans for how I was going to lose my pursuers, digging up every trick I ever learned. I figured I had a pretty good chance, too.

All that's gone now. None of those tricks will work on Mickey Free. They'll only slow me down.

Running won't work either. Coyote can outrun any horse alive, but the cavalry has resources I don't have. They can buy or commandeer fresh horses along the way. Eventually they'll catch us.

What does that leave me?

I could always surrender and hope they believe my story. But I already know that won't work. There's two dead people back there and one of them is a woman. The soldiers will be looking for revenge. It's likely they'll shoot me before I get a chance to talk.

Then it comes to me.

I have one chance. It's a slim one, practically nonexistent, but it's a darned sight better than no chance.

I have to catch the Apache Kid. If I can take him prisoner, maybe the soldiers will listen to me. Maybe they'll believe my story.

If I had time, I could track the Kid. Maybe I'm not as good as Free, but I'm no tenderfoot either. I've tracked rabbits through the sand. I've tracked lizards in the dust. With time, I know I could find him.

Unfortunately, time is something I don't have. Unless I cut the Kid's trail right away, Free and the cavalry will catch up to me long before I catch up to him. My only hope is to guess where he's going to go and then hope I can surprise him.

Which leaves just one question: where would he go?

Even a wanderer like the Apache Kid has a favored place where he can go to ground, terrain that he knows like the back of his hand, where he can elude his pursuers. Along the Arizona-New Mexico border there are some mountains. It's a wild place, too rough for farming, too remote for ranching. The Kid has been known to hole up there when things get rough, losing himself in the tangled canyons.

I've been heading south and southwest, but now I change course, veering southeast. As I go, I watch for sign, hoping I'll get lucky.

The hours pass. Now and then I twist in the saddle and look over my shoulder. There's a small cloud of dust on my backtrail, rising from the broken hills. That's the cavalry. They're only a couple miles back and coming steadily.

In the afternoon I see a boy up on a hillside, tending to a handful of goats. He might have seen the Kid. I ride toward him. He backs away when he sees me approaching. I can see him looking on down the valley at a few rounded mud and stone buildings down there, probably his home. I know what he's thinking. He's wondering if he can make it there before I can catch him.

But it's too far and he takes cover in some rocks instead. I ride up slowly, keeping my hands up, trying to let him know I mean no harm. I can see him peering out at me, his eyes wide.

This is Navajo territory. The Navajo don't like the Apache much, so I don't try Apache with him. It will only frighten him. Hopefully he speaks a few words of English.

155

"I'm not here to hurt you," I call out. "I want to ask you a question."

His eyes show no comprehension. I try Spanish with the same results. Maybe if I simplify the English.

"Horse," I say, pointing to Coyote. "Man," I say, pointing to me. I hold out my palm and move the fingers of my other hand over it, miming a horse walking. Then I gesture at the surrounding area. "Horse? Man?" More walking with my fingers.

He seems to think what I'm doing is funny because first he smiles, then he laughs. His head pokes up out of the rocks.

I'm glad he's enjoying this, but it's taking too much time. I turn and look at the cloud of dust. It's getting closer every second.

"Horse? Man? Come through here?" I ask him.

To my surprise he nods suddenly. "Horse. Man," he cries.

"Where?" I ask. I hold my hand up like I'm shielding my eyes from the sun and look around, as if trying to see someone in the distance.

This makes him laugh some more and he mimics my action.

I'm going to have to give up soon. "Where?"

He comes out of the rocks then and motions me to follow him. He runs up the side of the hill, as nimble as a goat. He stops on top of the ridge and points down into the valley below. He points at the sun, then points straight overhead. From this I take it to mean the rider passed through around noon.

I thank him and ride on. Could it really be that easy? I wonder. Am I that lucky?

There are tracks in the bottom of the valley. I don't know if they belong to the Kid, but I follow them anyway.

I follow the tracks clear through the rest of the day. If it really is the Kid, he's not making much effort to hide his trail. Probably he doesn't think anyone is following him.

Or he expects someone to follow and is planning an ambush.

That's the thought that bothers me the most and it keeps coming back to me as the hours slide by. There are so many good places for an ambush. Sandstone spires and bluffs everywhere. More and more clumps of scrub oak as the land rises. If I had the time, I'd stop and scout each one, at least try and make it difficult for him to get the drop on me.

But I don't have the time. All I can do is keep moving and hope I get lucky. I'm caught between a bear and a cougar and there's no way out but forward.

The sun reaches the horizon and still there's no sign of the rider I'm pursuing. Though I don't see him and have no reason really to believe it's him, I become more and more positive that they are the Kid's tracks. I also believe that he knows I'm following him.

More than that, he is *expecting* me to follow.

I remember what he said last night. One more step to take and he'd be free. What did he mean by that? I thought about it a lot during the night and never figured it out. It still makes no sense to me.

There was something in his eyes when he said it, something not quite human, like there was something else in there, looking out at me.

All at once I realize something. He set this all up. He knew the cavalry was chasing him. He knew I would go to that canyon. He put me in a position where the only choice I have is to follow him.

But why?

I put my hand in the pocket of my duster. I haven't had anything to eat all day and there's a piece of jerky in there. But it isn't jerky that my fingers close on.

With a sick feeling in my gut I pull out a raven feather.

It's the one the Kid left in the bottom of the canyon. For a minute I can only stare at it stupidly. I have no memory of putting it there.

I feel things closing in around me. Is it the curse Knuze spoke of? Or is it larger than that? Do I have any choices left or is something else making them for me now? The world suddenly feels very dark.

38

I stop when it gets too dark to follow the Kid's tracks. I have a feeling that he is close, maybe even watching me, but it might be only my imagination, which has been working overtime since I found the raven feather in my pocket.

I climb down off Coyote and pat him on the neck. "At least I still have you, right?" He tosses his head and snorts.

"Sometimes you're no help at all, you know that?"

I strip his saddle and bridle and turn him loose to graze. He doesn't walk off right away, but stands there looking at me. I remember that Annie asked me once why I named him Coyote. I told her it was because he was the same color as a coyote.

Now I'm not so sure.

I don't actually recall deciding to name him that. It's more like the name popped out of my mouth one day shortly after we started traveling together.

Coyote raises his tail and poops, then walks away.

"One little raven feather and suddenly I'm seeing spirits everywhere," I mutter. "I wish you wouldn't have crapped right there. That's where I was going to sleep." But Coyote is already grazing and he ignores me.

I pick a new spot and stretch out on the ground. Tired as I am, it's hard to sleep. What is the Kid up to? Where is he going?

I go over the countryside in my mind. Somehow it doesn't feel like he's heading for the mountains. He's going somewhere else. Then it comes to me.

He's heading for Tseyi, what the white men call Canyon de Chelly. It's a huge, deep canyon hundreds—maybe a thousand— feet deep.

But why? Why is he going there?

It can't be because he plans to hide out there. Tseyi belongs to the Navajo. They won't react well to having the Apache Kid hiding out in their midst and they will soon figure out he's here, if they don't already know.

The sides of the canyon are mostly sheer, unbroken cliffs, completely impassable. He's going run into a dead end, with no way to go forward unless he flies.

I'm still puzzling over it when I fall asleep.

I sleep poorly, my dreams filled with things I don't want to think about. I rise at first light, saddle Coyote and hit the trail, chewing on some jerky as I go. Ahead of me the Kid is doing the same thing, as are the soldiers behind me. Will today bring an end to this bizarre chase?

It's late morning when I reach the great canyon. Ahead through a break in the juniper trees the ground disappears, dropping away into nothing. I slow down and draw my Winchester from its scabbard.

There's a gunshot and a bullet hisses past my ear. I dive off Coyote and hug the ground.

"I could have killed you then," a voice calls out in Apache. It's the Kid.

I scoot behind a rock, careful not to raise my head and give him a target. "Why didn't you?" I yell back.

"I told you. I don't hunt Apaches anymore."

"But you slaughter innocent settlers."

He makes a disgusted sound. "They're not innocent. They're locusts, swarming everywhere, devouring everything. They are here to steal our land. They deserve whatever happens to them."

I've had this same argument with Geronimo and the other *Netdahe* who follow him. Part of me agrees with him. Every year there are more and more of them. It seems they will never stop coming until the land is covered with them.

But Geronimo and his followers were not the only voices I heard while growing up. Grandfather fought the white man for a long time, but eventually he came to see that it was hopeless. This was a war we could not win, no matter how brave we were or how hard we fought. He saw that the best we could do was to try to find a way to live in the new world we found ourselves in.

My mother felt the same way. She led us to Pa-Gotzin-Kay not so we could use it as base from which to strike at our enemies, but as a place of refuge, from which we could enter the world on our own terms.

"They'll never stop chasing you," I say.

"They're not chasing me. They're chasing you."

"Why did you do it?"

"Kill the settlers? I already told you."

"Not that. The raven feather. Why did you leave it where I could find it? Is it because you wanted me to follow you?"

When he speaks again, his voice is different. He sounds sad. "I didn't leave it. I lost it."

"I don't believe you. You left it as a message. But I don't know what the message is."

"That feather is strong medicine. I would never leave it." For the first time he doesn't sound as sure of himself.

While we've been talking I've been scanning the terrain. I think I know where he is now. There's a gnarled cedar beside a sandstone boulder. I think he's behind that. But he hasn't shown himself yet. I shift to where I can cover the spot with my rifle.

"It's not mine anymore," he says. "It left me. It chose you. It's yours now."

I don't like the sound of that at all. "You're wrong. Raven and I have never gotten along."

"Your problem is you don't know who you are, Ace."

That jars me for some reason. "I know who I am."

"No, you don't. You're caught between two worlds, trying to make them fit together, to make sense. But they won't. They never will. You have to choose one or the other, but you can't."

"Are you stalling, Kid? It sounds like you're stalling. What I can't figure out is why. There's nowhere else to run."

He stands up then, his hands where so I can see he's not holding his gun.

"I'm done running. I've arrived at my destination. I waited for you because I have something to tell you."

I stand up, keeping my rifle pointed at him. Even emptyhanded I don't trust him a lick. "There's nothing you have to say that I want to hear."

He smiles. His eyes are very bright. "I see you, Ace. The old spirits are thick around you. I saw them the first time I met you at the stronghold. I saw them again last night at your camp. That's why I didn't kill you and your friend. There's something special about you, some purpose you have before you. The old ways are strong in you. You could be a great leader for our people, greater even than Cochise."

His words hit me like a punch in the stomach. I'm having trouble swallowing. Something black flies across my vision, but when I look it's not there. I try to shake it off, to focus on the Kid. He's trying to trick me.

"You know the truth of my words, don't you? You don't want to, but you can't deny it."

His words are like wasps flying around me. They sting for some reason I don't understand.

"Raven led you here, Ace. He wants you to see what comes next."

I manage to find my voice. "What comes next is the cavalry will be here soon, Kid. There's nowhere for you to run."

"I won't be running, Ace. I'll be flying."

"You think you're Raven now, is that it?"

"Remember last night, when you named me Has-kay-bay-nez-ntayl?"

I don't like where this is going. I glance over my shoulder. I wish the cavalry would hurry up and get here. Soon it will be too late.

If it isn't already.

"It's only a name," I say.

"No, it's not. You know Dee-O-Det better than that. He is a great shaman, one of the greatest ever. He gave me that name because it's true. When I die, it will be in a mysterious way."

I'm sweating. The rifle is heavy in my hands. I feel angry suddenly. "Dammit, Kid, whatever you're about to do, don't. The cavalry's going to be here soon. They think I killed those settlers. If you care about your people at all, don't leave me to answer for your crimes."

"You'll be all right, Ace. You always are. The spirits watch over you. You are important to them for some reason."

He takes a step back. I could shoot him right now, but he's too close to the edge. He'll fall over. I want him up here and I want him alive.

I walk toward him, keeping the rifle pointed at him. "Come away from the edge."

His smile is feral. His eyes are blazing now. "Hold onto that feather," he says.

"I don't want the feather."

"It doesn't matter what you want. Raven chose you for a reason." He looks over his shoulder.

"Kid, don't..."

It's too late.

He spreads his arms and takes another step back. I start running, even though I know it's hopeless. He drops over the edge and out of sight.

I'm there a second later. I stand at the edge of the cliff and look down. It's a tall cliff, six or seven hundred feet high. I should be able to see him falling.

Instead I see nothing.

I look around, wondering if he tricked me, maybe jumped down to a hidden ledge. But the cliff is sheer. There's nowhere for him to have gone. He's simply disappeared into thin air.

I hear a bird call and turn. A raven flaps its black wings and rises into the air. It flies past me, fixing me with its yellow eye.

A voice comes from behind me.

"Drop your rifle and turn around real slow or we'll shoot."

39

I turn around slowly. There's about twenty soldiers facing me in a half circle, all of them pointing guns at me.

"Drop the gun and put your hands up!" the same man barks. There's faded gold braid on his coat, so he must be an officer. Mickey Free is standing next to him. He's the only one not pointing a gun at me. He's standing with his arms folded over his chest.

When I hesitate the officer grins. "Go ahead," he says. "Try it. It will be my pleasure to blow you straight to hell."

I drop the rifle and raise my hands.

"Disarm him," he orders Free, who detaches from the line and ambles forward.

I've never seen Free up close before. He has flat eyes and an impassive expression, yet somehow he looks disappointed.

"Not much of a run," he says.

"I wasn't running. I was chasing the Apache Kid."

His eyes on my face, Free leans in and reaches for my pistols. I want to act. I see the exact spot on his wrist where I could grab and twist. In a heartbeat I could have his arm behind his back, crouching behind him for cover. My eyes flick up and meet his and I can see he knows what I'm thinking. One eyebrow rises fractionally, asking me what I'm going to do.

I let him take my guns without resisting. The soldiers will not hesitate to shoot us both down. It is why the officer sent Free instead of one of his men. Free knows this as well as I do. Nothing will be accomplished except to get both of us killed.

Free shakes his head when he steps back and again I get the feeling he is disappointed.

"Private Barnes, cuff him," the officer says.

A soldier comes forward carrying manacles. He's young, maybe only sixteen. His uniform looks new. Probably this is his first patrol. He's heard about the fierce Apaches, but he's never seen one up close. He looks at me with deer eyes, like he's ready to bolt.

When I feel the cold steel click shut around my wrists something inside me howls. In the sound of metal on metal is contained everything I fear most about the white man and his world. The horizons are suddenly gone and hard stone walls take their place. I take a look over my shoulder at the cliff. I can see the raven flying out there in the emptiness, mocking me with his freedom. My muscles twitch with the desire to leap.

Barnes grabs me and pulls me away from the edge. "It's a long ways down," he says.

The officer looks me up and down and his lip curls. "I'm taking you to Phoenix now, where you will stand trial for your crimes. I hope you don't make it that far. I hope you try something between now and then so I have an excuse to shoot you down like the dog that you are. I'd shoot you right now, take your head back in a sack, but the new general's softer than Crook. He wants to see renegade Indians face justice. He thinks it will calm the reservations." He spits on the ground. "He's a damned fool with no understanding of the savage mind. Only violence works with you people."

It's hopeless, but I have to try. "I didn't kill those settlers."

"You speak English," the officer says, sounding surprised, like I was a horse walking on its hind legs or something.

I try again. "I didn't kill those settlers."

"So you were riding along, minding your own business and happened to find them there, conveniently already dead?" he sneers. "Is that what you're saying?"

"It was the Apache Kid who killed them. I saw the smoke and went to investigate."

"And while you were there you figured you'd help yourself to their scalps. Is that it?"

"They were already scalped."

"If you're innocent, why did you run? You got an answer for that?"

"I knew you wouldn't believe me. I was chasing the Kid. I thought that if I caught him, I could prove my innocence."

"But you didn't. Catch him, that is."

"I did."

The officer looks around. "Then where is he?"

I gesture with my chin. "Gone. Over the cliff."

"So afraid of you he jumped over a cliff, eh? Barnes, go have a look."

Barnes goes to the edge and looks over. "I don't see a body down there."

"He flew away," I say. I look at Free when I say this and he nods like I confirmed something for him.

"Save it for the judge, boy," the officer growls. "I'm done listening."

"We could go back," I say, that feeling of the walls closing in rising up again. "Give Free time to read the tracks. He'll confirm what I say." Except that I don't know if he will. Free's animosity toward all Apaches is well known.

"Sure. And how about we get you a nice steak dinner on the way?" the officer says. "Where's your horse? Or would you rather we just dragged you?"

I whistle and Coyote comes trotting up. He rolls his eyes at the officer and snorts.

"Easy, brother," I tell him in Apache.

"Damned ugly beast," the officer says. I tense, hoping Coyote won't stomp him for his words. I don't want to see my brother get hurt.

The officer looks back at me. "One thing you should know, before you get on. If you try to run, we'll aim for the horse first. We'll shoot him right out from under you."

I lower my head, knowing that, for now at least, I'm beaten.

40

There are times during that day when I see my opening, places where the trail passes through broken terrain, where Coyote and I could suddenly take off and be out of sight in moments. But I let them all pass. I can't risk getting Coyote shot. Whatever happens to me isn't as important as his safety. After all, it was me who got us into this mess, not him. I won't have Coyote paying the price for what I did.

I spend much of the day thinking about people I've known. My mother. Grandfather. The old shaman Dee-O-Det. I think about Victoria and Blake. I think about Doc Holliday. One-eyed Lou. I wonder if Ancil and Pearl got together. I even think about crazy old Virgil.

Most of all I think about Annie. I wonder what she's doing right then. I imagine her out in her garden, getting it ready for the spring planting. I can almost see her, the sun on her hair, her flashing green eyes. It helps and hurts at the same time.

We ride south and west, passing through harsh, bleak country. There are almost no trees, not much vegetation beyond dried grasses and brittle, dead-looking shrubs. The washes are baked hard and dry. Even the sandstone here seems to have given up. Gone are the impressive buttes and cliffs, replaced by small hills and ridges, the sandstone so brittle it crumbles underfoot.

We make a dry camp that night in a flat area roughly bordered by crumbling sandstone and shale hills. A few dead bushes cluster at the feet of the hills. I climb down off Coyote and when Private Barnes starts to reach for his bridle I say, "I wouldn't do that. He bites."

He jerks his hand back, his eyes widening. "Really? Or are you just saying that?"

"He bit off a man's finger once." It's true. I went into the mercantile in this no-name town in southern Arizona. The man thought he'd steal my horse while I was in there. Now he only has nine fingers.

"I don't want to lose any of my fingers. Why don't you unsaddle him?"

I strip off Coyote's saddle and bridle. When I start to reach into the saddlebags Barnes draws his gun out and points it at me. "What are you doing?"

I hold my hands up. "I'm getting out a brush. To brush down my horse."

"Or you're going for a weapon."

"You boys already searched everything. Remember?"

That doesn't seem to make him feel a lot better but he waves the pistol to let me know I can go ahead. I dig out the old brush I carry and start brushing Coyote down.

In Apache I tell him, "I think our time together may be coming to an end, brother."

Coyote snorts and stamps his foot.

I take hold of his muzzle and look him in the eye. "When the time comes and I tell you to run, you run. Understand?"

Coyote pulls his head away and tosses it. He opens his mouth and clamps down on my hand, but he doesn't bite me. He just holds on for a few seconds, then lets me go. It makes me feel better, knowing he understands me.

Captain Davis puts sentries up on a couple of the surrounding hills. A soldier fetches a chain from one of the pack animals. He runs it through my manacles and around a large stone, securing it with a padlock. It doesn't look like I'm going anywhere tonight.

For dinner a soldier named Harris brings me a shapeless lump of hard tack. When I reach for it he drops it on the ground. He smiles and steps on it. He's a big man with a thick neck and the swagger of a bully. "Oops. Looks like I stepped on your food."

He pulls his foot back. I don't move. "Ain't you going to pick it up?" he asks.

I know where that leads. "I'm not hungry."

His eyes narrow. He doesn't like me spoiling his fun. "Pick it up," he growls, putting his hand on his gun.

I bend down for the bread, but I know what's coming so when he tries to kick me I slap his foot aside and he stumbles a little. He points his gun at me, his eyes flashing. "I could kill you for that."

167

I don't reply. What is there to say? A few of the other soldiers are watching but it's obvious none of them are going to intervene.

"Pick up the damned bread," he says.

I don't slap the kick aside this time, only turn my body a little so he doesn't catch me solid with his boot.

"Watch yourself, Injun," he says and walks off.

My bedroll is still tied to my saddle, which is lying out of reach of my chain. Asking for it isn't going to do any good, so I stretch out on the ground. It will be cold tonight, but not too cold. I've made it through worse. One thing it won't do is stop me from sleeping.

Before I can fall asleep Mickey Free comes over and sits down beside me. It's dark by then and he is only a silhouette. I sit up.

"I've heard of you," he says in Apache. "The half-breed who fights with two guns. They say you faced John Hardin and Killin' Jim Miller at the same time and gunned them down."

That was in Lily Creek. They were gunslingers hired to kill me.

"I told them it would be best if they left town. I even offered to buy them a slice of pie," I reply. "They should have taken the pie."

"They say other things as well. They say Mustang Gray and his Scalphunters chased you in Mexico. He lost half his men that day."

"I wish we'd shot them all. The world would be a better place." I shift the manacles to a more comfortable position. "I've heard of you too. I heard you brought Pedro's head to General Crook in a bag."

A large number of Apaches got tired of being cheated out of their rations by their Indian agent and went on the warpath. Crook crushed the rebellion by offering rewards for the heads of the leaders. Mickey Free was the first to bring one in. For that they made him leader of the scouts.

"Pedro tried to run. He didn't run far enough or fast enough," Free replies. "I thought you would be different. I thought it would be hard to catch you."

"You know I didn't kill those settlers."

"I know. I read the tracks."

"But you won't tell the captain."

"No."

"Why not?"

"I always get my man."

It takes me a moment to realize what he means by this. "The Apache Kid was your man."

"You let him get away," he says.

"He jumped over the edge and disappeared. I think he turned into a raven."

"Or he was a raven who became a man," Free says. He has a strange, almost dreamy way of talking.

"So you believe me, that I saw him jump and disappear?"

"My eyes are not closed as theirs are. I know there is more to the world than they say there is."

"Why do you do this? They have no respect for you. To them you're just another Indian. They would have killed you today without thinking about it."

"I do it because I can. Because there is no one who is better at it."

"That's not much of a reason," I say.

"It's enough for me."

"You were born of the Mexican mother, raised by the Apaches and you work for the white man. All of them hate and fear you."

He shrugs. "It is my path. Three worlds and I belong to none of them. It is for me to find my own way."

"Why are you here, talking to me?"

"I came to see if there is still life in you. I came to see if you would run."

I hold up my manacled hands. The chain clinks when I do so.

"Men have escaped manacles before." He stands up. "Your medicine is stronger than you know, Ace. I will keep my eye on you. You may yet escape and give me a real chase." He walks off into the darkness and disappears.

41

We ride for two more days. We leave the eroded sandstone hills behind and emerge onto high plains where the only mountains are far in the distance. Sagebrush and stunted mesquite trees dot the plains. The wind blows steadily.

The town is called Bitter Creek. The creek in question has no water and is choked with desert broom and pack rat nests. The largest tumbleweeds I have ever seen blow down the town's one dusty street.

The town is there because the railroad is there. The tracks stretch away to the east and the west. Beside the tracks is a sagging, unpainted ticket station and a water tower. Nearby is the livery and corral. A train is sitting in the station, smoke belching from it.

"Finally, I can get off this horse," Barnes says. The officer must have assigned him to me because he's always nearby. He's not a bad kid, really. He's the only one of the soldiers who will actually speak to me. Over the last couple of days his fear of me has mostly disappeared and he talks to me sometimes. "I hate this horse. I think I hate all horses."

I get that feeling of the walls closing in again. There's no livestock car attached to the train. Even if there was, there'd be no reason for them to bring Coyote along. He's not the one going to face a judge. It feels like there's a stone in my chest. The time I've been fearing has come.

We ride on into the corral. I slide down off Coyote, unbuckle the cinch and strip the saddle, quickly before any of the soldiers realizes what I'm doing.

"What're you doing?" Harris says. "No one told you to unsaddle your horse." He shoves me. Since the first night he hasn't missed a chance to shove me or punch me. "The livery man will take care of the horse. Captain wants you on the train pronto."

I take off Coyote's bridle, grab his head and pull him close.

"Hey, you got a hearing problem or something?" Harris says, grabbing my shoulder and trying to pull me away.

I grab a couple fingers and give a good, hard twist. There's a pop as one dislocates and he jerks back with a cry of pain.

"The time is here, my brother," I whisper to Coyote. It's hard to make my voice work. I have tears in my throat. "Time for you to go." I let go of him and push him away.

"Hold on there!" one of the soldiers says, reaching for Coyote. Coyote snaps at him and he pulls his hand back, his eyes wide.

"Go!" I yell.

Coyote sidesteps, still looking at me, unsure.

"Close that gate!" someone yells.

A man runs for the gate and starts dragging it closed. Coyote looks at the closing gate, then back at me.

"Go!"

Coyote bolts for the gate. Realizing he won't get the gate closed in time, the man jumps in front of Coyote, shouting and waving his arms. It doesn't work.

Coyote runs over him, knocking him flying. Then he's out the gate, but still he doesn't run off. He stops and looks back at me again.

Harris is cursing. I feel a terrible pain in the back of my head as he cracks me with the butt of his gun, dropping me to my knees. He hits me again once I'm down but I pay him no attention. My eyes are fixed on my brother.

There's a cowboy outside the corral and he's shaking out a loop in his lasso. He twirls it around his head a couple times and then throws.

But Coyote's too smart for that. He sees the rope and dodges it, then runs off a little further.

More blows follow but I feel none of them. Coyote is free and that's what matters. Hands grab me and drag me out of the corral, to the waiting train. The sliding door is open on one of the cars. They lift me and toss me inside. It's a cargo car, empty except for two waiting soldiers and several heavy chains bolted to the floor. They loop one of the chains through my manacles and padlock it. They kick and hit me a few more times, then jump down out of the car.

The train starts moving. I sit up, looking past the soldiers as they wrestle with the balky door. Out beyond the last buildings of the town, out on the open plains, I can see Coyote. He's standing there, looking back at me.

"Be free," I whisper to him.

The door slides shut and I can see him no more.

42

The train picks up speed. My head is pounding from where Harris hit me with his pistol. I am alone and when I get to Phoenix, they will hang me.

I will never see Coyote again.

Somehow that hurts the most.

The train car smells like an outhouse. There are no windows. The floor, walls and ceiling are thick wooden planks. The chain is securely bolted to the floor. There's a small door in the far end of the car, but the chain is too short to reach that far.

I stand up and have to grab onto the wall to keep my balance. My vision is blurry. Waves of nausea wash over me. When I touch the lump on the back of my head my hand comes away with blood on it.

I try to sit down and end up falling. Darkness crowds my vision. I don't fight it. I want the darkness to take me. I'm a dead man anyway, why not simply let it end here, now? My helplessness is so thick I am choking on it.

But I don't die. I don't get the easy way out. I never do.

Lying there, sick and sore and bleeding, a memory comes to me.

I was very young and I asked Grandfather one day why it was he had made peace with the white man. Why had he given up the fight?

"I quit because I saw that there was no way to win, that so long as we continued to fight the white man by his rules, we would inevitably lose," he said. "The answer lies in finding a new path, somewhere between hopeless war and crushing surrender."

"Where is this new path, Grandfather?"

He shook his head. "I don't know. I haven't found it yet." He put his hand on my shoulder and turned me to face him. "I am old. I do not believe I will find it in my time. That will be for you to do. You must find the path and show our people the way."

He died only days later.

I roll onto my side and sit up. I look up at the ceiling of the car.

"You were wrong, Grandfather. There is no path."

I see this clearly now. Geronimo was right all along. There is only *Netdahe*, the path of endless war. The only other choice is abject surrender and the slow, crushing death it brings.

I tried to live in their world, by their rules, but they wouldn't let me. They made sure there was no way I could ever win. Every choice could only lead to death in the end.

I make a decision then. I can't win. No matter what I do, they are going to kill me.

But I can go down fighting. I can hurt some of them before the end.

The pain in my head recedes, replaced by a new clarity. Gone is the nausea, the blurred vision. Those were but signs of my weakness and I have no more time for weakness.

The hours pass. The train slows and comes to a stop. Voices outside. The door slides open and a sheriff sticks his head in.

"Got some company for ya, some fellers to keep you from getting lonely on the long ride to Phoenix," he says with a tobacco-stained grin. "Not sure how much you're gonna enjoy them, though. They put up quite the struggle while we was arresting them. They seem to have a lot of what you might call frustrations they need to work out. I'm thinking a murdering Injun will fit the bill right nicely."

He turns and speaks to someone I can't see. "Get a wiggle on, Lem. I don't want to stand out here all day."

The deputy comes into sight, herding three prisoners, and you know what?

I already know them.

43

It's Jesse James and Cole and Bob Younger. The last time I saw them they were running screaming through the forest, sure my ghost was chasing them.

The sheriff turns to Jesse. "Put out your hands." Jesse holds his hands out and the sheriff takes off his manacles. "Get in the car," he growls.

"You gonna put them in there without no handcuffs?" the deputy asks. "Ain't you worried they'll escape?"

"Once they get on this train they ain't my problem anymore," the sheriff says. "And I'm not giving up all my manacles. You know how long it will take me to get some more?"

"You're the boss," the deputy says. They uncuff the Younger brothers too and stuff them all in the car. The door slides shut and the train starts rolling out of the station.

I'm sitting against the wall, not moving, and the car is dim so it takes a moment before the men see me. I tilt my hat back so they can get a good look at my face. Jesse's the first one to realize who I am. His eyes get wide.

"It's that Injun we hung." He takes a half step back and reaches for a gun that isn't there. "You're supposed to be dead. How'd you do that?"

I simply stare at him.

"You ain't a ghost, are you?" Jesse asks.

"What kind of fool question is that?" Cole says. "Of course he ain't a ghost."

"Then how come he ain't dead? People die when you string 'em up."

"How should I know? Maybe the rope broke. We shoulda put a bullet in him, just to be sure. But that doesn't matter now. What matters is he didn't die and here he is, all chained up waiting for us."

"You're right," Jesse says. He seems to be getting his courage back. He swaggers over closer to me. "You made us for fools

175

back there. It took two days to round up the horses and all our gear. Frank was mad for a week."

The other two come up to stand beside him. Bob cracks his knuckles and scowls at me. "Because of you I got peed on and had to take a bath. I don't take kindly to that."

All three are staring down at me. I still haven't moved or said anything.

"Why's he sitting there like that?" Jesse says. "How come he don't move or talk? You sure he ain't a ghost?"

"Quit talking like that!" Cole says. "It makes me jumpy."

"Would a ghost have handcuffs on?" Bob says.

That seems to make sense to Jesse because he nods. He comes a little closer. "You're gonna be sorry," he says. "There ain't nowhere you can go. You're trapped in here with us."

"You sure about that?" I ask. They all look startled. "You sure you're not trapped in here with *me*?"

Jesse gets a confused look on his face. While he's sorting out this new thought, I act.

When they walked over to me they stepped over my chain. Probably didn't even see it. I take hold of it and give it a good, hard jerk.

Jesse and Bob go down. Cole keeps his feet, but just barely.

And then I'm all over them.

The black rage boils up inside me and I welcome it. I kick Cole in the knee, hard enough that I hear something crack and he goes down squalling.

Jesse is just getting up and I kick him under the chin. His jaw snaps shut and blood flies from where he bit his tongue. I follow with a double-fisted blow to the side of the head. The extra weight from the manacles and the chain gives the blow more power and he staggers off to the side, arms pinwheeling.

Bob grabs me from behind, getting me in a headlock. I back up and slam him into the wall. Then I come forward, grab onto his thumb and twist until it cracks. He cries out and his hold loosens. I flip him over my shoulder and slam him onto the floor, then drop down and slam my fists into his face. His nose breaks in a spray of blood and the manacles gouge deep cuts in his face.

Cole is trying to get up and I kick him in the knee again. He howls and collapses. I jump and come down with my full weight on my elbow, driving it into his gut. All the air whooshes out of him.

I stand up and Jesse charges me, swinging wildly. A couple of his punches land but I don't feel them. I stomp down on his foot and when he steps back I hook my other foot behind his heel and trip him. Then I jump on him and start slamming him in the face over and over.

It all gets blurry about then. There's no thought, only action and reaction. I'm holding nothing back. I want to make these men hurt. I want to kill them.

At one point I've got Jesse down on the floor and I'm choking him with my chain. I'm dimly aware that the other two are down and not moving anymore. The chain bites deeper and Jesse's struggles to get it off are getting weaker and weaker.

The door at the end of the car bangs open and a couple soldiers run in. They start hitting and kicking me, but it's not until one clubs me on the side of the head with his rifle that I let go of Jesse. Jesse rolls away, gasping and choking.

I come to my feet and charge the soldiers then, but they're no idiots. They fall back to the door and when I hit the end of that chain they're about two feet out of my reach.

"Goddamned savage," one of them says. "We should shoot him now."

The other one is looking at the three outlaws. "He took down three men by himself," he says in awe. "And him manacled and chained."

"He's an animal," the first soldier says. "Look in his eyes. There ain't nothing in there but killing. We should be killing them all, not putting them on reservations. Dying's the only thing that'll fix them." He turns to the other one. "Go tell the captain. We're going to need to post a guard in here."

44

A little later a handful of soldiers comes in. While one keeps a gun on me, the others manacle the three outlaws and then padlock them to the other chains. The outlaws complain a lot while they do this, whining about how much everything hurts. The soldiers leave, except for one who stays to guard us.

By then I've gone back to sitting against the wall. The outlaws huddle in the corner as far as they can get from me, whispering among themselves and flashing me scared looks now and then. I ignore them. I'm lost in dark thoughts, running over the mistakes I've made in my life. I see everything I should have done differently, every fork that was a mistake.

Every few hours the guard changes. They sit on a stool at the end of the car. I can't reach them but that doesn't seem to make them feel any better. Every one of them sits with his gun out, watching me closely. They pay no attention to the outlaws at all.

About dark the door at the end of the car swings open and Barnes comes in carrying a lantern. "About time," the soldier he's relieving says. "I couldn't see nothing." He hurries from the car.

Barnes holds the lantern up and peers at the three outlaws. He whistles softly when he sees how banged up they are. "Damn, Ace, you really went to town on them boys."

I look at him but don't say anything.

He goes and sits down. "The whole train is talking about you, how you whipped three men and you all chained up. I thought they were exaggerating, but now..." He whistles again. "The ones who found you reckoned you'd have killed them all if they didn't stop you." He leans forward and puts his elbows on his knees.

"Would you? Would you have killed them?"

"Yes. I'd kill them now if you weren't here."

The outlaws look alarmed at this and turn frightened looks on Barnes like they're afraid he's going to walk out and leave them.

178

"So you *are* a killer, then." He sounds disappointed. "And here I was starting to believe you, that you didn't kill those settlers."

"I'm an Indian," I say grimly. "That's all we ever do is kill, right?"

Barnes thinks this over. "Maybe Dan is right. Maybe we'll never be safe until we kill all the redskins off."

I turn away. I've got nothing to say to him. I manage to sleep that night, but my dreams are full of darkness and violence. There's a door inside me I tried all my life to keep closed and now it's open. It's pure poison and hate in there and it's spilling out freely.

It's the next day, late morning, and the train is climbing a hill and running slow. Then it comes to a complete stop. The soldier guarding us stands up, a frown on his face. "We're not supposed to stop here," he says.

Suddenly a barrage of gunshots come from outside. The soldier draws his pistol and crouches down. Jesse looks at the Younger brothers. "That's Frank. I'd bet my life on it. Frank's come to break us out."

Then he looks at me. "You'll be dead in a minute, Injun. Frank will see to you. I'll spit on your corpse."

I don't respond. The truth is, getting shot sounds a whole lot better than a trial and a hanging. Let whatever's coming come. I don't care anymore.

There's a couple of shots from right outside the car. The door quivers with the impact. Then comes the sound of the broken padlock being taken off and the bolt sliding back. The door slides open a few inches.

The soldier fires his six gun at the opening, fanning the hammer with his free hand. Six quick shots and then the hammer clicks on empty. He starts digging out more cartridges and trying to reload, his hands shaking so bad he drops several of them.

A rifle barrel slides through the opening. A couple of quick shots, flame and smoke, and the soldier slumps to the floor, bleeding from his chest and stomach.

The door slides open further. It's Frank James all right. I recognize the cold look, the gold tooth. He fires another round

179

into the soldier, then climbs into the car. He glances at his brother and the Youngers, then turns to me.

"Well, I'll be damned," he says. "I knew you weren't dead. I knew these knuckleheads were seeing things, going on about ghosts and such. I never believed it for a second."

"It wasn't our—" Jesse begins, but Frank cuts him off.

"Don't start up again, Jesse. Swear to god I can't listen to it anymore. You boys got drunk and he played you. That's all there is to it."

"Are you gonna search that soldier for the key?" Cole asks, holding up his manacled hands. "These are pinching something awful."

"He isn't going to have a key, you dimwit. You think they'd leave a key in here where you could get at it? The army's dumb, but they aren't that dumb." Frank has a pry bar stuck in his belt and he pulls it out and tosses it to them. "Use that to pry out the bolt fixing the chain to the floor. And make it quick. We don't know how many soldiers they got on this train." As if in response to his words another round of gunshots goes off outside. It sounds like someone on the train is shooting back.

While Cole goes to work on the bolts, Frank walks up and stands looking down at me. "You've been a whole passel of trouble, Injun, you know that? Those boys didn't sleep right for a week and they spent nearly every minute talking about the vengeful spirit that attacked them. I told them it wasn't no spirit, but they wouldn't listen to me. I don't know why you aren't dead, but I aim to fix that right quick." He turns the rifle on me.

I stare down the barrel. It's close enough that I can probably slap it aside before he fires. I might be able to twist it out of his hands and use it on him. But I feel a strange weariness. Maybe it would be best to have everything over and done with. No more running. No more fighting.

Behind Frank the door in the end of the train car flies open. It's Mickey Free, standing there with a shotgun pointed at Frank's back. Frank starts to turn and Mickey says, "Don't try it. I'll cut you in half."

Frank freezes halfway through his turn.

"You're not killing him," Free says. "Take the others and go. I don't care. But he lives."

This puzzles Frank. "Why?"

"You wouldn't understand."

Frank looks back at me. "They'll hang you for good this time and make sure you're dead. You'll get what you deserve."

I shrug. "So will you. Someday."

Cole has finished prying up the bolts by then. The boys gather up their chains and limp to the door. A minute later they're gone.

"You wasted your time," I tell Free. "Unless you're planning on cutting me loose, you're never going to get that chase you want so bad."

Free lowers the shotgun. "We'll see about that."

A couple of soldiers come hurrying into the car, guns out. "The other three escaped," Free says. "But we still have this one."

45

When the train stops in Phoenix, it's Harris who comes and unlocks me from the chain. Perfect. I've been looking for my chance for a little payback. Before he can stand up I club him on the side of the head with my manacles. Blood wells out of his ear and I jump on him and club him twice more as fast as I can.

That's all I get because the other soldiers pile on then, kicking, hitting me with rifle butts. It hurts, but the sight of Harris curled up on the floor with blood pouring out his head in a few places makes it all worth it.

They slap me around some more and drag me into the jail. It's bigger than other jails I've seen, with half a dozen cells. All of them are full. They take off my manacles and shove me into a cell with four other men. The men stand up and come for me, hard looks on their faces.

I don't waste any time. Hardly has the cell door swung shut than I go at them. I use every dirty trick I know. Head butts, eye gouges, groin punches. I take a lot of blows—four men in a cramped space is too much for any one man—but I deal out even more. It's dirty, brutal and painful.

A couple minutes of this and then one of the men says, "Enough! Stop! You let us be, we'll let you be." He's bleeding from his mouth and one of his fingers is sticking sideways. One of the men is down on the floor, not moving. The other two look like men who stumbled into a bear's den by accident.

I back away and sit down against the wall, retreating into myself. For the two days I'm there I don't look at them, I don't talk to them. They give me a wide berth.

The trial comes and it seems word has gotten around because the jailers put manacles on both my hands and my feet. Another chain links everything together. The chain on my foot manacles is short and I have to take tiny steps so I can't go very fast. "Get a move on," one of the jailers growls and shoves me, hard enough that I almost fall. I spin on him with a snarl and he backs up so fast he trips. After that they leave me alone.

The courtroom is bigger than the one in Pueblo and it's in an actual stone building. The windows have bars over them and the wooden floors have been sanded and polished.

The courtroom is packed, so full that people are standing in the back. Mostly men, but a handful of women too, wearing big hats, holding lace hankies to their faces. No one's wearing a gun—the deputy at the front door takes them before they're allowed in—and from the look on the men's faces it's a necessary thing. They'd like nothing better than to shoot me down.

The jailers prod me down the aisle and to a chair sitting up against the wall to the side of the room. Once I'm in my seat I take my time and scan the room, trying to look into their eyes, glaring murderously at them. They came here to see a bloodthirsty savage, I'll give them one. Most of them can't take it and quickly look away.

Across from me is the jury, twelve men sitting in two rows. Most of them don't have much luck meeting my glare, but one of them, a short, white-haired man in a vest, bares his teeth and draws his thumb across his throat in a throat-slitting gesture.

The judge comes in and everyone stands up except me. He's a tall man with sunken cheeks and close-cut hair. He's old, with deep lines in his face and a flap of extra skin hanging from his throat. He puts on a pair of gold-rimmed spectacles and looks me up and down.

"Let's get this over with," he growls. "First witness."

It's Harris. One eye is still swollen mostly shut from the beating I gave him and he's got a few bandages wrapped around his head. He flashes me a triumphant look as he walks up to the chair sitting beside the judge's bench. The bailiff swears him in. A man in a suit walks up to him.

"Tell the court what you saw that day," he says. He doesn't look at me. He sounds bored.

"It was morning. We'd been tracking a renegade Apache for two days and we knew we were close. We rode up to the edge of the canyon and when I looked down into it I saw that Injun right there down in the bottom. He was standing over the body of a dead woman, holding her scalp in his hand."

A gasp rises from the women in the audience and hankies flutter.

"It was dripping blood and everything. The woman was sprawled out like this—" He spreads his arms to show the room. "On her face. She'd been trying to get back to the cabin when he cut her down. Her man was dead off to the side. He wasn't armed or nothing."

The man in the suit asks, "And you're sure it was this man?"

"Sure as I'm sitting here."

"That's good enough for me. No further questions, Your Honor."

The judge looks around the courtroom. "Where's the defense attorney?"

Someone from the crowd pipes up. "I saw him earlier, Your Honor, down to the Silver Dollar Saloon. He was passed out."

The judge swears.

"Who needs him anyway?" someone in the audience calls out. "It's clear the redskin's guilty!" Cries of agreement greet his words and the judge has to bang his gavel for order.

He points the gavel at the man who spoke. "You speak out again and I'll throw you out of this courtroom. Do you understand me? We're going to do this the proper way. This isn't a lynching, it's a trial. And in a trial the accused has the right to a lawyer."

A groan goes up from the audience. This isn't what they wanted to see.

"Unless…" The judge turns to me. "Unless you waive your right to counsel. Do you?"

I'm not sure what that means, but I don't care. There's no way I'm getting out of here as anything but guilty. Might as well get it over with. I nod.

"Does the prosecution have any more witnesses to call?" the judge asks.

"I could call them, Your Honor. But they're all going to say the same thing."

The judge nods. "The jury will retire to reach a verdict."

One of the jurors stands up. "Your Honor, we don't need to retire." He glances at the others, who are all nodding. "It's plain this Apache savage is guilty. Any fool can see that." He sits back down.

The judge turns back to me. "The common sentence for this sort of crime, the brutal murder of two people, is hanging. And no doubt that's what the good people in this courtroom want to hear. But I've got something else in mind for you."

Angry mutters arise from the audience and the judge bangs his gavel for quiet.

"Hear me out!" he barks. They settle down and he continues. "I've a mind that hanging's too quick and easy. One quick snap and it's all over, right? To me that doesn't hardly seem fair, in light of what you took from those folks. What do you think?"

I think I'm a dead man no matter what. I stare at him expressionlessly.

The judge gives me a cadaverous smile. "We'll see if you still have the same attitude in a few years." He bangs his gavel. "I sentence you to twenty-five years in the Yuma Territorial Prison."

46

A couple days later they chain me up again and haul me out to a waiting stagecoach. There are already three men inside. The jailers shove me in and slam and padlock the door. The only open seat is next to a large, fat man. He's bald and sweaty and he gives me a pig-eyed glare.

"There ain't room," he says. "Sit on the floor."

My reply is to jump on him. I get the chain on my manacles wrapped around his fat neck and I push with everything I've got. His eyes bulge out and he tries to fight back, but his arms are beneath mine so he can't hit me in the face. The chain is biting too deep into his flesh for him to get his fingers under it. He can't throw me off because I've got my heels jammed against the far wall of the stagecoach. All he can do is hit weakly at my ribs.

By and by his struggles get weaker and his eyes kind of glaze over, but I don't let up. Then one of the other prisoners says, "Let him be, Ace. He don't know better."

At first I ignore him. I want to kill this man. He stands for everything I hate.

But then the air goes out of me and I pull back and sit down. The fat man starts choking and gasping and rubbing his throat.

"He sure enough knows now," the other prisoner says. I glance over and see that I recognize him from one of the other cells in the jail. The man next to him looks familiar too. The fat man must have been held somewhere else.

I settle back in my seat and withdraw into myself. The driver cracks the whip and the stagecoach starts out. The fat man presses himself against his side of the coach as tight as he can. His eyes roll in his head like a frightened mare's.

It takes a few miserable, long days to get to Yuma. By then the stagecoach smells like a hog died in there. I'm in a foul mood from bouncing around inside that stifling wooden box and none of the other prisoners dare even look at me.

The prison is set into the side of a hill where the Gila and Colorado Rivers come together. The wall is a good twenty-five feet tall, made of large, rough-cut granite stones mortared together. There's a guard tower on top of the wall. The entrance is a tall archway blocked off by a pair of metal gates made of overlapping strips of metal. The gate creaks open and the stagecoach rolls through into the prison.

The prison guards open the door of the stagecoach and we stumble out, blinking in the bright sunlight. We're in a big yard. There are four long, rectangular buildings that I guess are cell blocks, each made of the same rough-cut granite as the outer wall. Set into the sides of the buildings every ten feet or so are barred cell doors. There's also a large square building with a smaller one adjoining it.

Next to the cell blocks a new one is being built. Scores of prisoners wearing black- and white-striped clothes are working on it, mixing the mortar, wrestling the stone blocks into place. Several dozen more are quarrying new blocks of stone from the hillside. They are watched by a number of guards carrying shotguns.

The door in the small building opens and a man wearing a suit and a bowler hat comes out, followed by two guards carrying Winchesters. He is short and round. The guards line us up and he walks down the line, peering at each of us in turn. When he is done inspecting us he stops and faces us with his hands behind his back.

"Gentlemen, welcome to the Yuma Territorial Prison. I'm Warden Gates. It is my object to elevate rather than depress the men who have been put under my supervision. I wish to inspire you to hope, to revive the principles of true manhood which lie dormant within you. It is my greatest dream that you see the light and leave this place a changed man. To this end, the rules here are simple. No fighting. No cursing. Work hard. Church on Sunday. Follow these rules and your time here will go easy."

"So there's no rule against escaping?" one of the prisoners asks. He's a wiry little guy with a perpetual sneer on his face. "That's okay then?" He snickers a little at his own wit.

The warden smiles. "I'm glad you asked. This is my answer. Is there a need for a rule against flying? Against walking on water? No, there is not. And why is that? Because there is no need for a rule against that which is impossible. Your cells are solid stone with iron doors. The wall is twenty-five feet of unclimbable stone and guarded night and day by men who will shoot to kill.

"Feel like digging?" He stomps his foot. "We stand on a granite outcropping. You'll need dynamite and mining equipment to go that way, both of which are in short supply.

"But suppose you are clever enough or determined enough and you do find a way out of here. What then?" His smile gets darker. "Why…nothing. We won't even chase you."

One of the guards accompanying him chuckles. All of them are smiling.

"You see, gentlemen, escaping from the prison itself is the easy part. Beyond that wall lies a hundred miles of sand and desert in every direction. On foot, with no water, there's no chance of crossing it alive."

He wags his finger at us. "Some of you may still think you can make it. So I wish to tell you of one final obstacle. Indians. A dozen or so. The number varies. They live along the banks of the river, waiting, watching. When we ring the bell up there in the guard tower they know it is time to go to work.

"I have a standing reward offered for any escapee they capture. A twenty-dollar golden eagle. They don't need to return the whole prisoner, either. The head alone will do fine." He looks at the prisoner who asked the question. "Does that answer your question, sir? I'm glad you asked it, really. I'd rather save you the inevitable suffering and likely death you would incur in the attempt." He puts his hands in his vest pockets and rocks back on his heels.

One of the guards standing next to him leans in and whispers something in his ear.

"It appears that I have forgotten one important detail, gentlemen. Punishment. Around here there is only one. The cage." He points. On one end of the rock face where the prisoners are quarrying stone there is an iron door. "See that? Behind that is a shaft carved into the living rock. At the end of that shaft is a room and in that room is a four-foot square metal cage. Break the rules and you will end up in that cage, alone in the darkness until we let you out."

He digs his pocket watch out of a vest pocket and consults it, then turns to the guard who whispered to him. "Elmer, if you would? I believe it is time for Mr. Jackson's release." To us he says, "Witness."

Elmer walks over to the metal door. He unhooks the ring of keys hanging on his belt and unlocks the door. He disappears down the shaft and reappears a couple of minutes later, dragging a prisoner behind him. The prisoner is shaking and moaning. When he hits the sunlight he flinches and puts his arms over his head.

"I understand it is quite an unpleasant experience," the warden says. "Think long and hard before you cause problems in my prison. Good day." With that he turns on his heel and goes back inside.

Elmer and the other guard take off our manacles and Elmer glowers at us. "It don't take much," he says. "Believe me. Give me a reason and in you go. Keep that in your minds. Follow me."

He leads us into one of the buildings. Inside, there's a guard behind a desk. Behind him are shelves filled with clothing, blankets and such. One by one he calls us forward and we each receive a striped prisoner uniform. We're told to change into the uniform. We're allowed to keep our hats and shoes, but everything else is bagged up and taken away.

From there we are led to a big room filled with tables and benches. Along one side is long table with several large pots of food on it. A few prisoners already have their food. The rest are standing in line. The man behind the table serves me a bowl of something I don't recognize, though it doesn't smell too bad. I take my food and sit down.

Across from me is a man with a wicked scar running down the side of his face. It pulls his mouth up on one side in a grimace. He reaches over and grabs my bowl.

"From now on you give me half your food," he grunts.

I stand up. "This is going to hurt," I tell him.

"You're right about that," he says and comes over the table at me. I duck his first punch and smash him with a left in the ribs. He tries to get me in a clinch but I swivel my hips and throw him to the ground.

When he tries to get up I kick him back down. I jump on him and start slamming his head on the floor.

Guards charge over and start clubbing me. I shrug off the first few blows and keep pounding the scarred man, but finally there are too many of them. They pull me off the man and drag me from the room. Outside, they slam me up against the wall and hold me there while one of them fetches Elmer.

"That didn't take long," he says when he gets there. "You got here, what, a half hour ago? And already you're headed to the cage. Must be some kind of record."

"You'd have found a reason to put me there sooner or later," I tell him. "This way saves time."

"I got a feeling you're one of them that won't rehabilitate."

"I can't change what I am."

"No, I don't suppose you can. Reckon we'll see what the cage does to you."

And they drag me away.

47

The lantern lights up a room about fifteen feet across, carved out of solid rock. Sitting against the back wall is a rusted metal cage. They put me inside and lock it.

"You're not going to like it in here," Elmer says. He picks up the lantern and walks out, leaving me alone in the darkness.

He's wrong. The darkness around me matches the darkness inside me. I welcome it. I belong here.

Time loses all meaning. I might have been in here for hours and I might have been in here for days. I can no longer tell if I'm asleep or awake. I may be dead even. The darkness stretches around me, infinite and timeless.

At some point a light appears. Tiny at first, it grows. Within it I see a shimmering figure. The figure resolves itself into a giant raven. It draws closer. I try to run from it but I can't move. It swoops down and envelops me.

We fly up into the sky. The land is spread out below me. We race faster and faster, clouds zipping around us, the land below a blur. Days and nights pass in flashes of light and dark, too quickly to separate. At some point the flashes of light and dark slow down and stop. Raven glides toward the ground.

It's night time. A large fire is burning. Around the fire is a village, several dozen huts roofed with palm fronds. Trees grow thickly all around the village. Around the fire are gathered the villagers, wearing loin cloths and necklaces of seashells and black beads. The village is on the seashore, on a small bay. Long canoes are drawn up on the beach, well out of reach of the water. Out in the middle of the bay is anchored a large sailing ship.

In the midst of the villagers is the chief. He is an old man, bent by the years. He wears a headdress adorned with brightly-colored feathers. Standing before him are a half dozen sailors from the ship. They are wearing loose-fitting pants and long-sleeved shirts. Swords hang on their hips and their captain has a pair of single shot, black powder pistols stuck in his belt.

The chief tilts his head back and drinks from a bottle he is holding. It must be empty because he lowers it and peers into it unhappily. The captain nods to one of his men, who opens a large wooden box by his feet and takes out another bottle. The captain hands it to the chief.

"Here you are, my new friend," he says in Spanish. "Drink to celebrate our new friendship."

The chief takes the bottle and holds it up. He calls out something unintelligible, a cheer goes up from the villagers and bottles are raised. Many of the villagers are visibly staggering.

There is movement out in the darkness and from my vantage point above the village I can see rowboats leaving the ship and pulling up on the shore. Men carrying swords and wearing metal helmets get out of them. A number of them carry firearms as well. They move swiftly to surround the village. None of the villagers seems to notice them.

"The pearls," the captain says. "If you want to show your friendship, tell me where you got the black pearls."

I realize then that those aren't beads on the villagers' necklaces, they're pearls. I know what I'm seeing now. The captain is Juan de Iturbe. It is his ship that Beckwourth and I were searching for.

"I cannot," the chief says. He takes off his necklace and hands it to de Iturbe. "You may take all we have, but I can give you no more. They were a gift from Xela, god of the sea. I do not know where they come from."

"And I believe you are holding out on me," de Iturbe says, a dark gleam in his eye. "I will give you one more chance and then we will have problems."

For the first time the chief seems to realize that he is in trouble. He looks blearily around, sees that he is surrounded by grim-faced men with swords in their hands. He shakes his head sadly. "If only I could."

De Iturbe draws one of his pistols and points it at the chief's wife. There is an explosion, a cloud of smoke, and the woman falls over, bleeding from her head. Screams go up from the villagers. Some draw flint knives, while others run for their huts, to the spears and arrows they keep there.

More gunfire and the flash of swords. A half dozen men fall dead. The rest throw up their hands and go to their knees.

"Tell me where to find the pearls," de Iturbe says.

"I cannot," the chief weeps. He's on his knees, begging. "They were a gift from the sea!"

De Iturbe draws his other pistol and points it at a child. "This is your son, is he not? Too bad he will not grow up to be chief one day."

"Stop!"

De Iturbe turns his head. A young woman has emerged from one of the huts. She walks through the kneeling villagers, her head held high, her expression proud. She is beautiful, her hair long and as black as the night, flowing down around her shoulders. A greedy look comes onto de Iturbe's face.

"Who are you?" he asks.

"She is my daughter. Please, don't hurt her," the chief moans.

"I am Roana," she says, coming to a stop before de Iturbe. "I will show you where the pearls are. Pearls enough to fill your boat."

"No, Roana! Don't do this! You are promised to Xela." The chief holds his hands up to de Iturbe. "She doesn't know what she's talking about. There are no more pearls unless they are at the bottom of the sea."

De Iturbe touches the maiden's hair, his eyes drinking her in. She doesn't flinch away from his touch but stands emotionless, remote, as if she is too far above him to be affected by him.

"Leave them be and I will show you where the pearls are."

"You'll come with us. As my hostage." His eyes glitter as he runs his fingers over her bare shoulder.

"No," the chief moans. "You cannot do this." He tries to grab de Iturbe's leg, but the man kicks him away.

Then Raven and I are once again shooting skyward. Days and nights pass in rapid succession before we once again settle earthward.

We land on the ship. There is the whisper of wind in the sails, the creaking of timbers, the humming of ropes drawn taut.

In the bow of the ship stands Roana, de Iturbe beside her. His face is dark. The ship is near shore. In the distance lies the mouth of a river. He gestures at it.

"You say to sail up the river, but pearls come from oysters and oysters come from the sea."

"These are black pearls. They are not like any others you have ever seen. Is this not correct?"

He growls and pulls on his mustache. "If you are lying to me, if this is a trick, an attempt to make me ground my ship…" He touches the sword at his waist. "I will carve you into pieces. After my men use you. Then I will return and slaughter your entire village."

She looks down at him. She is taller than he is. Next to her he looks small and grubby and hunched over. He knows this and it angers him. "I know this," she says. "The pearls are there."

De Iturbe glares at her, then calls the order to his crew. Sails are raised, the wheel turns, and the ship begins to move toward the mouth of the river.

The winds are favorable and the ship sails swiftly up the river. But this does not seem to please de Iturbe, who looks blacker and blacker the further they go. Over and over he asks her how much further and every time she tells him it is not much further. He looks like he badly wants to strike her down, but his greed is strong. If there is even a chance to find more of the pearls he will not let it get away.

For most of the day they sail upriver. The banks of the river are covered by sand dunes, stretching as far as the eye can see, broken here and there by stone buttes and fists of rock that jut up from the sand.

"This is it," she says at last. "We are there."

The captain orders the sails furled. The ship glides to a stop. He stands at the railing, peering into the water. "The water is muddy. How will we find the pearls?"

When she does not answer he turns to her. She is standing with her arms upraised, calling out in a strange language. Her voice sounds of the sea, filled with wild, crashing sounds. In her words lies the storm and the crushing blackness of deep water.

"I'll kill you," de Iturbe says, drawing his sword. But when he moves toward her there comes a shout from the lookout high in the main mast. Every eye turns to look downstream.

A huge wave has appeared out of nowhere. It races swiftly toward them. It is wild, swirling. Within its depths there seems to be a face, huge and angry.

Cries of alarm rise from the sailors. They run frantically in all directions, but there is nothing they can do, nowhere they can go.

With a curse, de Iturbe raises his sword and charges at Roana. But now a fierce, shrieking wind has risen. It pushes him back. Some of the sailors are blown overboard. Through it all Roana stands tall, untouched, as if in the eye of the storm. She stares unblinking at de Iturbe.

The wave rises over the ship, blotting out the sun. De Iturbe gives up trying to get to the maiden and wraps his arms and legs around one of the masts.

The waves crashes over the ship. More sailors are swept overboard screaming. Sails and rigging are ripped away. The mast de Iturbe clings to cracks in half. The ship tilts dangerously.

But it does not sink. Instead it is lifted high into the air as the wave continues inland, carrying the ship like a toy far from the river. Several miles it carries the ship, then the wave recedes. The ship is dropped onto the sand. The water sinks into the sand and disappears.

Roana walks to the captain, who is still clinging to the broken mast. "This is what comes when you anger Xela, god of the sea."

"If I'm dying here, then you are too," he snarls. He tries to charge her but she raises one hand. Ropes snake around him, binding him to the broken mast.

"You will never leave this place," she says.

She makes her way across the debris-littered deck and jumps down onto the sand. De Iturbe fights against the ropes but it is no use.

She gestures and the ship begins to sink into the sand, taking its captain with it.

Once again Raven carries me into the sky. Days and nights flash by in rapid succession. We begin to spiral back toward the earth but this time I resist. There is something I must know before Raven carries me back to the prison.

Take me to Coyote!

Raven veers to the side and we fly lower. Then, in the distance, I see him. Coyote is standing in a meadow by a stream, grazing. We get close and Coyote looks up. I get the feeling he sees me. I try to call to him, but I can make no sound.

48

I open my eyes to darkness. I'm back in the cage. I never truly left.

What happened? I wonder. Was it a vision or simply a hallucination? The darkness, the solitude, they do things to the mind. Probably I imagined the whole thing.

Except that I have the feeling it was real. Raven took me back and showed me the past. I have this feeling I know where de Iturbe's ship is now.

And I think that was really Coyote I saw. It eases my heart to know that he is safe. My other mistakes don't matter if he is free.

Seeing Coyote, whether or not I actually did, has left me feeling different. The black rage is gone. Well, not exactly gone. I can still feel it, but it is at a distance. It no longer poisons and controls me. There is power there and I can tap into it if I wish, but only if I choose to.

I understand something now. The true prison was the one in my own heart, built by me, fiercely guarded by my rage. My freedom was not taken from me; I gave it up. I chose to let myself be imprisoned by my hatred. All I ever needed to do to be free was to make a different choice. Which I have done.

Now it is time to escape the other prison, the walls of stone and iron that seek to hold me here.

I hear the door open. Footsteps approach, along with a bobbing light. Elmer stops at the cage and holds up the lantern.

"You ready to come out and settle down?" he asks.

"I am." It's true too.

"You seem awful calm for a man who just spent five days in the cage," he says.

"I needed the time to think."

"Must be something to do with the Injun blood," he mutters, more to himself than to me. He unlocks the cage door.

I follow Elmer out into the bright sunlight of late afternoon. The sun is warm on my face, warmer than it was when I went in. Spring is here. From the sliver of moon overhead I can see that there's still time to make it for the ship's appearance on the full moon, but not much time for delay. I will have to leave today.

49

Elmer takes me to the prison cafeteria. He stops at the door and turns to me. "Think you can eat supper without beating someone half to death?" he asks.

"I'll do what I can."

He stares me down for a minute, then shakes his head and opens the door. When I step into the room the place goes silent and everyone looks at me. Elmer waves one of the guards over.

"When he's done eating, show him his bunk. Put him in with Mel."

The guard's eyes widen. "With Mel?"

"You heard me."

"Okay," the guard says.

I head over to get a bowl of food. There's a few men in line when I get there but they all back away and so I don't have to wait. I get my food and sit down at a table with a few men sitting at it. They get up and leave quickly. I guess this means I'm famous. Or infamous. I never really understood the difference between the two.

I don't see the man with the scar while I'm eating. No one bothers me, which is good because it turns out I'm actually pretty hungry and now that I'm not so angry I'd a lot rather eat than fight. When I finish the first bowl I go up for another. The man ladling out the food looks like he wants to say something to me, maybe refuse me a second helping of food, but he ends up not saying anything. He fills my bowl the whole way and even gives me two rolls. I stuff the rolls inside my shirt. I'll need the food after I escape.

When I'm done eating I stand up and here comes the guard Elmer was talking to. "Come on. I'll show you to your cell."

We leave the cafeteria and head toward one of the cell blocks. "I take it Mel isn't a popular roommate," I say.

The guard gives me a sidelong look. "That's one way to put it," he replies.

The cell he opens has four bunk beds in it, but only one man, who is lying on his side on one of the bottom bunks, facing the wall. Of course, he's big enough to be two men. The metal bed frame creaks alarmingly when he rolls over. A hand roughly the size of a bear's paw pulls a pair of spectacles onto his face. They look absurdly small against that great mass of flesh.

"Oh, a new roommate," he says. His voice is soft and somewhat high.

He levers himself up off the bed and the guard quickly slams the cell door and locks it. "Good luck," he says to me and hurries off.

Mel bends over to get a better look at me. The sun is down now and the light is fading quickly. "You don't look so bad," he says. He seems to be completely hairless. Not only is he bald, but it doesn't look like he even has eyebrows.

I resist the urge to back up. There's really nowhere to go anyway.

"You don't look so bad either."

"I'm Mel," he says, holding out his paw. "I don't get a lot of roommates."

My hand disappears in his. I hope I get it back. "I'm Ace."

"I think the other prisoners don't like me." He sounds kind of sad. For all his size, he has a baby face. His cheeks are pink and his eyes are a faded blue color. It looks like tears are gathering in his eyes.

"They probably just don't know you," I say. Probably they do know him and they're afraid of him. I don't know him and I'm afraid of him. But I keep that to myself.

He hangs his head. "I've done things. That's probably what it is."

"We've all done things. That's why we're here."

"Not like I've done."

"How bad can it be?"

"I ate my wife."

I have to admit, that surprises me. I do my best not to let my mouth hang open, but I'm not sure how well I do. "You *ate* you wife?"

He nods. A tear slides down one chubby cheek.

"*All* of her?"

"Pert near. There was some parts I just couldn't get down, like the eyes." He wrinkles up his face. "Maybe it's just me, but there's something wrong about eating eyes."

There's something wrong about eating your wife, I want to say. But I don't. He seems like the kind of person you don't want to upset.

"Left the bones too," he adds. "Threw 'em out back for the pigs. They ate them right up."

"Why?"

"I don't know. Pigs'll eat about anything."

"No. I mean, why did you eat your wife?"

"I didn't like the way she cooked. Told her so and she said I couldn't do any better. Guess I showed her."

"She probably meant chicken or beans or something. Don't you think?"

"Now I do. The judge thought the same as you. Didn't seem so clear at the time though." His head sinks a little lower. "It gets worse."

I don't want to hear this, but I kind of feel I need to. "How so?" I ask.

"I liked the way she tasted. I learned something. People taste better than cows and pigs and such."

That's alarming. I ease away from him a bit. The next question is an obvious one, but that doesn't mean I want to ask it. "Are you thinking about eating me?"

He scratches his ponderous belly, thinking. "No. Not yet, anyhow."

"I'd take it kindly if you didn't. Probably best for you too."

He gives me a quizzical look. "How so?"

"I'm Apache."

"Apache taste different from white folk?"

"It's the diet. We eat mostly cactus, rattlesnakes and scorpions."

"Really? I hadn't heard that."

I nod. "Centipedes too. All we can get."

"That's sure some strange eatin', mister."

Says the man who ate his wife. "If you was to eat me, it'd probably make you sick."

"I can see where that would be a consideration," he says solemnly. "I'll keep it in mind."

"So I reckon that's why you have this cell all to yourself," I say. "On account of your, uh, diet."

"It seems to bother them all right. Waking up with bites missing gets them all kinds of worked up."

"Some people are funny that way." I definitely have to escape tonight. I'd like to keep all my parts. I walk over to the door to have a closer look at it. Breaking out of the cell is the part of escaping that I think is going to give me the most trouble.

"What're you doing?" he asks.

"Trying to figure out how to open this door. I don't like being cooped up."

"It's not so bad, once you get used to it. I've been in the cage six times now. It's right nice in there, dark and all."

I look over my shoulder at him. It's getting dark. I can't really see his face now. I hope he's not licking his lips. Did he even get dinner? "I imagine you spend a lot of time in there, what with biting people and all."

"You heard the same rules I did," he says, sullen now. "The warden didn't say anything about no rule against eating people."

"I expect it was implied."

"Mister, I don't even know what that means."

"It's one of those things you're supposed to just know."

"Well I know now, don't I?"

"But you keep doing it. Trying to eat people."

"And they keep sticking them in here with me. Seems we all got bad habits we can't seem to break." He comes toward me suddenly.

It occurs to me right then how small this cell really is. Not a lot of room to move around in here if it comes to fighting. I drop into a fighting crouch and get my hands up.

"Don't be so touchy. I'm only trying to help." He pushes me gently out of the way and takes hold of the door. He gathers himself, then lifts and jerks on the door at the same time.

The door pops open.

I stare at him, dumbfounded. "That was mighty impressive."

"Not as much as you think. That lock's been rusting a long time. They should fix it."

"How long have you known you could open the door?"

He shrugs. "I don't know. A while."

"And you never tried to escape?"

"Naw. It's probably best I stay here. You know, on account of that problem I got? I'd only get in more trouble."

"Why don't you put the door back the way it was for now, Mel? I'll get further if I wait until people are asleep."

"Good idea," he says, and bangs the door shut. "I knew you were a thinking fellow."

He goes back and lies down on his bunk. I take one of the other ones. In a little while I hear him snoring.

I wait until around midnight, then I get up. First I try the door myself, thinking maybe I won't need to bother Mel. But it doesn't budge at all. Reluctantly, I approaching the snoring mass that is Mel. I poke him in the side.

A big hand flies out and clamps on my arm. It's a hard grip. Mel's got a lot of fat, but there's muscle under there too. I don't think I could get loose if I tried.

"Easy there, Mel. It's me, Ace. I'm ready to go."

"I'm hungry," he says.

Real quick I dig the two rolls out of my shirt and hold them out near where I think his face is. "Take these," I whisper. I feel his lips on my fingers and it sends a chill down my spine, but I force myself to hold my hand still, hoping I'm not about to lose a couple of fingers.

He takes the rolls and chews them loudly. "Better than nothing," he says. "But not much."

"I'd give you more if I had it."

"True," he says. He's still holding my arm. My hand is going numb.

"The door?" I say.

He sighs. "Doing the right thing is hard. It makes me hungry." But he lets go of my arm. I step back and he hauls himself to his feet. He goes over and jerks on the door again. It pops open.

I step through the door and turn back. "Why are you doing this, Mel? Why are you helping me?"

He ponders this for a moment. "You don't belong in here," he says finally. "You can fly."

50

I head out into the darkness thinking about his last words. And it occurs to me that he's right. I *can* fly.

I run to a corner of the wall and without hesitating, without thinking or questioning, I go up it. I trust my hands and feet to find the small cracks and protrusions that I can use for holds. I climb like I climbed when I was a kid, scaling the rocks around Pa-Gotzin-Kay for fun.

Seconds later I'm at the top. There is no outcry. No one seems to have noticed.

It's a long drop down the other side and I tuck and roll when I land. It hurts, but when I come to my feet nothing is broken or twisted so it came out well enough.

I head into the small town of Yuma, sitting on the banks of the Colorado River about a quarter of a mile away. I have to find different clothes. These striped things I'm wearing stand out too much. Also a gun if I can get one.

I wish Coyote was here. That brief glimpse of him in the vision was so real that it still hurts. I feel like a part of me is missing. If I had him I'd make a run for it, count on him to outrun any other horses that the bounty hunters would have.

But I don't have Coyote and I'm not going to try and steal a horse. A horse leaves too many tracks and is too hard to conceal. Since I don't have speed, I'll go for stealth, counting on my ability to hide to elude the bounty hunters.

The town is quiet, only a few lights on. I consider breaking into a home to steal clothes, but that's a good way to get shot. The saloon, of course, is all lit up and noisy and that gives me an idea. I find a spot outside where I can stay hidden and watch the door. All I need to do is wait for someone to head home and then I'll follow him and steal his clothes. The drunker he is the better.

It takes about an hour and I'm getting antsy, when a man comes out the door. He's about my size and from the way he's weaving he's plenty drunk. This should be no problem at all.

I follow him toward the edge of town and when he leaves the main street I figure this is my chance. It's easy to sneak up behind him. He's humming to himself and paying no attention to anything. What I should do is hit him over the head and knock him out. That would be the safest thing.

But for some reason I can't. This man has done nothing to me. It doesn't feel right to hurt him. Bad enough I'm stealing his clothes.

So instead I tap him on the shoulder.

He stops and turns around. He's wearing a gun, but he doesn't reach for it. He peers at me. There's not much light. "Who're you?" His words are slurred and his breath smells powerfully of cheap whiskey.

"I need your help," I say.

A big smile comes on his face. "Well, you came to the right hombre, pardner. Lucky McGraw they call me. What can I do to help you?"

"I need your clothes."

That throws him. He wasn't expecting me to say that. "I don't understand," he says. He leans in and peers closer at me. "Oh, I see. You're a prisoner up in the…up in the…" He waves his hand toward the prison, the word not coming to him.

"The prison."

"Yeah, the prison. That's why you need clothes."

His voice has risen and I'm worried someone will hear him. "Not so loud. I don't want anyone to hear."

"Oh, right. We don't want that." He puts his finger to his lips. "Shhh. Quiet as a mouse." He starts giggling. "That's funny. You want to know why?"

"Not really."

"Because mice…there's one lives in the walls of my house. He's not quiet at all. Running back and forth all night. That's why I have to drink so much. So I can sleep."

Sure. That's why you drink.

"I had a cat. But he ran away. Or the mouse got him. It sounds like a big mouse."

I can't spend the whole night listening to him. I want to get as far away by daylight as I can. "Can we get on with this?"

"On with what?"

"Your clothes."

He scratches his head, confused. I'm starting to realize that he's a lot drunker than I thought. "What are we doing?" he asks.

"I'm escaping. I don't know what you're doing."

He gets a big, loopy grin. "That's easy. I'm being drunk."

"You're very good at it."

"I have—" He hiccups. "I practice a lot."

"Clothes?"

"Right. Because of the escape. I've never escaped before. I keep forgetting."

"You're getting loud again."

"Shhh!" he says loudly. "We don't want anyone to hear." He starts laughing and puts his hand over his mouth in an attempt to stifle it.

I really should have hit him over the head.

He starts fumbling with his shirt. "I always hated this shirt," he says. "The buttonholes are too small." He stops as an idea hits him. "Or the buttons are too big. Do you think that's it?"

"I think this is taking too long."

"Oops. Sorry. The escape. I have to remember that." He goes back to working on the shirt. He gets down to the last couple of buttons and then makes a frustrated sound and simply rips the last couple off.

He hands me the shirt. It doesn't smell too good, but I shuck the striped one and put it on. Next he unbuckles his gun belt. I hold out my hand.

"I'm going to need that too."

"Okay." He hands it over. "Little secret though."

"What?"

He motions me closer and leans in. He looks around to see if anyone is listening. "It doesn't work," he whispers loudly. "It broke the first time I used it."

I'm getting irritated. "Why are you carrying it then?"

He nods very seriously. "For protection."

"That makes no sense. It's broken."

"Ah!" he says, holding up one finger. "But other people don't *know* it's broken. And this way I don't accidentally shoot myself."

"You can keep the gun."

"Good. I wouldn't feel safe without it. You never know when someone will try and rob you."

"Like I'm doing right now."

He nods. "Exactly." He reaches for the gun.

"Why don't I hold onto it? Until you get your pants off?"

"Oh, good thinking." He taps his temple with his finger. He starts fumbling with the buttons on his pants. "I may need some help here," he says after a bit.

Nope. I'm not messing around with his buttons in the dark in this alleyway. I have my limits.

"Wait. I got it." He drops his pants around his ankles. "Dammit. I forgot to take off my boots first." He lifts one foot and promptly falls down. This brings on more giggling.

I'm beginning to think I'll never get out of this town. This whole thing is starting to feel unreal. "Let me help you," I tell him. By then he's rolling around in the dirt, trying to get a hold of his foot. I grab one of his feet. "Hold still."

"Good idea," he says. "When did my feet get so far away?"

At first the boot won't budge. "They're a little small," he says. "But they look nice."

I have to really yank to get the boots off. Then I figure, what the heck. I've come this far. I take hold of his pants and pull them off too. I'd like to not still be here come sunrise. I put his pants on. They fit okay.

He tries and fails to stand up. After the second try I give him a hand. He stands there, holding onto my arm. "Thanks. That was close."

Close to what? I wonder, but decide not to ask.

"You want my johnnies too?" he asks. He's wearing one-piece long underwear, like we wore up in Montana during the winter.

"No. Not really."

"You sure?" He turns around. "See, they have a butt flap and everything. It's handy when you have to poop."

"It's all right. You keep them." I'm ready to go, but now I'm wondering if I should tie him up, maybe gag him. "You going to keep quiet about this?" I ask him.

He clamps his hand over his mouth and looks around guiltily. "Am I being too loud again? I can't tell."

"You're fine. I need to know if I should tie you up somewhere."

He straightens up and salutes me. "They'll get nothing from me. I swear. Wild horses couldn't get me to talk."

"What are you doing?"

"Showing—" He hiccups. "Showing you that you can trust me."

"All right." I may regret this, but now I want nothing but to get out of this town.

"I actually wish I was going to remember this," Lucky says suddenly. "It's the most fun I've had in a while." He sounds kind of sad now.

"You won't remember this?"

"No. I'll wake up and wonder where my clothes went. I do things when I'm drunk that I don't remember. One time I woke up in a hog pen and found out the sow had eaten my finger." He holds up his hand so I can see the missing finger. "You'd think something like that would wake a man up."

"You'd think." I start to walk away.

"Good luck with the escape," he calls after me.

From a nearby house someone yells, "Goddammit, Lucky! Shut your ass up or I'll come out there and put a hole in you!"

Time to leave.

51

I head off, following the Colorado River north. Bedbug shouldn't be more than a few days upriver from here, though I'm not exactly sure how far it is. And it's been a while since I traveled much on foot so I've kind of lost touch with how much slower it is. Fortunately I'm wearing my moccasins. They're a lot better for walking in than my boots would be.

What little moon there is is far in the west. I'd say ten days to the full moon and the appearance of the ghost ship—that is, assuming Knuze wasn't making the whole story up. With luck we'll still make it.

I walk in the river whenever I can, leaving it always in deep sand or on bare rock. My pursuers are going to guess that I'm following either the Colorado or the Gila Rivers, but they won't know which one unless they find my tracks leaving the town and I was careful to hide those. That means my pursuit will be split in half.

I'd like to swim across the river, but it's running pretty high from the snow melt up in the mountains and there's a decent chance I'd get myself drowned, so I don't risk it. I wish I had some food, but I should be able to go for some days without it. I've done it before. At least there's no lack of water, even if the Colorado is pretty muddy.

I travel until about an hour after sunrise, then start looking around for a place to hole up during the day. I can't travel during daylight hours. I'll be too exposed.

There are patches of thick brush growing along the river and I find an especially dense one and crawl as deep as I can into it. I make myself more or less comfortable and go to sleep.

Along about midafternoon I hear voices and wake up. I don't recognize the language. They're taking their time, looking for sign. They never come close to where I'm hiding and after a bit they go back the way they came, trying to figure out where they lost me. It's like I thought. They're good trackers, but not good enough to follow me. So long as I haven't badly misjudged the distance to Bedbug, I should make it there all right. Even if it's further than I thought, I'm sure I can scrounge something to eat along the way.

Once it's dark, I head out again. The river cuts through some low mountains here and the going gets harder. The banks are narrow and choked with thick brush. Cliff walls fifty or a hundred feet high rise on both sides. It wouldn't be good to hole up here. Someone on the cliff above could look down and spot me and there'd be nowhere to run. The canyon walls are fairly sheer, with a number of ledges, so I could probably climb them. Otherwise, the only ways out of the river along here are up side canyons, all of them lined with pretty good cliffs as well.

Along about midnight I suddenly get a feeling and come to a stop. I don't know how, but I feel utterly certain that I'm not alone. I turn and look back down the canyon but I don't see anyone. Who's back there? Who could possibly be good enough to track me in the dark like this?

And then I know.

It's Mickey Free.

Who else could it be? Who else has the skill to follow me?

My blood runs cold at the thought. There's no way I can lose him. And he's sure to have supplies so there's no way I can outrun him.

I'm going to have to set a trap for him.

I turn up the next side canyon. I walk up it a couple hundred yards, then I scale one of the sides until I get to a ledge about fifteen feet up. I crawl out on it and lie down in the shadows where I can watch the canyon. The canyon is narrow here. He has to pass right below me. When he does, I'll jump down on him. With luck I won't get killed.

A whole lot of luck.

A few minutes later here he comes. I can just see him, a dark silhouette making his way cautiously up the canyon. He's smart. He can smell an ambush. But he also knows his best bet is to flush me out. If he tries circling around to come at me from above he risks me slipping away.

He stops when he's about fifty yards away.

"I know you're in here, Ace," he says in Apache. "I can feel your spirit."

He draws his pistol and I get a bad feeling. I start backing along the ledge, putting distance between us. A couple seconds later he fires. Right at where I was. The bullet ricochets by my head. That was way too close.

I turn and, moving as fast as I can without making too much noise, I scoot along the ledge. The canyon doglegs just ahead and I get around the corner about the time he fires a couple more shots.

I jump down off the ledge and hightail it up the canyon. More shots ring out behind me. After a few hundred more yards I come to a scree slope where the canyon wall has collapsed and I hurry up it to the top of the canyon.

Once there I consider running. But there's not much cover. I'll be too exposed, especially once the sun comes up. No, one way or another, this has to end now. Come daylight he'll hold every card.

I peer over the edge of the canyon and see him come into sight down below. He pauses, looking at the scree slope, thinking maybe I left that way. That's no good. I don't want him coming up this way. I get an idea.

I back up from the rim so he won't see me, then pick up a rock and throw it as far as I can up canyon. He turns toward the sound, then starts to head that way. But when he gets to the base of the scree slope he stops, looks up.

"That's not going to work, Ace. Surely you know that."

He starts up the scree slope and I look around for other options. If only I had a boulder I could roll down on him. There are some big rocks, but none close enough to the edge. Once again I consider running, but there's just no good cover out here.

I duck behind one of the rocks close to the edge. Maybe he'll get careless and I can jump out and get my hands on him before he can shoot me.

Small chance of that. But what other choice do I have?

I hear him getting closer. He's careful, taking his time. He seems to know I'm waiting up here for him, which means my chances of surprising him are practically nil. If only I had a gun of my own to even the odds.

He's almost at the top when the rock he puts his foot on rolls under him, causing him to stumble. It's not much, but it's an opening. I rise up and leap at him. He's swinging the gun around toward me when I punch him in the side of the face. He stumbles backward and comes very close to falling down the scree slope.

But then with catlike agility he regains his balance. He points the gun at me but I grab hold of his wrist and his shot goes high over my shoulder. He punches me twice in the ribs while I hammer at his face.

Suddenly he changes tactics. He lowers his shoulder and drives into me. I lose my footing and fall backward. But I keep my hand locked onto this wrist and he falls with me. The gun goes off right by my head, setting my ears to ringing. The bullet whines away into the night.

We roll around in the dirt along the edge of the cliff, neither of us able to get the upper hand. I'm on my back, him on top of me, when he twists his free hand away and tries gouging my eyes. But I get my head turned and his nails dig into my cheek instead.

I land a punch on his chin, rocking him back enough that I can flip him off of me. On top now, I slam his wrist repeatedly against a rock until he loses hold of the gun. We both go for it but it skitters away and goes over the edge of the cliff.

I elbow him in the face and feel his nose break. He hammers me a couple times in the ribs, then I catch of glimpse of him grabbing for something at his belt.

Moonlight flashes off his knife blade as he stabs at me. I'm too slow to deflect it and it bites deep into my side at the lower edge of my ribcage.

There's a burst of white-hot pain and I go berserk.

I break free of him and jump to my feet. Blood's running down my side and the pain is unbelievable.

As he starts to come to his feet I kick him in the side of the head. He staggers and I charge him, swinging as fast and as hard as I can. I feel the knife cut into my forearm but somehow it doesn't matter. All that matters is killing him.

He tries to take a step back, but he's forgotten where he is.

His foot goes over the edge of the cliff.

I hit him again and again. For an instant he hangs there, trying desperately to keep his balance, then he topples over and is gone.

52

I stumble to the edge of the cliff and look down. He's about fifteen feet down, lying on a ledge. His leg is bent at an awkward angle. He rolls over and looks up at me.

"My leg is broken," he says.

"Better it was your neck," I growl. Part of me wants to jump down there and bash his head with a rock until he quits moving.

"I knew you had more in you," Free says. His tone is calm, conversational. "That's why I followed you to Yuma and waited. I knew you would escape."

"Don't ever come after me again," I say. "Next time I'll kill you. I promise you that."

"I think I'm done with this business now," Free says. "I already quit the army to chase you."

"I should kill you now anyway."

"But you won't. You're not a killer. And you've nothing to fear from me anymore."

I take off the stolen shirt and wrap it tightly around my torso, hoping it will stop the bleeding.

"That's quite a wound," Free says. "You'll find it hard to escape now. Too bad you don't have a horse."

"Where's yours?"

"I didn't bring one. I saw you were on foot and chose the same."

I figured he didn't have one, but I was hoping. Without another word I start walking. Bedbug won't get any closer on its own.

I haven't gone far when I realize I'm not going to make it. I've lost too much blood and I'm weak. I have no water and no food. I have enough strength to make it back down to the river, but then I'll be too weak to climb back out again and the way the canyon's been narrowing I expect it won't be long until I come to a place where I'll either have to swim or traverse the cliff along the side. Neither of which I can do in this condition.

There's no point in worrying about it. I bite down on the pain and set myself to walking. I'm not giving up. I've come too far to give up.

A couple of hours pass. The blood continues to leak out of me. Every step is agony. I feel light-headed, dizzy. My thoughts run in disconnected circles. I'm having trouble remembering where I am or what I'm doing.

I trip over something hidden in the darkness and fall down. I land hard and have to bite off the scream that wants to burst from me. I'm done. I can't walk any further. I roll over on my back. I want to look at the sky as I die.

But something large and dark blots out the sky then. There's a soft whicker and a big head, coming down for a closer look at me.

It's Coyote. His eyes look like they are glowing in the dim moonlight.

Except that it can't be him. I'm delirious is all. So I just lie there.

Coyote nudges me. When I still don't respond he bites me on the shoulder.

"Ow." I shove him away. "Is that really you?"

He paws at the earth by my head. He's telling me to get up.

"I don't know if I can."

He makes a low rumbling sound and paws again, closer this time.

"Okay, okay." It hurts, but I make myself sit up. The pain's a lot worse when I stand and the only way I'm able to make it the whole way is by grabbing onto Coyote's mane. I wrap my arms around his neck.

"It *is* you. I missed you, brother," I tell him, my face pressed against his neck. "It was too long."

He whickers again.

"Your timing is awful, you know. A couple hours sooner and I wouldn't have this hole in my side."

He stamps his foot and swishes his tail. Coyote isn't much for conversation.

Climbing on his back takes the pain to new heights, but somehow I manage it. I lie forward and wrap my arms around him, hoping I can stay conscious and alive long enough to get somewhere, anywhere.

53

I don't know how long I'm on Coyote's back. I know that day comes, the sun shines hard on my back, and then the sun goes away. Whether this happens once or twice I don't know. I'm delirious, drifting in and out of reality and hallucination. In my hallucinations I see all kinds of people and talk to them. I talk to Annie. I talk to my mother. At one point I even talk to Roana, the maiden who lured de Iturbe to his death. She is trying to tell me something important but I can't seem to fix it in my mind.

At some point Coyote stops. I raise my head and see that we're in a town. When I try to dismount I lose control and fall on my side, which causes new colors of pain to burst behind my eyes. Vaguely I'm aware of someone bending over me.

"James Beckwourth," I whisper. I repeat it two more times and then I drop my head to the dirt again. I feel hands on me and nothing else.

When next I open my eyes it's to bright sunlight coming in through an open window. I'm lying on a bed. I start to sit up and a stab of pain goes through me. There's a bandage wrapped tight around my middle.

"No, Señor," a woman's voice says. Soft hands try to push me back on the bed. The hands belong to a young Mexican woman with her hair tied back in a ponytail. She hands me a glass of water and I drink greedily. I seem to be parched all the way through.

The young woman disappears and a minute later who should come in but Beckwourth himself. He doesn't bother with hellos but starts right in to talking, like we only saw each other yesterday.

"I knew you weren't in any danger," he says. "Why it was just a scratch. I've seen men with wounds twice as bad dancing around the fire that same night. One time I was so stuck with arrows I looked like a pincushion and I—"

"I take it this is Bedbug." If I don't cut in there's a real danger he might talk all day.

"One and the same. It's not only a name either." He scratches his side. "I've got bites all over me. I should've made my own camp outside town."

"I'm not dead, so I guess you found me a doctor."

"Not just a doctor. The best doctor in town."

"Probably the only doctor." Something occurs to me. "How did you pay him?"

Beckwourth gets a pained look on his face. "He didn't need them anymore. Not really."

It takes me a moment to figure out what he's saying. Probably I'm still fuzzy from blood loss. "You stole Knuze's pearls."

He winces. "I took them while you were digging. I didn't have any money and what reason to bury them with a dead man?"

He has a point there. It doesn't make any difference to Knuze, that's for sure. The only real problem I can think of is the attention selling something unusual like those pearls is bound to draw. Too often it's the wrong kind of attention, the sort that gets you drygulched by people wanting to cut your claim. But what's done is done.

"What day is it?" I ask.

"We still have a couple days until the full moon. I have to tell you, I was starting to think you weren't going to show up."

"I had some problems." That's putting it mildly.

He looks at my bandage. "At least one that I can see. You got lucky. Whoever stabbed you didn't poke a hole in anything important."

"I know where the ship is. Exactly."

His face lights up. "You do? How?"

That's a good question. I wonder if I really saw what I think I did. "It's hard to explain. Can I get some grub?"

"I already ordered for you. Figured you'd be hungry. Got some oats for your horse too." He rubs his arm. "He bit me."

"Don't worry about it. That means he's likes you."

"But the last time he bit me you said—"

"Don't overthink it. You'll only confuse yourself."

"I was powerfully worried about you, to tell the truth. I take it you managed to elude the cavalry?"

"Not exactly. They caught me. I went to trial. The judge sentenced me to the Yuma prison."

His eyes get big. "I have to hear everything. But let me get my book first."

"You're going to put this in your book?"

"I won't if you don't want me to..." I can see how hard it is for him to say that.

"You can use it. But don't use my name, okay?"

He hesitates. "I wasn't planning to."

"Wait. You were going to write it like it happened to you, weren't you?"

He looks sheepish. "Maybe."

54

"This is the spot."

"Are you sure?"

I close my eyes and picture the terrain again as I saw it in the vision. In my mind I can see the black butte that looks like a tombstone and the low jagged hills off to the west. I open my eyes. "It is."

Beckwourth looks around. "I thought it would be closer to the river. It's hard to believe that a wave could carry a ship so far."

"It was quite a wave." Not for the first time I wonder if I should tell him about my vision. I can imagine how excited he'd get. But I decide not to. He'll just pepper me with questions and want to write it down in his book. Maybe later I'll tell him.

I check my gun. Beckwourth had some money left over from selling the pearls so I was able to buy a used Colt revolver. I was able to buy a decent saddle and some boots that mostly fit too. I miss my duster, but if all goes well here I'll have enough to buy another and plenty of other stuff as well.

I know. Big "if".

The sun drops below the horizon. At the same time the moon rises. It's orange and looks bigger than I've ever seen it. Dusk seeps in with the shadows.

The ground shakes.

"Did you feel that?" he asks.

More shaking. About a hundred yards away the sand starts to shift, roiled from underneath.

Beckwourth shudders. "The hair on the back of my neck is standing up."

I know what he's talking about. I feel like I'm in the middle of a lightning storm, like electricity is running over my skin.

Something appears out of the sand. It's a mast. There's a grinding, crunching sound and it rises into the air. Ropes and bits of tattered sail dangle from it. Another mast breaks through and then the stump of a third. Finally the body of the ship appears.

It's bigger than I'd imagined it would be, but then, the only boats I've ever seen are canoes and ferries and they are tiny compared to this thing. Cannons stick out of ports along the side. At one end there are windows. The thing is in surprisingly good shape, though I'm not sure what I really expected. I mean, who knows what to expect from a ghost ship, right?

My eyesight seems to flicker and everything goes blurry. When the blurriness fades the ship looks different. It's no longer old and decayed. The sails are intact, all the rigging in place. The broken mast is whole. I see men moving about on deck, engaged in various tasks.

I blink and the image is gone. Once again the ship looks dead and abandoned.

Oh great. It's the temple of Totec all over again. I look at Beckwourth. "Be careful. There's a chance I might start acting weird."

He looks at me. "What? I don't understand."

"I'm saying that if I try to sacrifice you to an Aztec god or something, feel free to shoot me."

Now he really looks confused. As he should be. "What in the world does that mean?"

"I don't know. I wish I did." I pick up my rope. "Let's go. We don't know how long we have. I don't want to be on that thing when it goes back down."

We walk over to the ship. It's a good thing we have a rope. I don't know how else we'd get up there. It's not like there's a ladder or anything.

It's a long throw, but I manage to toss a loop over one of the railing posts. I go up the rope first and take a quick look around. Everything looks quiet. "Come on up," I call to Beckwourth. A minute later he's on deck too. I don't have to help him either. I'm continually surprised by how strong and fit he is for a man his age.

"This is incredible," he says. "I can't believe I'm standing here, on the deck of a ship buried hundreds of years ago." He shakes his head. "I don't...I don't know what to think. Such a thing shouldn't even be possible. I never really believed Knuze when he said those things and now that I'm here I still don't know what to believe."

I clap him on the shoulder. "That's the problem with the white man. You want everything to make sense. You think you have the whole world figured out and when something doesn't fit it upsets you."

"Hey, only half white, remember?"

"Yeah, I forgot."

He looks around. "So none of this...you're just okay with it?"

"Maybe, maybe not. But right now is the time for action. Thinking can come later. If I spend too much effort trying to figure out how I feel about it, I'll be dead and it won't matter." I point to the other end of the ship. "I saw windows down there."

"Doubtless those were the captain's quarters," he says.

"So that's probably where we'll find the pearls. Let's go."

We've only gone a few steps when we pass an open hatch. Beckwourth looks in and calls out to me.

"Wait! Look what I found."

"We don't really have time," I say, turning back. "This thing could go back underground at any moment."

"That's gold down there, Ace. I'm sure of it."

Reluctantly, I look. I think he's right. Down in the dimness I see a glitter that can only be gold. I turn away. "Forget it. We're here for the pearls, remember?"

"And who's to say they aren't down there? Who's to say we can even find them? But one thing we do know for sure. There's gold down there. We should at least take a closer look."

"We don't know what else might be down there. Knuze said the captain killed the three men with him."

"If the captain is anywhere, don't you think he'll be in his quarters?" Beckwourth asks. "Tie the rope around me. Lower me down. If it looks dangerous, you can pull me right back up."

"I still say it's a bad idea."

"It will only take a couple minutes. Humor me." He hurries over and retrieves the rope which is still hanging over the side. He ties one end around himself and hands the rope to me.

"I'm not going to talk you out of this, am I?" I say.

"No. You're not."

"Let's get it over with then." I toss the rope over a yardarm, take up the slack and get a good hold on it. "You ready?" He nods.

He steps over the edge of the hatch and I begin lowering him. As I let him down I keep a sharp eye on him. If I learned one thing from my little adventure in Totec's temple, it's that anything can happen. And probably will.

He gets to the bottom. "It's gold all right!" he calls back up.

"Grab some and I'll pull you back up. I have a bad feeling about this," I call down to him.

"Give me some slack," he says. "There's something else down here. Some kind of big statue. I want to take a closer look at it." He tugs on the rope until I give him slack and he disappears from sight.

"Oh," he says. "This is really incredible. I never expected anything like this."

Suddenly he yells. The yell is cut off abruptly. There's a hard tug on the rope, hard enough that I lose my grip and it races through my hands, giving me rope burns.

Then the rope goes still.

55

I pull on the rope but there's nothing on the other end. I don't waste time yelling for Beckwourth. If he could speak, he'd still be yelling.

I tie the rope around a mast and then shinny down it, my pistol in one hand. I go fast and hit the bottom hard. As soon as I let go of the rope I spin, ready for the attack I'm sure is coming.

Nothing moves in the dimness. There's no sign of Beckwourth. No blood either, which I'll take as a good sign.

Near my feet is the open chest of gold coins that Beckwourth saw from above. About ten feet away, barely visible in the gloom, is the statue. It's about half again as tall as I am and appears to be some kind of monstrous being. I step closer, peering at it in the dim light and when I realize what it is my gut clenches.

Not again.

It's a statue of Xipe Totec, the flayed god. What in the world is that doing here? Beckwourth said that de Iturbe sailed clear around South America looking for treasure. He must have picked it up along the way.

There's no time to think about it now. I have to find Beckwourth. I can wonder about the statue later.

Patches of moonlight filtering down through the deck provide a weak illumination. The hold is filled with stacks of crates and barrels, all lashed down securely. There's an aisle down the center between the stacks. Dust lies thick over everything, but in the aisle it has clearly been disturbed. It looks like someone dragged a body down the aisle. Hopefully a living body.

"Hold on, Beckwourth," I say. "I'm coming."

Scanning the stacks of cargo, I start down the aisle. It bothers me that I can't see what's on top of these stacks. I'm vulnerable to anything up there that wants to jump down on me.

Soon I hear the scurrying of small, clawed feet. It sounds like rats. I can't pin down where the sound is coming from. It sounds like it's coming from multiple places.

Something small darts across the aisle in front of me, moving fast. I catch a glimpse of it before it disappears, see exposed bone and flaps of shriveled, dried skin. It looks like a rat, but one that's been dead for some time.

Great. Knuze didn't say anything about undead rats. Why does there have to be undead rats? If I get out of this, I swear I am never going after lost treasure again. I don't care what reason someone gives me. A man could get killed doing this. Most importantly, *I* could get killed.

From the corner of my eye I catch movement above and to my right. Instantly I step back and bring the gun up. Flame stabs from the end as I fire into the shadowy figure that's leaping down at me. I fire twice more quickly, the second time into the head.

And it doesn't slow down at all.

Then it moves into one of the patches of moonlight and I can see what it is.

It's a dead man. A skeleton, really, though with scraps of clothing and withered flesh still clinging to it.

This could be trouble.

My bullets did nothing but chip some bones. They don't look like they hurt it at all. Even the head shot, all it did was punch a hole. What difference does that make to something that's already dead?

He's carrying a sword and he swings it. I duck and the sword whistles over my head. It sticks for a moment in the side of a crate and that gives me the opening I need.

I hammer down on the skeleton's wrist with the butt of my gun. There's a crack of snapping bone and his hand breaks clean away. It's still gripping the sword, but it's no longer attached to the rest of him.

He charges at me, clawing at my face with his remaining hand. I club him in the head with the butt of my pistol and knock him back, then I grab the sword and wrench it free of the crate.

The skeleton comes at me again so there's no time to peel off his hand, which still has a tight grip and is twitching. I hack madly at him with the sword. The first blow crashes down through his ribcage, parting rotted cloth and shattering bones.

He falls to the floor, but there's no quit in him. He's looking up at me. One eye is completely gone, but the other is still there, sunken and shriveled, but clearly fixed on me. His bony teeth clack together as he grabs my ankle with his remaining hand and tries to bite me.

I kick him and his head comes off and clatters down the aisle.

That seems to settle him down. At least he finally quits moving.

I peel the skeletal hand off the hilt of the sword and take a couple practice swings with it. It's rusted, but seems pretty sound. I reload, then holster the pistol. Looks like it's time for a change in weapons.

More scurrying sounds as I continue down the aisle. I don't want to think about how many rats there are down here. Hundreds at least. Maybe thousands. Another good reason to get out of here quickly.

Up ahead is an intersection of sorts, where an aisle runs perpendicular to the one I'm in. I don't have to see them to know that two more dead men are waiting for me there, one on each side, swords upraised to cut me down. I pause, considering what to do.

I could climb up on top of one of the stacks of crates, try to drop down from above. But that's going to slow me down. I don't know what kind of trouble Beckwourth is in or how much time he has.

A muffled moan from up ahead settles it for me. I decide for the direct approach.

I take off running. Right before I get to the intersection I go into a slide.

They're not expecting that. Their swings go over my head and instead of hitting me, they hit each other. As I slide between them I slash with my sword and take one of them at the ankles. Dried tendons part and he goes down, missing his feet.

I jump to my feet right as the other one jerks his sword free of his fallen companion and stabs at me. I slap the blade aside with my own and reach forward and grab his wrist. I jerk him toward me—one thing I've already learned about these skeletons, they're pretty light, what with all the flesh and such gone—and smash him in the side of the head with the hilt of my sword.

His skull shatters into a thousand pieces and he drops to the floor. The other one is still writhing around, trying to get at me, but I dodge his feeble attack and stomp on his head, putting him out of my misery. Stomping is one thing that boots are really good at. Glad I chose to wear them instead of my moccasins.

I've never held one before today, but I've decided that I like swords. They're really handy weapons. I pick up another one. If one's good, two must be better, right?

Now properly armed, I start down the aisle once again. From the dimness ahead I hear Beckwourth cry out.

"Ace! Help me!"

That's it for sneaking around. Time to charge this thing and end it one way or another. I start running.

Two more skeletons jump down in front of me but I don't even slow down. I'm too close and moving too fast. I simply lower my shoulder and crash into them, basically smashing a path through them. What's left of them collapses to the floor.

Charged now, I let out an Apache war cry. "You'll have to do better than that, ghost ship!" I yell.

What was the point of that? I wonder. There might have still been something on this ship that didn't know we were here yet.

At the next intersection I don't even slide. I hold my swords up as I go through and the skeletons' attacks bounce harmlessly off them. As I pass between them I swing backwards with both blades and remove two more heads.

You know, I'm getting pretty good at this.

At the far end of the hold is another cleared area. The hatch above must be open because the cleared area is lit up by a large square of moonlight.

Beckwourth is lying on the floor. At least I assume it's him. It's something shaped like Beckwourth, but it's completely covered by a mass of the skeletal rats so I can't tell for sure.

I skid to a stop, not sure what I'm going to do. I can't very well start hacking at them. If Beckwourth is still alive he won't appreciate that at all.

More scurrying feet and I look around to see that the hold is swarming with the things. They're all over the walls and the floor of the hold in every direction. I wish I had a torch or a lantern. Maybe I could light them on fire.

I decide my best bet is to grab Beckwourth and drag him out of here. While hacking at the rats as best I can. It's not much of a plan, but I don't really see a lot of options.

Then from the shadows on the other side of the cleared area something moves. It steps into the moonlight.

At first I think it's just another skeleton, but then I see there's something different about this one. He's mostly intact. His hair is long and there are finger bones tied in it. He's wearing a long black coat and heavy boots. One cheek is exposed bone, but the rest of his face is covered in rotting flesh and the eyes that look out at me are almost human. He has a sword in one hand. I'm guessing it's the captain himself.

His mouth opens. "You should never have come," he says in a hissing voice. "You will never leave."

"We'll see about that."

I can see no reason to stand about chatting with him, so I charge him. I block his first blow and slash at him with my other sword, taking him on the shoulder. But he's made of tougher stuff than the other ones and though the blow bites deep, it doesn't seem to hurt him all that much. I hack at him a few more times, but he shrugs them all off.

He's also faster than I expected. Somehow he gets a hand around my throat. I hack at his arm, but I can't get a good enough swing to cut through it and he doesn't let go. He lifts me into the air. His grip is horribly strong and I can no longer draw breath. I have to get him off me or this is going to be one short fight.

I lift one sword, flip my grip on it, and jam it through his eye. It goes through easy enough and pops out the back of his skull.

That gets his attention.

He makes an eerie howling noise and drops me, reeling back and clawing at the blade, which I leave buried in his skull.

While he's preoccupied with that, I wind up and let him have it with the other blade, aiming for his knee.

This blow goes all the way through and he staggers to the side, then falls down. One more hard blow and his head comes free of the rest of his body and he goes still.

The rats are all staring at me. Maybe they're impressed by what they just saw. Or maybe they're just dead. Whatever.

I start sweeping them off Beckwourth. I get a few bites, but nothing serious. I hope dead rats don't carry diseases like live ones do.

At first I think he's dead, he's so still. But then Beckwourth stirs. His eyes open and he looks up at me.

"Ace? What happened?"

"I killed the captain. Saved your life. It was pretty heroic. But there's time enough for that later. Can you walk? How about run?" I grab his arm and jerk him to his feet. "It doesn't matter. We have to go."

I pull my other sword out of the captain's skull. "Follow me."

Beckwourth recovers his wits quickly and stumbles after me. A few more skeletons pop up along the way, but I've figured them out by now and they're no real problem to deal with.

We get to the rope. "Can you climb?" I ask Beckwourth. He nods and starts up the rope.

I stare up at him, willing him to go faster. I can feel some new bad thing is about to happen and I want to be out of this hold when it does. But I can't go anywhere until he gets out of the way.

He reaches the top and pulls himself laboriously over the edge. Finally. I stick one of the swords through my belt and get ready to leave.

And right then the wooden statue of Totec explodes.

56

Splinters fly everywhere. Something huge stirs itself, then takes a step toward me. Something that was, I don't know, *trapped* inside that carving?

Goddammit. I knew this was going to happen.

"I don't have time for this right now," I tell the thing. "I have places to go."

It doesn't seem to care. It growls and takes another step. The ship shakes under the impact. It's got to be eight foot tall and naturally it looks like Xipe Totec, down to the flayed skin coat, the long, sharp teeth and the cruel eyes. At least I hope it only *looks* like Totec. Surely it's not actually him. The stench coming off it is awful. It growls again and its lips peel back, making sure I get a good gander at how long and sharp its teeth are.

Scary teeth. I get it. Let's see how scary they are once I chop you into pieces.

I back up as far as I can, then sprint toward it. Once I get up to speed, I jump and catch hold of the rope. I swing toward the thing and hit it in the chest with both feet. That staggers it a bit, but doesn't knock it down.

I let go and hit the floor. Thinking this might be a good time to try my pistol again, I draw it and fire six shots into its head, as fast as I can.

It howls and claws at its face. Some kind of yellowish fluid leaks out of the holes. But, once again, it doesn't go down.

It shakes off the wounds and comes for me. A clawed hand slashes at me. I duck under the attack and roll. When I come out of the roll I'm behind the thing. Before it can turn I whip out my sword and hack at the closest hamstring, or where a hamstring should be.

The sword bites deep and clearly there's something important under there because the monster howls again and staggers. But the thing makes sure I know there's no time to relax and pat myself on the back by righting itself, lunging forward, and slashing at me with a clawed hand. This one gets a little close for comfort. It shreds the front of my shirt and I feel the claws bite into my flesh.

I should have some nice scars from that. Assuming I live long enough.

I whirl and climb up one of the stacks of crates. It slams into the stack a second later, shaking the stack. With the sword I slash at the rope securing the crates until it parts. Then I pick up one of the crates, hold it over my head, and slam it down on the thing's head.

This time it goes down.

Quickly I snatch up another crate and throw it down on top of the thing. I get lucky and hit it in the head. It seems dazed.

I follow with another crate and then another. While the thing is preoccupied, I figure it's time to take my exit. I jump down, run to the rope and shinny up it as fast as I can.

It recovers pretty quickly, but not fast enough to catch me. Fear is a wonderful motivator. I climb that rope faster than I've ever climbed anything in my life. I feel one of its hands slap at my foot, and then I'm up and over the edge.

57

Beckwourth slams the hatch shut and then we start piling whatever we can find on top of it. Below, the thing is howling and jumping at the hatch, which fortunately seems to be out of its reach. Hopefully it's not smart enough to stack crates to stand on.

Beckwourth and I drag a rusted old anchor over and pile that on top of the other stuff.

"Think that will hold it?" he asks. His face is pale, but his eyes are lit up and there's a half smile on his face.

"You're enjoying this, aren't you?" I say.

The smile goes away. "A little."

I swear at him. "Do you see now why I didn't want you to go into the hold?" I yell at him. Maybe I shouldn't be yelling, but nearly getting killed a few times has gotten me a little worked up. Yelling seems like a good way to let some of it out. "Do you?"

"Maybe it wasn't the best idea after all."

"It was a damned stupid idea. I don't mind so much doing stupid things, but I prefer it when they're my idea."

"Thanks for coming to get me."

"Next time I'll leave you."

"I sure hope the pearls aren't down there," he says.

"Me too. Because if they are, they're staying there. Can we go search the captain's quarters now, or do you want to find some more monsters to play with first?"

"Don't be sore. You have to admit it was pretty exciting."

I want to choke him, but there isn't time. Maybe later. I stomp off toward the other end of the ship.

There's a little set of stairs leading down from the deck a few feet, then a landing and a heavy door that's nicely carved. Sword ready, I slowly turn the door knob, then fling the door open.

Nothing. The cabin is quiet.

As it should be. I already killed the captain, after all. But it's good to know there aren't other nasties lurking in his bedroom.

With Beckwourth following close behind, I step into the room. It's well lit from the moonlight that floods in through the large windows. To one side is a heavy desk with a chair behind it. There's a large globe in a stand beside the desk. A large bed is against the far wall. Decaying rugs cover most of the wooden floor and there are tapestries hanging on the walls, along with an assortment of weapons, swords, spears, even some ancient black-powder rifles and pistols. Everything is rusted. A thick layer of dust lies over it all.

"I think there's something on the bed," Beckwourth whispers.

I take a closer look and swear under my breath. He's right. It looks like a man is lying there, under a blanket. I guess that wasn't the captain I killed after all.

I soft foot it over there. The blanket covers the figure completely. He's not moving yet, which is good, but that doesn't mean he'll stay that way. I need to make sure he does.

I start to reach for the blanket, then pause. The swords on the walls look a lot better than one I'm carrying. I toss my sword down and take one. It's heavy, with a thick, curved blade. Around the hilt is a curved basket of metal, meant to protect the fingers I suppose. I swing it a couple of times to get the feel of it.

Then I turn back to the bed. With the tip of the sword I reach out and flip the blanket back, then raise the blade, ready for an attack.

The man lying there looks almost peaceful. He has black hair cut short and a thin mustache. He's wearing a long coat with gold braid on the shoulders and ruffles of lace at the cuffs. His hands are folded across his chest. He looks like he's sleeping, like any minute he'll get up and stretch and look around.

Which is what I'm afraid of.

Cautiously, I poke him with the sword. When he doesn't move, I jab him. The sword goes in a few inches, but still he doesn't move. Is it possible? I wonder. Could there be one thing on this ship that isn't waiting to attack me?

"Look at this," Beckwourth says. He sounds excited. "I found them."

I turn halfway, still keeping one eye on the captain. "You found the pearls?"

He's behind the desk. "I think so." He lifts a small chest and sets it on the desk. He opens the lid and his eyes light up.

"Unbelievable," he says. He sticks his hands into the chest and when he pulls them out they're filled with black pearls.

I give the captain another jab. Still nothing. I back away, certain that at any moment he's going to come to life, but strangely he doesn't.

I walk over to the desk. "Close it up and let's go before anything else bad happens."

"It's too late for that," a voice says from the doorway.

58

Five men come into the room. Naturally they're all pointing guns at us. I forget what it's like to run into people who aren't pointing guns or something deadly at me. Maybe I'm in the wrong line of work.

"Damn, you have a way of popping up," one of them says, looking at me.

"Do you know these men?" Beckwourth asks me.

"We're old friends," I reply. To the man who spoke I say, "It's great to see you again, Frank." I look over the other four. "I see you're still toting around too much dead weight though. When *will* you learn?"

Frank's expression darkens. "Don't talk about my brother like that."

"Or what? You'll follow me onto a ghost ship and shoot me? But wait, you're already doing that. Spare me your threats. What are you doing here anyway? I thought I'd seen the last of you."

Frank smiles and I can see his gold tooth. Before he can speak, Jesse cuts in. "Arizona was too hot and we was headin' for Californy when we stopped in this nowhere town and heard tell of a man who was selling black pearls. We did some asking around and then out of nowhere you show up. All we had to do was follow you boys and you led us right here."

I knew it. Sell something like that and you're bound to attract the wrong kind of attention. There's always vultures around.

"Sorry about that, Ace," Beckwourth says. "I should have been more careful."

"Don't worry about it. Someone needs to snuff out these varmints. It might as well be me."

"Shut up!" Frank barks. He and his gang have fanned out in an arc facing us. Cole is limping badly and using a crutch. That knee I broke isn't going to heal overnight. Bob's right hand is all bandaged up so he's holding his gun in his left hand, and it doesn't look all that steady. Most men can't shoot with their off hand.

With their injuries that evens the odds a little, which makes me feel better about our chances. Of course, they have the drop on us, but a man takes what he can get.

A distraction would sure help right now.

"What you want to do now," Frank says, "is pull out your guns nice and slow and toss them over here on the floor."

"No funny business, neither," Jesse says.

His eyes are darting around the room and I can see he's jumpy. All of them are jumpy. Except for Frank, who maybe has ice water in his veins. I don't imagine it would take much to set them off.

That gives me an idea.

"Okay, we'll hand them over," I say. I start reaching for my gun, then freeze and stare over their shoulders. I raise a shaking hand and point. "For the love of god, what is *that*?"

It works. Jesse and the Younger brothers all jolt and spin around. Cole moves so quick he falls down. Only Frank doesn't turn around, but he turns his head slightly and that's all the opening I need.

My hand drops to my gun and as Frank's head turns back toward me I draw it. It comes out clean and I squeeze the trigger.

The gun misfires in a flash of light and a cloud of smoke.

Frank fires, but he misses me. The bullet whizzes by my head and hits the wall behind me. I drop down behind the desk. Beckwourth is already there.

The gunshots come fast and furious as the boys empty their guns at us, firing as fast as they can. But the desk is solid and it stops the slugs. The worst we get is wood chips from the ones that hit the wall behind us.

There's a break in the firing and I peer over the edge of the desk. They're all reloading. Jesse is shaking so much he drops his gun.

But it's not them I'm looking at. It's the movement behind them. A shape is rising up off the bed.

I point. "Behind you," I say.

"What kind of durned fools do you take us for?" Cole says. He's down on one knee, trying to force shells into his gun but dropping most of them. "We ain't dumb enough to fall for that again."

"Don't say I didn't warn you."

Bob hears the dead captain first. He turns. When he sees the captain looming over him his eyes bulge out of his head and strangled noises come out of him. His muscles twitch, but he seems to be paralyzed by fear.

"What the hell, Bob?" Jesse says. He turns too and when he sees de Iturbe he screeches and points, which makes the rest of them turn.

While everyone stares openmouthed—facing down a dead Spanish sea captain isn't the sort of thing most people's lives prepare them for—de Iturbe grabs Bob by the throat and lifts him into the air. I've got a clean shot which probably wouldn't do old Bob any good anyway, but I don't take it. You could say I'm not feeling kindly disposed toward any of these boys. Frankly, I'm sick of them trying to kill me.

For a few seconds that seem to go on forever, Bob thrashes in de Iturbe's grip. Then he shrivels like a dead frog left in the sun, his skin turning to old leather, cracking and peeling to expose the bone underneath. De Iturbe tosses his dead body aside and turns on the rest of them.

That breaks their paralysis.

They all start shooting like crazy. Except Jesse, who it seems never got around to reloading his gun. He throws the empty weapon at the captain, then he runs for the door.

The bullets aren't having much effect on the captain, except maybe to slow him a bit. Frank and Jim are backing away as they fire, but when Cole tries to stand up his knee gives out and he falls hard. He loses hold of his gun and it skitters away. The captain reaches for him.

"Help me, Jim!" he yells, trying to crawl away.

But there isn't anybody who can help him.

De Iturbe gets hold of his leg and picks him up. Hanging upside down, he's still hollering for his brother when his screams break off abruptly. He spasms once and goes still, shriveling and drying like his brother.

The ship lurches suddenly and tilts to one side, then sinks a couple of inches.

"Time to go," I say, grabbing Beckwourth's collar. I drag him toward the door and we run out of the cabin. Behind us I hear someone else start to scream.

We run up the steps to the main deck and there's Jesse. He's got his knife out and he's waving it at us.

"You stay away from me!" he yells. "I'll cut you!"

The ship shudders, tilts a few more degrees and sinks deeper into the sand. We don't have much time.

Right behind Jesse is an open hatch, probably the one right above the spot in the hold where I rescued Beckwourth. Dead rats start pouring out of the hatch. Beckwourth yells a warning. Jesse looks down just as they start to swarm up his legs.

"Oh, come on!" he yells.

He starts stomping and slashing at them with the knife but there's too many and they're too fast. They crawl up into his pant legs and under his shirt. They start chewing on him and he screams and tears frantically at his clothes. He staggers backwards, catches his foot on the lip of the hatch—

And falls backward into the hold.

"Poor bastard," Beckwourth says.

Beckwourth and I run for the other end of the ship, where I left the rope. I'm glad I had the sense to pull it out of the hatch before Beckwourth closed it. I tie the rope off and throw the end over the side. The ship shudders again, tilts further and settles down another foot. It's tilting upwards on our side and the motion causes me to stumble toward the hatch we piled all the stuff on. I have to grab onto the railing to keep from sliding over there.

"Go!" I yell at Beckwourth.

It's hard because the ship is moving pretty much constantly now, but he manages to climb over the railing and start climbing down the rope. Before I can follow him here comes Frank.

He's got wild eyes and he's lost his hat, but he's still all kinds of mean. "Not so fast!" he yells. "You're not getting off this ship alive."

He's got me dead to rights, but when he pulls the trigger the ship shakes again and he stumbles. The shot goes wild.

"Why don't we finish this down on the ground?" I yell. The ship is groaning and creaking loudly.

"It ends now!" he yells back.

He raises his gun again and I tense for the leap over the railing. There's always the chance he'll miss again.

But right then the hatch cover explodes upwards and my old friend Totec rises up from the wreckage.

His eyes bulging, Frank spins toward the thing. He fires into it and then tries to back away, but the ship tilts again. He loses his footing and stumbles right into the thing's waiting arms.

Goodbye, Frank. I wish I could say it's been a pleasure.

I jump over the railing and get out of there.

59

Beckwourth and I stand at a safe distance and watch as the ghost ship settles back into the sand where it came from. In a few minutes it is completely gone. There's no sign it was ever there.

"Was that enough adventure for you?" I ask Beckwourth. "Think you'll be able to finish that book now?"

His eyes are shining. He looks like he's just had the time of his life. "That was *incredible*!" he bursts out. "It was better than I could have imagined."

"Better? Are you loco? You know we almost got killed like ten times, right?"

"But we didn't. That's what's so incredible." He starts clapping me on the back, his excitement too much for him to contain. "We did it, Ace. We went into the ghost ship and we emerged to tell the tale."

"Too bad we didn't get the pearls," I say. "It would have been nice to have something to show for our, well, *my* troubles."

Grinning, Beckwourth sticks his hands in his coat pockets. When he pulls them out, they're full of black pearls.

"We did get something," he says.

60

It's around midnight but we're both way too wound up to sleep, so we mount up and start riding toward Bedbug. We let the horses go at their own speed and they walk slowly. While we ride, Beckwourth transfers all the pearls from his pockets to a leather pouch.

"I don't think I'll ever understand what I just saw," Beckwourth says when he's done.

"Some things aren't meant for understanding. Some things simply are."

"You're too young for the wise old Indian thing, you know."

"I'm trying it on while I can. If I keep getting caught up with people like you I won't live to be old enough."

"Don't blame your life choices on me. I didn't know you when you decided to whack that old grizzly bear on the ass."

"I guess you have a point," I concede.

Beckwourth hefts the leather pouch. "So, about this here treasure. There's something you should know."

"Is this the part where you point a gun at me and tell me you're keeping it all?" I say it jokingly, but I was half expecting to see him reaching for his gun.

"Close, except you're completely wrong," he says, then flips the bag to me.

I catch it. "What's going on?"

"I want you to have it all," he says. He opens his hand and shows me two in his palm. "I kept two for souvenirs, but the rest are yours." He pats a bulge in his pocket. "I also kind of picked up some of that gold, so I should have enough funds to, you know, get me to the end."

I'm stunned. Maybe I'm a little gun shy where treasure and rewards and such are concerned, but I've gotten used to thinking that something is always going to get between me and the gold. "I don't understand."

"'Some things aren't meant for understanding. Some things simply are.'"

"Throwing my own words back at me already?" I say.

He smiles. "I couldn't pass up the chance. Truthfully, though, they're not much use to me." He winces and reaches into his saddlebags for the little brown bottle. "I'll be dead soon and I can't take them with me, as they say. Someone else, someone who had no part in this, will get the money then. I'd rather you have it."

I'm genuinely touched. I remember my black rage, my desire to strike back at the world which I thought was filled with people who did nothing but treat me poorly. How could I have forgotten that the world also had people like Beckwourth, people like Annie and the townsfolk of Lily Creek, in it? "I don't know what to say."

"Eh, forget it. You talk too much anyway." Beckwourth laughs at his own joke. "What are you going to do now?"

"I haven't really thought that far ahead," I say. "Mostly I've been trying to survive. Maybe I'll go visit my family. I haven't seen them in a while. I'm going somewhere out of Arizona anyway. They're going to be looking for me for a while."

We ride in silence for a bit. Then Beckwourth says, "I want to thank you, Ace."

"It was nothing."

"Don't say that. It's not true. You didn't have to go on this crazy adventure. You could have gotten yourself killed. But you did it anyway. You did it for an old man who talks too much. You're a good man, Ace. One of the best and I'm proud to call you my friend."

He sticks his hand out and I take it. I feel choked up. "I am proud to call you my friend as well."

He pulls out his pipe and starts packing tobacco in it. "Did I ever tell you the story about the time my horse died and I had to ride a buffalo back to camp...?"

The End

Ace's story continues in
Ace Lone Wolf and the Hidden Fortress

Available now on Amazon.com

(Author's note: Although this is a work of fiction, some characters and events are based on fact. There are some historical notes at the end if you're interested.)

NOTES ABOUT THE STORY
Although this is a fictional tale, there are elements of historical fact mixed into it.

Ace's character is very, very loosely based on an actual historical figure named Niño Cochise. (And I mean *loosely*. For one thing, Niño was full-blooded Apache.) Niño Cochise was the grandson of the famous Apache chief Cochise. Under the leadership of his mother (Cochise was already dead by then and his father was in Washington, D.C.), Niño's clan slipped away while the Chiricahua Apaches were being transferred to another reservation.

They fled to an old Apache stronghold in the Sierra Madre Mountains in Mexico (which is described more in *The Lost Temple of Totec*). There they lived for several decades, trying to stay hidden from the world as much as possible, forming alliances with American ranchers in the area, Tarahumara Indians, and even with their old enemies, the Yaqui Indians. In the 1900s the stronghold was gradually abandoned as Niño's people moved out into the world.

All of this is detailed in the fascinating autobiography called *The First Hundred Years of Niño Cochise*, told by Niño Cochise to A. Kinney Griffith. I think what I like best about it is that theirs is a story of hope. While most Native Americans were forced onto reservations, they were able to remain free. When they did enter the larger world, they did so on their own terms and by their own choice.

Most readers are probably familiar with the notorious outlaws Frank and Jesse James. The James-Younger gang was an actual gang, though all similarities end there.

Horace Tabor and both his wives are actual historical figures. How Horace earned his money, as well as the divorce and most of the information about Leadville is accurate.

Old Mose was an actual grizzly bear who roamed central Colorado for many years, and he was credited with the killings I wrote about here, including the killing of the hunter.

James P. Beckwourth was an early mountain man and trapper. His autobiography is called *The Life and Adventures of James P. Beckwourth: Mountaineer, Scout and Pioneer and Chief of the Crow Nation of Indians*. The stories his character relates are taken from his book, though they are changed and

243

mashed together somewhat to fit my story. While relating those stories I attempted as much as possible to capture the same overall tone and word usage that Beckwourth used in his book. The information about his parentage is accurate.

The Army scouts the Apache Kid and Mickey Free were also historical figures and the information about their background is correct.

The Yuma Territorial Prison was the most feared prison in the West, with perhaps the exception of Alcatraz. It was built pretty much as I described it, including the solitary confinement cage in the room cut out of solid rock.

The earliest tales of "the lost ship of the desert" surfaced after the Colorado River flood of 1862. A colonel reported seeing the ship in 1863 and the Los Angeles newspaper had an account of it in 1870. The ship was reported to be somewhere north and west of Yuma. It was believed that a freak tsunami lifted the ship out of the Colorado River channel and deposited it inland. Some believed the ship to have belonged to a Spanish explorer named Juan de Iturbe that was actually carrying a fortune in black pearls. Other accounts claim it was Thomas Cavendish's ship *Covenant*, filled with pirate treasure. Still others believed it to be the Spanish ship *Iqueue*, which was taken by mutineers.

ABOUT THE AUTHOR

Born in 1965, I grew up on a working cattle ranch in the desert thirty miles from Wickenburg, Arizona, which at that time was exactly the middle of nowhere. Work, cactus and heat were plentiful, forms of recreation were not. The TV got two channels when it wanted to, and only in the evening after someone hand cranked the balky diesel generator to life. All of which meant that my primary form of escape was reading.

At 18 I escaped to Tucson where I attended the University of Arizona. A number of fruitless attempts at productive majors followed, none of which stuck. Discovering I liked writing, I tried journalism two separate times, but had to drop it when I realized that I had no intention of conducting interviews with actual people but preferred simply making them up.

After graduating with a degree in Creative Writing in 1989, I backpacked Europe with a friend and caught the travel bug. With no meaningful job prospects, I hitchhiked around the U.S. for a while then went back to school to learn to be a high school English teacher. I got a teaching job right out of school in the middle of the year. The job lasted exactly one semester, or until I received my summer pay and realized I actually had money to continue backpacking.

The next stop was Australia, where I hoped to spend six months, working wherever I could, then a few months in New Zealand and the South Pacific Islands. However, my plans changed irrevocably when I met a lovely Swiss woman, Claudia, in Alice Springs. Undoubtedly swept away by my lack of a job or real future, she agreed to allow me to follow her back to Switzerland where, a few months later, she gave up her job to continue traveling with me. Over the next couple years we backpacked the U.S., Eastern Europe and Australia/New Zealand, before marrying and settling in the mountains of Colorado, in a small town called Salida.

In Colorado, after starving for a couple of years, we started our own electronics business, because electronics seemed a logical career choice for someone with a Creative Writing degree.

Around the turn of the century we had a couple of sons, Dylan and Daniel (I say 'we', but when the hard part of having kids came around, there was remarkably little for me to do). Those boys, much to my surprise, have grown up to be amazingly awesome people, doubtless due to their mother's steadying influence during their formative years, and not to the endless stream of bad jokes and puns spewing from their father.

In 2005 we shut the business down and moved back to Tucson. I am currently writing full time.

Made in the USA
San Bernardino, CA
28 January 2019